Cannibal Eliot and the Lost Histories of San Francisco

CANNIBAL ELIOT

Cannibal Eliot and the Lost Histories of San Francisco

BY HILTON OBENZINGER

MERCURY HOUSE
SAN FRANCISCO

Copyright © 1993 by Hilton Obenzinger
Published in the United States by Mercury House
San Francisco, California

This is a work of historical fiction. With obvious exceptions, names,
characters, places, and incidents either are the product of the author's
imagination or are used fictitiously. Any resemblance to actual events,
locales, or persons, living or dead, is entirely coincidental.

"The Kiss" previously appeared in *Bastard Review* and "Spite Fence"
appeared in *Oxygen.*

United States Constitution, First Amendment: Congress shall make no law
respecting an establishment of religion, or prohibiting the free exercise
thereof; or abridging the freedom of speech, or of the press; or the right
of the people peaceably to assemble, and to petition the Government for
a redress of grievances.

Mercury House and colophon are registered trademarks of
Mercury House, Incorporated

Printed on recycled, acid-free paper
Manufactured in the United States of America

Library of Congress Cataloging-in-Publication Data
Obenzinger, Hilton.
    Cannibal Eliot and the lost histories of San Francisco /
Hilton Obenzinger.
       p.   cm.
    ISBN 1-56279-047-1
     1. San Francisco (Calif.) — History — Fiction.   I. Title.
PS3565.B36C3   1993
813'.54 — dc20
                                  93-12722
                                  CIP

5   4   3   2   1

for Isaac and my parents

Contents

The author gratefully acknowledges the help of the staffs and resources of the Bancroft and Doe Libraries of the University of California, Berkeley; the San Francisco Public Library, especially the San Francisco History Room; the Leonard Library of San Francisco State University; the Sutro Library; the Chinese Historical Society; the California State Library in Sacramento; and the Green Library of Stanford University.

Grateful acknowledgment is given to books used in researching *Cannibal Eliot and the Lost Histories of San Francisco*, including: *San Francisco or Mission Dolores*, by Zephyrin Engelhardt (Chicago: Franciscan Herald Press, 1924); *Anza's California Expeditions*, by Herbert Eugene Bolton (Berkeley: University of California Press, 1930); *The Writings of Fermien Francisco de Lasuén*, translated by Finbar Kenneally (Washington, D.C.: Academy of American Franciscan History, 1965); *Who Killed Mr. Crittenden?* by Kenneth Lamott (New York: Ballentine, 1973); *The Indispensible Enemy: Labor and the Anti-Chinese Movement in California*, by Alexander Saxton (Berkeley: University of California Press, 1971); *Madams of San Francisco*, by Curt Gentry (San Francisco: Comstock Editions, Inc., 1977); *Let Justice Be Done: Crime and Politics in Early San Francisco*, by Kevin J. Mullen (Reno: University of Nevada Press, 1989); *San Francisco Murders*, edited by Joseph Henry Jackson (New York: Duell, Sloan and Pearce, 1947); *Sam Brannan: Builder of San Francisco*, by Louis J. Stellman (New York: Exposition Press, 1953); *Sam Brannan and the California Mormans*, by Paul Bailey (Los Angeles: Westernlore Press, 1943); *Denial of Disaster: The Untold Story and Unpublished Photographs of the San Francisco Earthquake and Fire of 1906*, by Gladys Hansen and Emmet Condon (San Francisco: Cameron & Co., 1989); *The San Francisco Earthquake*, by Gordon Thomas and Max Morgan-Witts (New York: Stein & Day, 1971); and *The Barbary Coast*, by Herbert Asbury (New York: Knopf, 1933).

Cannibal Eliot and the Lost Histories of San Francisco

Introduction
The Victor Archives

Cannibal Eliot and the Lost Histories of San Francisco is composed of never-before published diaries, memoirs, interviews,
and other firsthand accounts of San Francisco history from the
first clash between Spanish soldiers and native people in 1776
to the Great Earthquake and Fire in 1906. All the manuscripts
presented here had been lost, and all were recovered under
remarkable circumstances only within the last few years. The
fragment by William "Cannibal" Eliot, "Cannibal in California," was accidentally found by his brother's great-great-
granddaughter Rainbow Eliot-Cohen in 1989, and I relate the
story of its discovery and what little is known of his life in that
section of the book. The rest of these manuscripts are from a
previously unknown collection of documents called the Victor
Archives, and the story of this collection demands telling now.

While facts about the Victor Archives are few—and the
reason for their disappearance still baffling—I can reconstruct
at least the outlines of the project's history, which begins with
Mrs. Frances Fuller Victor, one of the researchers and writers
employed by Hubert Howe Bancroft in his "history factory."

Hubert Howe Bancroft was a highly successful bookseller
in San Francisco in the 1860s who amassed an enormous,
extraordinarily rich collection of books and manuscripts on
California and Pacific history (which the shrewd businessman
eventually sold to the University of California and which is
now housed in the Bancroft Library on the Berkeley campus).
In the 1870s he began producing history books, fashioning
what became known as a "history factory" in his library: many

researchers and writers would pore over documents on revolving tables invented by Bancroft, drafting books that the wealthy bookseller would then rewrite or edit. In many respects, Mr. Bancroft introduced modern industrial techniques to researching and writing history, supervising numerous assistants to index, analyze, and draw upon the vast resources at his disposal in order to compose exhaustive chronicles of California and all the lands between Alaska and Central America.

While all of theses volumes were signed by H. H. Bancroft, the bookseller offered not a single acknowledgment of his collaborators' efforts. Mrs. Frances Fuller Victor, like the other researchers and writers, labored over ten hours a day, six days a week for little pay, yet received no recognition for the fact that she had written major portions of Bancroft's histories, sometimes complete books. For example, two volumes on the history of Oregon were written entirely by Mrs. Frances Fuller Victor—with Bancroft taking no hand in the work except to affix his signature to the title page.

Eventually, some of the researchers rebelled, such as Henry L. Oak, who unsuccessfully demanded monetary compensation. For her part, Mrs. Frances Fuller Victor denounced Bancroft as a literary criminal, displaying several of "Bancroft's Works" with her own name printed on their title pages at various literary exhibitions, including the book exhibit at the 1893 Columbian Exposition in Chicago. "That is her way of claiming her own," wrote satirist Ambrose Bierce,

> and it is to be hoped that the same thing will be done at Chicago by not only her but every living writer whose work Mr. Bancroft claims as "his" because he paid for it. Most of the names are now adorning little headboards out in the cemeteries—a result of Mr. Bancroft's scale of wages. It was he who, estimating the number of his hack-writers who were dead of overwork and undereating, wept to think that Nature allowed him nothing for their skulls as "returned empties."

Mrs. Victor "claimed her own" in other ways as well. Even before the open rupture with her employer, she embarked on her own project, secretly collecting a variety of manuscripts independent of Bancroft. Mrs. Victor readily bent her employment with the bookseller to her will, even to the point of conducting interviews under false pretenses as Bancroft's agent (the interview with Charles Crocker in "Spite Fence" may well be an example). She had begun to revolt against the strictures of Bancroft's "history factory" even before his self-aggrandizement became unbearable; but when she did break with Bancroft she turned what had been perhaps nothing more than a diversion into a clandestine institution. Mrs. Victor began seeking manuscripts with zeal, collecting interviews, journals, diaries, and unpublished (often unpublishable) books, all of which she kept hidden in her home.

By the time Mrs. Victor moved back to her beloved Portland, Oregon, in 1893, she had amassed a considerable collection, which she handed over to her colleagues. Her friends, inspired by her idea, vowed to maintain and expand the secret archives, setting out to document important aspects of the city's life that Mr. Bancroft would never have deemed worthy of attention. They began gathering interviews and memoirs of prostitutes, autobiographies of labor agitators, accounts of gamblers and Chinese merchants, and the like, all in an attempt to record the hidden history of the city. When Frances Fuller Victor died in 1902, the archivists elected to name the collection in honor of its founder.

The Victor Archives may have contained as many as twenty-five hundred items in 1907. Such a massive project must have involved scores of archivists—and yet their numbers and identities remain unknown: all chose anonymity, and no roll of the archivists' names survives. Internal disputes splintered the archivists into feuding factions after 1907, and the manuscripts were scattered and lost in the fury of bitter political splits. We have no idea whether the Victor Archives were destroyed by fire, by worms, or by human mischief; and the lack of even anonymous accounts by former archivists of the collection's fate only deepens the mystery.

One fragment of the Victor Archives that did survive was discovered by Dolores, the daughter of Henry O————, the archivist who wrote "Calamity and Crime" printed here. (In the spirit of the original archivists Dolores also requests anonymity.) Dolores, who still resides in San Francisco, did not realize that her parents had secreted away any files from the Archives until 1988, when, sending her long-deceased father's favorite chair to be reupholstered, she uncovered a large manila folder sewn into the seat.

I extend my grateful thanks to Dolores and her daughter Marina for allowing me to restore and publish selections of the texts they discovered. I also want to express my deepest gratitude to Rainbow Eliot-Cohen and the Eliot Family Trust for permitting me to print the fragment by William "Cannibal" Eliot. Owing to the generosity of both families, posterity can now claim these lost histories of San Francisco.

Finally, I want also to acknowledge Adam Raskin and Alicia Schmidt-Camacho for their professional service assisting me in Spanish translation and Sarah Blake for her many hours of research in the Bancroft Library.

The Kiss

From the Diary of Sergeant Juan Pablo Grijalva,
December 1776

When I visited the Mission I learned of the recent insolence of the savages.

Most of the Indians from the nearby area had fled across to the other shore, after their *ranchería* was burned down by their enemies from San Mateo, and only a few Indians would come to the Mission as they went to hunt for ducks on the nearby lake.

These hunters would be very shy, but they would offer the Franciscans some ducks, and Fathers Palou and Cambon went about their business of fishing for souls, offering their beads and delicacies in exchange. (I actually savored the little black ball of seeds the savages would give us. They tasted like toasted almond tamales. If by food faith is won, I might have been a convert to theirs on these tamales alone. *Jesus, Mary, and Joseph, forgive me for writing these things!*)

At any rate, one of these duck-hunting parties of savages grew so familiar that they became uncommonly bold, started stealing food, clothes, utensils—all sorts of things—as Indians do, stealing with no shame.

Then I was told that one of the brutes ran up to María Angela Chumasero, the wife of one of our soldiers, Domingo Alvisa, whereupon the savage suddenly kissed her on the lips!

When I heard this, my blood began to boil. Naked as Adam, this filthy beast ran up to María Angela, his member flapping like a banner in some holy procession, to kiss her on the lips! And when Corporal Alvisa sought to protect her honor, the savage shot arrows at him. The filthy beast had actually kissed her! I have seen many soldiers take their pleasures with Indian women, but never have I heard of such a thing right before the eyes of our soldiers!

At the same time, another of the duck hunters saw a neophyte from Mission Carmelo whom he must have thought was his people's enemy, for the Indian began to aim his arrows at him too, and began making threatening noises. Finally, they left, much to the relief of the Mission, after which María Angela was taken by the other women to the Fathers to revive her.

I was amazed and sorely troubled by this report. It so happened that a few days after I heard this, five Indians came to visit the Mission while I was there. Corporal Alvisa pointed out to me the one who threatened the neophyte from Carmelo. I ordered him arrested on the spot, and we took him to the guardhouse we had built of logs and tule, and there I gave him a few lashes.

Two savages who were hunting ducks in the lagoon heard his cries and came running up, jumping up and down, howling. Then they had the audacity to take their revenge by shooting arrows at us. We discharged two shots from our muskets to scare them off—and at the sound they began to run away, frightened. I followed them to the wooded mountain by the beach, and then I retired to the Presidio to take charge in Lieutenant Moraga's absence, as is my duty. There I made plans with the soldiers to search for the savages.

The next day we set out for the beach, for I suspected that they had not yet crossed over to the other shore, in order to have them flogged for shooting arrows in the Mission. My object was to fill their hearts with dread, for they must learn now, at the outset, a wisdom taught by all soldiers of the Crown, a wisdom as much a staple of their souls as the blessings of the Fathers. They must be made to feel fear.

On the beach we encountered the band of savages. By signs I asked them who had shot arrows at the Mission, and the savages readily pointed out the two guilty ones. The accused loudly protested their innocence, but when I dismounted to seize them, the two culprits fled, with two of our soldiers pursuing them. But then the other Indians suddenly turned on us and began to shoot arrows at us. One of the settlers, Pedro Pérez de la Fuente, had forgotten to wear his leather jacket, and he was slightly wounded by one of the arrows, as was also one of the horses.

I commanded that the muskets be discharged. One of the Indians fell dead by the water, killed by this same settler Pedro Pérez de la Fuente, while the others fled to some rocks isolated in the surf nearby from where they continued shooting arrows.

I then discharged my own musket, with the ball passing through the leg of one of the Indians and digging into the rock. With one dead and another wounded, the savages threw down their bows and arrows, pleading for peace. I threw down my gun in a similar fashion. But despite my gestures of peace, they would not return to the beach to pick up their belongings.

Meanwhile, the soldiers had captured the two culprits who had run away to the mountain. I charged them with the insolence of shooting their arrows in the Mission, and caused them to be whipped. Although they could not understand me, I believe they understood the flogging. After the lashes, I made cutting signs at my neck to indicate that if they were to commit their crime again, I would kill them. They quivered in fear, but I told them to gather up their belongings, as well as those of their companions, and that if they did not violate our trust again, we would be friends.

In the absence of our commanding officer, I took all of this upon myself, feeling that, as sergeant, it was my duty to conduct ourselves in this fashion, since it is our charge to protect the missionaries in their Holy labors of saving souls and keeping Russians from our land, and the necessity of swift punishment to serve as a lesson requires our utmost and immediate attention, otherwise the insolence of the savages would know no bounds.

Our situation—the necessity of soldiers to accompany the missionaries—can be compared to the banner I have seen Father Garces use to convert the Indians, a comparison which I will endeavor to explain.

Father Garces would show the savages the large painting of the Most Holy Virgin with the Child Jesus in her arms. The Indians would manifest great and noisy delight at the image, marveling at it, saying that it was good, and that they wished to be Christians in order to be white and beautiful like the Virgin. Father Garces would tell them that they could, at another time, but that at the present it could not be. Father Garces would then quickly reverse the banner, on which was pictured a condemned soul burning in Hell, whereupon the pagans would raise a great outcry and shrink back, saying that they did not like that! In such a way, Father Garces would introduce their catechisms, not allowing them easy baptism without learning at least the beginnings of reason. I have seen him do the same with the Opas and the Yumas, and I have admired his method, along with his phlegmatic ability to get along with these simple creatures.

In our situation, the Fathers are the bearers of Heaven, but we are the other side of the banner—the soldiers must be the tormentors of Hell. We can easily paint such a picture, particularly as the Fathers come from Spain, while we soldiers come from Sonora, so many from its jails.

As this was the first crime committed at the Mission, we needed to locate the culprits and to punish them swiftly in order for the Indians to understand that we have come to bring them either the blessings of the Church or the muskets of the King. In any case, the Fathers must be protected, no matter how these savages decide, and for that they spend their Pious Fund to feed us.

That night we sang the Alabado with Fathers Palou and Cambon, content in the exercise of our duties. I told Father Palou that I believed these Indians had never felt the stings of a flogging before. I told them they had been so surprised by the lash, that they howled as much in consternation and humiliation as in pain.

Father Palou looked saddened. The Father felt that these strange creatures were like his children, and he wept.

"Well," I said to Father Palou, for I wanted him to be relieved of his sorrow, "now that they know the lash, they will be able to approach reason. Soon you will have your flock."

The Demented Grin of Father Fernández

From *Noticias de la Misión de San Francisco de Asís* (1799) by Father Martín de Landaeta, O.F.M.

Father Lasuén, in light of Father Dantí's poor health, if for no other reason, allowed Father Antonio Dantí to retire early in 1796. I bade farewell to this outstanding missionary, with whom I had labored since 1791, and who had served six difficult years, and I shed tears for my stricken teacher and close companion.

At first, I eagerly welcomed the arrival of young José María Fernández, fresh from the College of San Fernando, and Diego García, although I must confess that even then I welcomed Father García with more reserve due to his strange reputation, which had preceded him.

But as soon as Father Fernández disembarked from the *Aranzazu*, I noticed his unsteady gait, his strange countenance of an almost stupid grin mixed with a grimace of pain. I learned that the poor Father had been struck in the head during a rough passage of the voyage and had begun to suffer severe headaches and, worse yet, hallucinations.

I was wary of Father García, who came to serve as supernumerary, because of the reports that he was difficult, irresponsible, disobedient, and troublesome. This Andalusian, while at Soledad, actually refused to sow seeds for crops one year, joining with the Indians in gathering native seeds, which, as he later explained to me, were more abundant and healthful than our crops, and in this way justified the indolence of the pagans with his own! When requested to join in the founding of Mission San José, Father García gave a thousand flimsy and fantastic reasons to justify his refusal. Oh, how I yearned for Father Dantí's experienced hand, for his firm treatment of the neophytes, and I prayed for guidance by God and deliverance from this bizarre pair before further sorrow should strike.

Soon it became apparent that Father Fernández could not exert himself strenuously without getting incapacitating headaches, although he made every effort to work. It also became apparent that Father Fernández was of such a kind disposition and filled with such love that, assisted by his strange countenance of smiling pain that attracted their attention, the Indians soon began to gather about him, laughing and playing like the birds and animals who would gather around our Saint Francis. Father Fernández would talk to them of our Savior's life with signs and the words of their language, which he had such facility in learning from the moment he had arrived. When Father Fernández witnessed for the first time the death of one of the Indians, he mourned so greatly that he impressed the neophytes, particularly as he joined the poor dead child's mother as she beat her breast with stones. I became concerned that Father Fernández was not taking the appropriate fatherly relationship of the missionary, but, touched by his sweet temperament, his innocence, and his popularity with the Indians, I did not voice my apprehensions.

Father García's reputation, however, soon proved all too true. As I exerted efforts for the Indians to labor with even greater zeal—for we required the construction of twenty new habitations for the Indians, a new granary, a ditch to enclose our pasturage and grain field, and many other projects —Father García acted as much a laggard as the uncivilized natives themselves. Once I even discovered Father García dancing with the savages, attempting to learn their crazy jumps and whoops. Despite my remonstrances, he continued his indolence, becoming increasingly impudent. I began to suspect that the Father would even enter into their *tamascals* to sit amongst their steaming rocks, perhaps learning the pagan idiocies which passed for their religion, and I grew fearful that the Indians were converting Father García rather than the Father teaching these ignorant savages the Gospel.

After only a month at the Mission, Father Fernández approached me after Mass, and, before an assemblage of neophytes, he began to berate me for my alleged mistreatment of the Indians with a passion I had never observed in him before. Seemingly unaware that his loud disagreement was in full public display, Father Fernández went on with his passionate accusations while I stood silently. I would not enter into an argument before the converts, so I simply rang the bell for work to begin without making any response. That night I tried to reason with Father Fernández, to explain the danger of public disputes and the wisdom of our policy, but he still remained agitated and inflamed, completely abandoning his mild demeanor. I reverted again to silence and marveled at the change in the Father. Father García witnessed all of these incidents, keeping silent himself, although I could see the derision and ridicule displayed on his face louder than any words.

Shortly thereafter, I learned that Father José María Fernández had chosen the irregular and disloyal course of writing directly to Governor Borica to level the most serious charges against me and Father Dantí, asserting that the desertion of the Indians was due to the ill treatment they had received at our hands! Soon thereafter, Lieutenant-Colonel Pedro de Alberni informed me that they would not allow soldiers to cooperate in punishment of the Indians unless requested by *both* myself and Father Fernández; then he declared that a formal, military investigation would be held on September 12th!

Imagine my horror, my dismay, to learn that the meek

Father Fernández and the dissolute Father García had banded together to sully my name, and in their ignorance had allowed the soldiers to assist in their conspiracy. For months the Governor had insisted on re-establishing the Royal Ranch at Buriburi after listening to false complaints from the soldiers that our cattle were scrawny and our prices inflated. Now these charges of misconduct would be used to knock down all the efforts of Father-President Lasuén and myself to obstruct this infringement on the rights of the Mission, which, of course, is also an infringement on the rights of the Indians themselves. And all of this damage done in the name of defending the poor savages!

Four soldiers gave their sworn depositions at the proceedings, each of them conveniently asserting that the two hundred Indians who had run away from Mission San Francisco last April did so because of what they called *"los tres muchos"* —too much work, too much punishment, and too much hunger.

I listened, again in silence, as distortions and lies flew from their mouths. Indians were punished, they said, because they absented themselves for days at a time to look for seeds they were accustomed to eat or to look for shellfish along the beach. They complained that the Indians were punished most especially for coming to the Presidio to carry water and wood for the soldiers, a service for which the soldiers declared they were customarily rewarded with food. My outrage grew as I listened to Sergeant Pedro Amador relate this nonsense, knowing well how I had complained to him that the soldiers—who refused to do any work themselves!—would distract the neophytes from their assigned labors. They then testified that the Indians ran away because, after becoming Christians, they were refused permission to return to their villages to visit parents and relatives (and yet they wanted us to prevent runaways!) while punishment of those who fled was overly harsh. Food was insufficient, and rations were cold, etc. Then Diego Olbeza, *mayordomo* since the founding of the Mission, declared that treatment of the Indians by Father Dantí and myself was the worst he had ever seen!

Los tres muchos! Yes, too much work seems very much a crime when spoken by these lazy fools who never do a bit of work themselves but choose instead to entice my Indians to do their own labors! I admitted that perhaps I drove the Indians hard, but I argued that our needs for construction required it. All the land and fruits of their labor are their property, which we hold in trust, and once they have fully become people of reason and civilized subjects of the Crown, all will revert to them. Consequently, all their labors are for themselves, and if I drive them with zeal, it is only in the exercise of my fatherly guidance, for they are very much like children who suffer excess in everything. (Besides, our buildings withstood the winter rains, unlike the Presidio—even their guardhouse blew away in a storm, the soldiers too lazy or too ignorant to tie beams together with rawhide to cope with the scarcity of nails!)

Punishments? Father Dantí and I never exceeded the twenty five lashes allowed to the religious, and our employments of imprisonment, the stocks, the shackles, and the whip were all according to custom. I never whipped the women in public, but only in their houses, so as not to incite the men. Father Fernández, it is true, would weep through his lunatic smile as I administered lashes for shirking work, but the floggings were nothing excessive. These savages had never understood calendars or time. They would eat when they felt like it, and they would only labor to search for something to eat. By choosing to live in the Mission as Christians they have chosen to live according to the divisions of the day as announced by the bells, and it is our duty to make them learn that they cannot wander off as they wish, that the tolling of the bells requires respect, whether for meals, work, or mass.

How frightfully deep is their ignorance! Why, these Indians have no idea of the Last Things. They do not think. They do not have any notions of Eternal Reward and Punishment. The most they will say is that they go to the sea when they die. They do not reflect on what they do. If they are questioned about Eternal Reward or Punishment, they will answer: "Who knows?" Naturally, they will not understand all that is required of them, since they have only just learned of Heaven and Hell. That is why the missionaries must guide them as a father guides his children, first with gentle rebuke, then with punishment. Certainly, the punishments we have administered are even less than those given to schoolchildren in Spain! As the teacher says, *La letra con sangre entra*—Letters enter only with blood. How can anyone object to our paternal ministrations when we are "merely" trying to have the Letters of the Gospel enter their hearts? Father Fernández, in all his hallucinations, would even weep at a schoolmaster flogging his students!

All of this ran through my mind as I heard these absurd charges, but I stayed silent. When they asked my response, all I said was that I would deal directly with either Father-President Lasuén or Governor Borica. "As for cold rations," I said, "even Father Junípero Serra distributed dry rations, and Father Dantí and I have been generous with barley, beans, and wheat. However, I would be most happy if I were supplied with cauldrons for *pozole*, for many of the Indians do not have anyone to grind the grain for them, and others are too lazy to do it."

Then the soldiers, when asked what might be done to improve the opinion of the Mission amongst the Indians, replied that all the Indians said that Father José María Fernández was full of kindness and gentleness and treated them well, and that if Father Landaeta left, as Father Dantí had already, and if another missionary like Father Fernández came, the Christian Indians who had fled would return and they would bring more pagans with them. I could not believe this insult as I stood before them, raising the demented Father Fernández as a banner to use against me! Such a transparent conspiracy, to collect so many accounts of cruel, enormous, and monstrous crimes in order to expel me!

The next week Father Lasuén arrived to investigate the situation himself. Fathers Fernández and García presented themselves to him in public, right before the officers of the Presidio no less, and demanded that I should leave the Mission, attributing to me all sorts of inhuman atrocities and other tall tales. Father Lasuén listened in silence, then moved to a private room. There, Father Lasuén explained that he was greatly concerned, and he read from Governor Borica's letter to him that this problem "deprives me of sleep at night and has me talking to myself." I could only raise my eyebrows at the Lord Governor's exaggerated concern, while I could see Father García smirk in satisfaction. "You must understand," Father Lasuén continued, "that this problem could very well result in a costly lawsuit that may undermine all of our efforts and burden us with added worries."

Father Lasuén then asked me if I fully appreciated the Governor's policy of peace with the Indians, considering the weaknesses in the defenses of the colony. I told the Father-President that I was well aware that neither we nor the Presidio could survive a concerted attack, that our situation was indeed perilous, particularly in light of an impending invasion by France or England, and that I concurred with the Lord Governor that the success of our ministry throughout Alta California could be gained only through cautious and careful relations with the natives.

After further questioning and inspection of the Mission, Father Lasuén assembled us again. He concluded that Father Dantí and I may have gone to extremes in disciplining. "I will not try to make saints out of you," he said, although I hardly felt worthy of such an aspiration. However, to my satisfaction, he stated that, previous to this scandal, he had neither witnessed such extremes, nor heard about them, nor received any reports about them.

He also said that it was clearly evident by the big projects accomplished in such short time that much of it must have been due to forced labor. He reprimanded me, and placed me under obligation to be more forbearing. "I am well aware that it takes as much effort to get you to work more slowly as it does to induce others to do enough work elsewhere. But you must learn, Father Landaeta," he said.

"What the Lord Governor wishes is that the work of the Indians be made light, that there be more moderation in punishing them, and that they be given their rations cooked. You should be much more kind in dealing with the Indians, and you should give them permission to go to their *rancherías* when they ask for it, if you had been imprudently refusing them before. And when you see that they are in declining health or becoming homesick, you should send them even if they do not ask permission."

Then the Father-President paused before continuing, "Father Landaeta, I expect you to put these changes into effect quickly and quietly."

"I would never put obstacles in the way of obedience," I replied, while Father Fernández once more evinced his lustrous, lunatic smile.

"However, as to the scandal," Father Lasuén resumed, turning to the demented priest, "I must instruct you, Father Fernández, never to make disagreements in public, especially before the neophytes, and certainly not before the soldiers.

Also, disputes between religious in anger that are described in detail or documented in a signed statement serve to make the altercation a matter of public record. I am sure you are well aware of our many enemies who seek to discredit the religious and to divert the riches of the Pious Fund to other, less worthy purposes than the salvation of pagans. I know that you are youthful, Father Fernández, and I grieve that you have been injured and that your judgment may have been impaired, but I implore you to exercise restraint and to use the proper methods for resolving such disputes.

"Finally, Father García, I hope that you are not piqued by any perceived slight regarding your treatment at Soledad or here, and that you carry out your duties as supernumerary with humility."

So ended our meeting. But while Father Lasuén was still at the Mission, it happened that several of the Indians who had run away came back. When questioned, they said they had not fled because of fear of punishment or aversion to the work but because of fear of disease. Despite the rebuke I had received, I was satisfied that these Indians had bolstered my case and that Father Lasuén's instruction would at least prevent Father Fernández's passion from being manipulated by the insolent Father García.

Father Lasuén spoke to me privately before he departed, at which time I unburdened my pent-up injuries. He reassured me of my good efforts despite what he called my "excessive zeal." I thanked him for his kind instructions, and he went on to reveal that the whole affair was "a cavillous machination directed towards a very unjust claim" and that he was well aware of the fanatical plots of the Reverend Fathers Fernández and García to expel me and to cloud the reputation of Father Dantí. He implored me to observe a strict and rigorous silence until the occasion would arise that would allow some motive or pretext to withdraw Father García from the country. For Father Fernández he felt more concern, hoping that his malady would be relieved, allowing him to return to his duties without delusions. "He is evidently a young man of great goodness, and I am loath to lose such a servant of God with so much potential," he said. I rejoiced that Father Lasuén could see through the subterfuge, and I agreed that Father Fernández had an extraordinary effect on the Indians and that all efforts should be made to cultivate his apostolic abilities.

How those two had conspired to expel me!—but now the Father-President had seen the truth! And I had but to pray and to wait.

Father Fernández, despite suffering more and more painful headaches, still poured his kindness upon the Indians. While his medications could not stop the contagion any better than mine, the Indians would flock to the man who smiled and cried, bringing their sick for his hapless cures and tearful prayers, and I prayed to God that their attraction to this strange creature would only serve to hasten their instruction in true religion and not be used by the Devil.

However, the changes Father Lasuén ordered only served to justify Father García's indolence, and he would loll even more with the savages, enjoying their games and their pagan stories. One day, perhaps to display his wit, he told me that the Indians all believe that they are descendants of a great Coyote. I told him that I was well aware of their childish fables. "Yes," he continued, "but are you aware from whom they believe the Spaniards have descended?" I replied that I was not so informed. "They believe that we are the children of a great *Mule!*" and then he roared with brazen laughter, catching the attention of some of the Indians nearby who came to inquire the cause of such mirth. Off he went with them, chattering in their own language and leaving me in utter bewilderment at his manner and angry at his unabated insolence.

Soon thereafter Governor Borica arrived to inspect the

Mission for himself—as well as to inspect the site for that insidious Royal Ranch. Satisfied that affairs at the Mission were conducted according to his wishes, he became aware that our permissive policy of leniency towards the Indians may have had untoward effect, particularly as the murderers of the seven Christian Indians who were killed when they were sent across the bay to bring back runaways in 1795 had as yet gone unpunished. The Indians were becoming restive, believing that the Spaniards would no longer subject them to reprisals for showing disrespect of our authority.

In order to impress upon the savages that they were required to perform their duties and pay proper respect to their superiors, His Lordship set out to make an example. He shortly had occasion to do just that.

One of the neophytes, Miguel, had stayed away from prayers, had been arrested by a soldier, and was being conducted to the Mission, when he turned upon the soldier, struck him down with a stone, and escaped. Miguel was subsequently arrested again and thrown into prison for a month. Governor Borica, upon hearing of this, pronounced the punishment insufficient and directed the commandant to inflict a further punishment of twenty-five lashes in the presence of all the neophytes of the Mission at the end of Miguel's imprisonment. After the flogging, the order from the Governor was read out loud that any further offense, being subversive of public order, would be punished with still greater rigor.

I was gladdened by the Lord Governor's firm hand, although I rankled that what he felt soldiers could perform we ourselves were prevented from so doing. Still, it was a wise decision that stopped the erosion of Spanish authority amongst the savages. This time the demented Father Fernández did not smile through his tears, although he kept silent and wisely did not protest, while Father García kept his eyes to the ground as if he were one of the chastised savages himself.

At the end of April 1797 Father Diego García—may God forgive him and grant him every happiness—was withdrawn from the country, and he was instructed to return to the College of San Fernando and thence back to Spain. Meanwhile, Father Fernández's headaches grew worse, and he would lie prone on the ground, his adoring Indians tending to him, and only for small snatches of time could he even stand. He could not say mass, nor could he work, so I knew it would not be long before he too would be withdrawn, for reasons of poor health.

How the Indians would weep at the departure of Father Fernández! But I was relieved, and my heart was lifted that I would no longer be plagued by that demented visage, for misguided kindness can come to no profit amongst savages in such a foggy, barren, windswept land, and could even undermine all good intentions. To be sure, I regretted the loss of the Father, for he proved to be so effective a glue to cement the neophytes to the Mission despite their fear of mortal contagion. Yet when Father José de la Cruz Espi, a native of Valencia and a man with many years of rich missionary experience in California, came as his replacement, I felt that God would allow our labors to save souls to resume.

Work at the Mission returned to normal until June 1797, when another misfortune occurred. A large number of fickle neophytes again disappeared, many of the fugitives belonging to the Cuchillones across the bay. Raimundo, a trusted neophyte from Baja California, asked Father Espi if he could search for the fugitives, and Father Espi, after consulting with me, gave his permission, whereupon Raimundo crossed the bay with thirty Christian Indians on balsas. They discovered the deserters in three gentile *rancherías*. Raimundo persuaded them to return unobserved while the savages were enjoying their heathen dances. The truants consented, but just as they were about to embark they changed their minds and refused to be led away. Suddenly the pagans appeared to come to the aid of their resisting tribesmen, and Raimundo and his companions were forced to make their escape without bringing back any of the runaways.

When poor demented Father Fernández heard of Raimundo's attempt and observed that he was not consulted in the transaction, he felt so incensed that he immediately reported the occurrence to Commandant Argüello and directed two long letters to Governor Borica, denouncing Father Espí and myself as the cause of all troubles. When Commandant Argüello demanded the particulars of Raimundo's attempt, we explained that the proposition to go after the fugitives came from the neophytes themselves, and they repeatedly assured us that there was no danger whatever. We consented to their request, as Father Espí explained, "solely in order to comply with the obligation of our ministry, and to alleviate in some measure a pastor who has to give an account of so many lost sheep, if by every means he does not exert himself in seeking them." Commandant Argüello just glared darkly at us and forbade us from making any more such excursions.

I helped Father Espí compose a letter to Governor Borica, explaining that the neophytes were eager to go and "there was no risk, because every day they go and come and deal with the Indians across the bay." We expressed that our love for the souls of the deserters impelled us to consent to the attempt of returning the backsliders. "We must acknowledge the Governor's concern," I advised Father Espí, and so he added a marvelous passage that answered His Lordship's suspicions even before they were voiced. "I know," Father Espí wrote, "that Your Honor will not be favorably disposed towards the practice, much less so after the disparaging criticisms which are based only on the lies and vile assertions of some of the neophytes"—No, no, we would not even mention Father Fernández's ravings, ha!—"but the truth of the matter is that those who went have returned without any harm, all without a scratch. If for what could have happened we erred, I am ready to accept any reproof and propose to amend . . ."

Wonderful, wonderful, "accept any reproof . . . propose to amend . . . for what *could* have happened," just the right tone. But we needed some kind of counterproposal, something that would advance our policy without contradicting the Governor's. "I have it!" Father Espí exclaimed, and he wrote, "But with all due respect we appeal to the tribunal of the well-known piety of Your Honor that, if the existing difficulties and disputes permit, Your Honor would furnish us with a little expedition, for the Indians are tractable. If they see four soldiers (and me, if I am permitted) with four sacks of wheat, I trust in the Lord that the savages will deliver the fugitives to us, and many gentiles will feel constrained to come along."

Yes, "a little expedition" was an inspired proposal that would surely prod the Governor towards a correct policy. Four sacks of wheat! Without Father García, it was the two of us against the one demented Father's ravings. We had outmaneuvered the madman!

As I expected, the Governor replied that, lest the savages be provoked to make war or the messengers come to grief, it would be "prudent" to forbid unarmed parties to go after fugitives. However, particularly because of pagan threats to kill the Christian Indians at Mission San José, Governor Borica ordered Sergeant Pedro Amador on an expedition to punish the Sacalanes and Cuchillones, to collect fugitives, and to dispel any ideas that Spaniards were afraid of the Indians. Sergeant Amador left Mission San José with twenty-two men with orders to fall upon the main *ranchería* at dawn and capture the chief and the deserters, avoiding bloodshed if possible.

I was delighted, although once more we had to suffer the Governor's rebuke. While Sergeant Amador's expedition was still gone, Commandant Argüello unexpectedly appeared at Mass on July 16th accompanied by the other officers, two corporals from the Catalonian Volunteers, and two leather-jackets. After Mass was over, Argüello assembled all the Indians, and, in the presence of all the Fathers and all the visiting military and naval officers and the soldiers, he made a speech.

Commandant Argüello explained to the Indians the new orders from the Governor. "On no account," he said, "are any of you Indians of the Mission to cross the bay to the other shore. Even if the Fathers of the Mission should send you across the bay, you are not to go! Even if it is to bring back fugitives from the Mission, you are not to go! No matter what the reason is, you are not to go! Do you understand me?" The Indians indicated that they did. "I hope you do, for punishment for disobeying this order will be rigorous. I am done now."

It was a brilliant display of military power, pomp, and oratory, and I was impressed, although I well realized that the effect was to humiliate Father Espí and myself before all the Indians and even before the common leather-jackets. I approached Commandant Argüello and said, "Commandant, I meekly submit to the decision, but I have one difficulty which I hope you can clarify for me. What am I supposed to do when the Indians who were born on the other side of the bay beg permission to visit their relatives? How am I supposed to satisfy them? Our instructions are to allow them to leave—but now our new instructions are to command them to stay. What shall I do?"

Oh, my manner was so meek, so mild, yet I had him in a snare as daring as any military stratagem! Commandant Argüello did not move a muscle, did not betray a quiver of agitation, but quietly he turned to me in his full military bearing and replied, "I will consult the Governor." Then, abruptly, he began his march back to the Presidio.

Meanwhile, Sergeant Amador's expedition ran into some difficulties. The Sacalanes, much to Amador's surprise, had dug three rows of pits, so that the soldiers were forced to dismount and attack with sword and lance. In the fight, two soldiers were wounded and seven natives killed. The Cuchillones were next attacked, but retreated after two of their number were killed. Two days after Commandant Argüello's speech, the expedition returned to Mission San José with eighty-three captured Christian runaways and nine gentiles, including five Sacalanes who were implicated in the murders of the seven Christian Indians in 1795 and three Cuchillones who had attacked Raimundo the previous month. Yes! Yes! This expedition began to turn the Governor's policy around despite all of Commandant Argüello's blunt oratory.

By this time Father Fernández was in constant agony, ranting to himself about the Indians, although his denunciations fell on deaf ears. Finally, Father Lasuén had no choice but to conclude that "his mind was somewhat confused," as he said. He ordered the demented Father back to the College of San Fernando because his attacks had rendered him "entirely unfit for this ministry."

He was ordered to return to México in the company of Father Antonio de la Concepción Horra of Mission San Miguel who had gone violently insane. I had heard of Father Concepción's violent outbursts and of his own mad ravings about the treatment of the Indians, and the frightening ways he menaced all about him with arrows and muskets. I was saddened that gentle Father Fernández, as demented as he was, had to sojourn with this maniac, while I also feared that the coupling of the two would only spell more mischief.

However, before Father Fernández departed, Governor Borica's new policy bore yet more fruit. First, Commandant Argüello returned with Governor Borica's reply to my question. The Governor ordered that Christian Indians who wanted to visit their parents or relatives across the bay should travel around the bay by land. A soldier would accompany them to Mission San José, whence they could proceed to their villages. "I am most appreciative of this clarification by the Governor. Thank you, Commandant Argüello," I said, with a humble demeanor, but inwardly I was smiling, roaring with laughter. Yes, if the Governor wanted to get involved in such nonsense, so be it. He will soon tire of it and allow those of us who must deal with these natives directly to go on with our ministry. "I am most appreciative of this clarification . . ."

Next, seventy-nine of the Indians who had run away two years before suddenly returned to the Mission—on their own! Such joy! This was like the return of the Prodigal Son, an unexpected surprise, almost a miracle. Yes, they had returned, now that the deaths from disease had abated.

However, Commandant Argüello launched yet another military investigation, and there, before Father Fernández, who was prone on a straw mat, Father Espí, and myself, José Argüello and three other soldiers asked the prodigals why they had fled.

Oh, such nonsense came from their lips in response. Tiburcio said he was flogged five times by Father Dantí for crying at the death of his wife and child. (Actually, he was flogged because he would not *stop* crying even days after the period of mourning, thereby avoiding his labors.) Magín said he was put in the stocks when ill. (He regularly faked illness to avoid work.) Tarazón visited his relatives and felt inclined to stay.

(At least this was an honest confession.) Claudio was beaten by the *alcalde* with a stick and forced to work when ill. (Nonsense. He was never forced to work if he was truly ill.) José Manuel was struck with a bludgeon. (As indeed he was, in view of the crazy way he started to scream during mass.) Liberato ran away to escape dying of hunger as his mother, two brothers, and three nephews had done. (Indeed, his family had died—but from disease and not from hunger!) Otolón was flogged for not caring for his wife after she had sinned with the *vaquero*. (I think this simply speaks for itself.) Milán had to work with no food for his family and was flogged because he went after clams. (No, Milán had plenty of food, but he dearly loved spending days looking for clams rather than working on building the granary.) Patabo had lost his family and had no one to take care of him. (The Mission would care for him as his own family!) Orencio's niece died of hunger. (Yes, his niece did die, although from disease and not hunger. Also, Orencio failed to mention his sinful relations with her *and* her sister as reasons for his flight.) Toribio was always hungry. (There is not one moment of the day when Toribio is not hungry!) Magno received no ration because, occupied in tending his sick son, he could not work. (Yes, he received no ration because he did not work. Others would have cared for his son while he worked, but he refused.)

On and on, I had to listen to these childish excuses, lies, distortions. I had already announced that none of the prodigals would be punished for fleeing the Mission, so I listened, content to await the conclusion of this farcical exercise and to get on with the business of saving souls.

Then Commandant Argüello asked the prodigals why they had returned. One after the other they replied in almost identical ways. They said they came back because they had heard of Father José María Fernández, that Father Fernández was a holy man, that Father Fernández loved the Indians, that

Father Fernández smiled even when he cried, that Father Fernández understood their sorrows, that Father Fernández —on and on, *ad nauseam!*

Father Fernández, upon hearing this, once more presented his silly grin, then said to the Indians that he thanked them and loved them but, because he was sick, he had to leave in order to recover. He assured them that he would get well and that he would return, but until that time they should listen to the words of the good Fathers and be good children of Jesus, Mary, and Joseph.

Then he spoke to them in ways I could not understand, in words of their own language which I had never heard before, although it seemed that they readily understood him, hanging on to his every word. Then, at the conclusion of his little homily, he made an odd noise, a sound akin to the braying of a mule, and all the Indians seemed delighted, roared at his bizarre braying. They crowded about him, laughing at his words at the same time that they wept at his departure. Laughing and weeping still, they stood on the shore as he waved farewell, his miserable smile getting fainter and fainter as the launch pulled out into the bay.

I could only gaze in amazement at the strange scene. Even after the Indians were sent back to the Mission and the bay was empty of boats, I stood there on the shore alone, transfixed, contemplating the past events. Father Fernández was a saintly man, perhaps, but completely unsuited for the rigors of Alta California. Then I began to laugh with relief that the last of the conspirators was gone, and I laughed and danced about the rocks, until I felt a sudden piercing in my heart, and I came to a halt with tears in my eyes. I could see the vastness of the bay before me, the azure of the cloudless sky whirling about me, and there in the bright sunlight I could also see the strange grin of the Father of the Mules as if the smile were right before my eyes. I fell to my knees to pray, but, like the other children he had left behind, I too could only whimper as I saw the sky tear apart with that maddening face. I began to sob, my chest heaving, my throat emitting husky, involuntary noises, until I was startled to perceive that my howls also sounded like the braying of a mule. Then I could not help but laugh at the absurdity of it all, how ridiculous I seemed, at the same time that I sobbed, standing there on my knees as I brayed like a mule at the sky above the bay.

But just as suddenly the vision was gone. I composed myself once again, and I prayed that God would return Father Fernández to a sound mind. Then I rose up refreshed, and I turned back to the Mission and to the labor of God's Word, never to see the demented face of Father José María Fernández again.

The Wall

Concerning the Murders of María Antonia
and Blas de Jesús Olivas on August 15, 1828

I can remember nothing of that night except a blackness, a deep, penetrating blackness, and a growl, as if some ferocious animal's roar blocked out all other sounds, all other senses, and filled the night with its violence. I cannot even say it was an animal, but rather it felt like some presence, a dark, indescribable substance, for I cannot remember seeing anything, although I can sense this presence even today, fifteen years after the murders.

That is all I remember. My parents told me that when they came into the house in the morning I was standing against the wall next to the body of my sister and across from the body of my brother. They said that I stood there laughing, laughing incessantly. When they asked me what had happened I told them that a very ferocious coyote had come into the house and that he killed María Antonia and Blas de Jesús.

I was only four years old, and I must have felt this to be true. Perhaps I said it was a coyote because, in my infant mind, that would be the only animal I could imagine to be as ferocious as the black presence that still lingers in my soul, but why I was laughing I do not know. My parents took me to the priest who thought perhaps I was possessed by the Devil or was simply driven to laughter from fright, and he prayed over me, blessed me, exorcised the Evil One until I was well. As I was the only one of their children to survive, my parents were relieved that my mind would be sound. But my ears still filled with the monstrous blackness, most especially when I pressed them to the wall. And so I must confess I am not so sure that the priest succeeded.

Today I am a young man, and I have resolved to stop the horrible roaring in my ears. I hope to leave this hideous nightmare behind, buried, if I may say so, with my poor parents and their children. That is why I have returned from San José to our old home. Although it is but a ruin, it yet stands, most especially the wall, and I have come to tear down the house and its wall. I intend to take each adobe brick and one by one crumble it into powder, so that I can no longer press my ear to that wall and hear the sound of darkness rushing from the blood on both sides.

But I am afraid I am confusing you with all of this, and I must tell you the story. Such a story is not entirely for your benefit or entertainment. I have my reasons for filling your ears with my tale. To succeed in tearing down this wall and the demons it encloses, I must enlist you in my endeavor with the fullest understanding of the vast good you will accomplish. Others must join me in order to win this liberation, or I will undoubtedly fail. Yes, I know, you are only humble *vaqueros*, tanners, sailors—but, although I am no wealthy *don* myself, I shall reward you handsomely with pesos and with plenty of *aguardiente* to drink. Then, after I tell you my story, you will join me in destroying the old house of Ignacio Olivas and his tormented family with full hearts and a promise of more pesos and drink.

Señor, bring us some more bottles of *aguardiente*!

My friends, you shall hear the history of the murder of my sister María Antonia Olivas, five years of age, and my brother Blas de Jesús Olivas, barely one year old. You shall also hear of the trial of the soldier Francisco Rubio and of his execution at the order of "the black governor" Manuel Victoria. Does everyone have a cup that is full? Good. I shall begin.

My father, Ignacio Olivas, was a soldier of the Presidio in

San Francisco. On the night of August 15th, a *fandango* was to be held at the house of Señora Viviana. Francisco Rubio, a soldier in the company, was twenty-six years old and originally from Los Angeles. He came to the door of our house early that night and asked my parents if they were going to the *fandango*. When my father replied that they were in fact planning to attend, Rubio asked if they were going to bring their children. No, they were not. Rubio then suggested that they would be making a gracious contribution to the *fandango* if they brought something to drink. My father knew that sometimes it was hard to find enough *aguardiente*, and he concluded that Rubio's conversation was all aimed at achieving this important result. Yes, my father would bring a bottle, and Rubio, satisfied, took off.

My parents left me and my brother and sister in bed, tied up the front door of our house with a rope, and went to the *fandango*. They danced and drank and celebrated until the break of day, at which time they made their way back to their home. A short distance from our house, near the house of Pablo Pacheco, they saw someone walking across the cement in front of the church, and as they drew near, they saw this person again. My father said that it must be Uncle Teodosio Flores, but my mother said, "What do you mean, Uncle Teodosio? Isn't that Rubio? Yes, that's Rubio."

They continued on to the house and found that the front door was tied as they had left it, but then they noticed that the back door was flung open. My father jumped in, and, as he went to the kitchen to get some light, he heard my mother scream, "Antonia is dead!" They found Antonia on their bed where they had left her, her clothes torn off and the sheet covered with blood; then they found Blas de Jesús dead in the bed that he slept in with me. That is when they discovered me, as I related earlier, laughing and talking of the coyote. When they brought the light closer they saw Antonia's blood had even splattered on the wall. Again, I remember nothing of this, but I tell you what my parents have said and what I have learned from the records of the investigation. I have heard it so many times that I feel that I do remember it, but I must confess that I am very much like you, my friends, a listener to someone else's tale.

The next day Lieutenant Ignacio Martínez, commander of the Presidio, began the investigation by having the Englishman Guillermo Richardson, who had some knowledge of medicine, do the postmortem in the company of two matrons. He reported that Blas de Jesús had many black-and-blue marks on the neck, demonstrating that he had been killed by choking with the hands. Antonia, very pale, had a pink mark on her neck about the size of a peso, indicating that, while she had also been choked, it was done with a cord. On her shoulders were some purple marks, showing that she had been pressed down by someone's hands, and she was scratched all over. The blood issuing from her genital area indicated that she had been raped. Señor Richardson concluded that her death was probably caused by the rape even before the strangulation. Am I being too exact in my description? Perhaps all you need to know is that they were dead and the girl was raped, but I want you to know the details of crime, the burden of it, as I have come to know it, and in that way you too shall seek release with me.

My father told Lieutenant Martínez that Francisco Rubio was the perpetrator of this vile deed. Rubio's question about whether my parents would bring the children to the *fandango* now seemed incriminating in light of the crime. The fact that my parents saw Rubio near the house, that my father testified that Rubio knew very well how to break into the back door, and that Rubio had a fight with my mother only a few days before—all of this cast Rubio in a guilty light.

Esteban, a baptized Indian from the Mission San Rafael,

told Lieutenant Martínez that he too was at the *fandango*. At about nine or ten o'clock that night Francisco Rubio called from outside, and he went to talk with him in the darkness away from the house. "Bring me a shirt!" Rubio cried. Esteban looked at him with some confusion. "Bring me a shirt!" Rubio hoarsely whispered again. "Bring me a shirt!" Esteban quickly took off the one he had on to change with Rubio. Rubio was covered with a *serape*, but Esteban could see he did not have a shirt. The way Rubio talked made Esteban very frightened, and he ran away, pushing through the people at the door, shaking from fear himself because he felt such terrible fright from Rubio.

Juan García told Lieutenant Martínez that the *serape* was his and that Rubio had asked to borrow it that night to dance with it at the *fandango*. Rubio left the *serape* with Rafael Pacheco, who returned it the next day. But Juan García said that when he lent the *serape* there were no bloodstains on it, and the next morning there were. Bloodstains were also found on a sash that Rubio wore around his waist, and bloodstains on the shirt for which he sought a replacement from Esteban.

Lieutenant Martínez ordered Rubio arrested. Nicolás Higuera reported to the Lieutenant that when he and Lázaro Peña took Rubio to the prison, Rubio asked him for some tobacco, which he gave to him. But Higuera's suspicions were aroused when Rubio's hands shook so much that he could not even make his own cigarette. He had never seen Rubio tremble so much, and he could always roll his own cigarettes before.

When they brought Rubio to the prison, Lázaro Peña measured the bottom of his foot to compare it to a footprint they discovered behind the back door of our house. When Peña bent to stretch the string, Rubio's foot trembled and shook so much that Peña had to hold it, which Peña also reported to the Lieutenant. Even more damning, the length of string measuring Rubio's foot matched the length of the footprint in the mud.

Then Rafael García told the Lieutenant that at the beginning of the *fandango* Rubio was quite happy, but some time between nine and ten o'clock at night he left, saying that he was going to look for some *aguardiente* that he had been promised. About two hours later Rafael García said he saw Rubio seated on a cot, covered by a shawl, his hat pulled all the way down over his eyes, and he seemed to be very sad. García went up to him to give him a sip of *aguardiente* and asked, "What's wrong? How come you're so sad? What happened with the brandy you were promised?" Rubio seemed very pensive, and after a little bit he replied that he would bring the *aguardiente* soon. Rafael García thought that all of this was very strange.

When Lieutenant Martínez asked the baptized Indian Esteban, of whom Rubio had demanded a shirt, whether Rubio was a good man, Esteban told him that he was a bad person who was always in jail. Others testified that Rubio had been jailed at San Francisco Solano for having violated an Indian woman named Machora, and he had done the same to another named Samuela. One soldier told the court that he knew of another girl that Rubio had raped and killed. And Sergeant Gaviola, who was assigned to defend Rubio, sought to be excused because he was the prosecutor against the prisoner in a case at the Mission Santa Inés concerning the death of an Indian. Oh, my friends, Esteban was most correct. Rubio was not a good man, and his bad reputation had earned him the nickname of *Coyote*. Yes, they called him by the name of the animal that I had said had come into our house, *El Coyote*. He was wild in his drunkenness, vile in his habits, and furious in his violence. Was he the one I meant when I said a coyote had killed my brother and sister?

When the court took his declaration, Rubio explained that

he was at the *fandango* at the house of Señora Viviana, that he was seated on a cot and was covered with a *serape*, but that when the soldier Rafael García came, he gave him a little *aguardiente* and told him that there was no more because the little bit he had been given was finished. García had promised him a jar, but instead he told Rubio to go get it himself, and so he left and went to the house of gunner Mariano Frías. On his way he met Chief Valencia, who asked him how the *fandango* was. "No good," he told Valencia, "there is no *aguardiente*." Then he continued to the home of Frías. It was about midnight when he got there, and when he looked in the window he saw that Frías was lying down, so he went to the house of Juan Martín to search for *aguardiente*, but he saw that he too was asleep, so he returned to his quarters and entered the kitchen of his captain where he saw the Indian Larios playing cards with someone. "Shall we play?" he asked, but Larios said he was already playing with somebody else. So Rubio told the court that he decided to lie down in the kitchen, and he covered himself over with the shawl. Then the Indians Achilles and Zacharias arrived, and he asked them if the *fandango* had ended. Although they said yes, he got up and went over to the house to discover that it was still going on. He found Rafael García at the door, who told him that there was no more *aguardiente*, but he said it was the morrow and they could get the next day's ration. They went in to the party, but after a little bit he left to go outside to the corner of the house of Chief Pablo to purge his bowels. You see, Rubio explained, this house is next to Ignacio Olivas' house and that must have been when Olivas saw him. Then Rubio went back into the party and called out to the Indian Esteban to try to sell him his shirt so that he could buy some more *aguardiente*. The stains on the shirt? The sash? Rubio told the Lieutenant that they were sheep blood. About three days before the *fandango* he had killed two sheep at the home of Marta Higuera, had dragged away one and left the other for Nicolás Higuera to drain the blood.

So much for the declaration by *El Coyote*. Marta Higuera declared that Rubio had in fact killed only one sheep at her house, and that it had been butchered five or six days earlier and not three, as Rubio had said. Besides, Juan García said he had lent Rubio the shirt only that day, so no blood from any sheep could have stained it whether it was butchered three or six days before.

No, I won't go on with more details. They brought Rubio face-to-face with the witnesses and asked him about all the contradictions, and Rubio answered that he had no hate or ill will towards my father, that he agreed with him except for the matter of his asking about the children, that he denied asking the Indian Esteban three times for a shirt, etc., etc. All of these proceedings took place within days of the crime. And then . . . nothing, nothing at all.

All sorts of irregularities had been discovered in the documents. The Lieutenant had forgotten to swear in the court secretary, words had been crossed out but had not been initialed—things of that sort—and, as a consequence, the proceedings simply came to a halt. Nothing much was done to correct the irregularities, and nothing more was done to prosecute Rubio.

I do not understand why this occurred, except that, as many explained, Governor Echeandía was not particularly attentive to criminal prosecutions, busy as he was with trying to wrest control of the missions from the friars. All I can say is that Francisco Rubio remained a prisoner, although he was allowed to roam about the Presidio even without a guard as he performed personal services for Lieutenant Martínez. He could have easily escaped at any time, but it seems he wanted to demonstrate his innocence, so he worked as a servant, gathering firewood and performing other chores. He was given his rations and was confined at night, but it was almost as if he were free. Perhaps he willingly passed his days in such a manner with the expectation that the Governor would eventually allow such penance to serve as punishment. I do not know why he ceased his notorious drunkenness and violent sprees—except that such excesses might have served to draw attention to himself and therefore forced the proceedings, irregular or not, to go on. Instead, he shuffled with his head bowed, seeking invisibility.

Years passed in such manner—whole years! I remember seeing Rubio walking by our house and my mother grabbing me and pushing me into the doorway. But I peeked out as the murderer of my sister and brother passed, and I could see his head turn, and I could see him smile at my mother with bright teeth, and she would glare at him, her silent fury so intense that I could feel fire spurting from her eyes.

It was during this time, also, that I first heard the wall. I don't remember exactly how it happened, but one day I pressed my face to the wall where the blood had splattered, and it was as if I had cupped a seashell to my ear. I heard roars like the surf as it breaks again and again, and I heard the darkness, and I felt the palpitating presence, the hideous animal presence, and I thought I heard the screams of María Antonia, and I shouted and cried, and I insisted that my mother press her ear also to the wall to listen, but she could hear nothing, nothing but the silence of whitewash on adobe. Although I would shake with fear, I would creep back and press my ear to the wall, trying to hear the sound, listening if I could discern my sister's screams above the din, until I could take it no longer and threw myself to the floor.

My parents showed alarm when I told them of the wall, so I would not listen to it when they could spy me. But when I was alone I would creep to the wall and press my ear against its surface. Instantly I would hear the roar again and, faintly, I could hear my sister's screams. I imagined that the monster and my sister were both trapped in the wall and that my poor sister was trying to escape, that she was calling for me to help her, to pull her from out of the darkness between the inside and outside surfaces. But how? I could do nothing but press my ear to the wall and taste the darkness, breathe the evil, touch the roaring, until I could bear it no longer and would fling myself away.

One day the screams and roar reached a crescendo of deafening magnitude. I could suffer no more and threw myself to the floor. When I got up, I saw *El Coyote* walking past our window with some carpentry tools on his way to repair something for the Lieutenant. I stepped up on the table to look out the window. Rubio saw me and turned towards me, smiling like a saint. For the first time I did not feel afraid of Rubio. For a moment I even thought that perhaps he was not the beast after all. But the moment passed, and I jumped off the table and ran under it.

Time flew—Rubio walked past our house—my ear surreptitiously sought out the voice of my sister—and justice was left forgotten—that is, until General Anastasio Bustamante became president in Mexico City, a man who sought to cool the radical ardors of the republicans. Consequently, a new governor was appointed who would reflect his views, Manuel Victoria. Governor Echeandía, goaded by his *ayudante inspector* José María Padrés, attempted his *golpe de estado* by declaring all the missions to be "secularized" before he left office, so that when Manuel Victoria came, he was *forced* to place all of Alta California under military rule. You know well enough the intrigues that ensued. How the Osios, the Alvarados, the Vallejos, and all the rest of the *dons* hated Victoria. Yes, Victoria was spat upon as a tyrant—but I believe he was wronged!

I have befriended Governor Juan Bautista Alvarado. He has spoken to me at length of those days in '31, and of his hatred of Governor Victoria, and I have learned much. "His Excellency and the reverend friars understood each other perfectly." Don Juan Bautista told me as we sipped our wine at his *rancho*. "Victoria was prepared to issue arbitrary orders, to ignore the rights of the people, to trample upon the immunity of the deputies, provided he was given gold, while the friars were willing to part with their gold, provided the governing authority would close the doors of learning to the people and would preserve to themselves the rights and privileges which had been granted them by an imbecile monarch!" Yes, yes, how Don Juan Bautista hated Victoria as an agent of the Spanish friars!

There were other reasons, of course, why Victoria was detested, which I learned when we beheld his Excellency the first time he came to San Francisco. Everyone gasped in shock as he rode in for his inspection, although by this time we had been forewarned, for, as Don Juan Bautista put it, "my black boots are white when compared to the color of the executive whom President Bustamante sent to govern our poor country!" No one had ever seen a man so black before—we had heard that there was a woman slave from Perú and maybe a prisoner from the French somewhere in the south, and we heard that at Los Angeles some of the settlers were black—we were stunned. I stood frozen in horror, for the only time I had seen such blackness was when I put my ear to the wall and could feel the night of the murders once again. Was Governor Victoria the animal who had come into our home? Was he the beast that raped my sister? Such a thing was absurd, not only because he was such an important man, but simply because he was not even in California when the crimes were committed! Yet his blackness recalled the terror, made me shrink from him as if I had seen the beast within the wall itself. Of course, my parents thought I recoiled for other reasons.

But besides his blackness, the great *dons* hated Victoria

because of their offended sense of democracy and justice. It is true that Victoria did not convene the *diputación*, and it is also true that the governor eventually exiled hotheads like Padrés. But he also came and said, "The laws must be executed, the government obeyed, and our institutions respected" (although Don Juan Bautista, an honorable man, remembers the governor's order more as, "I am the government, and the government, it is I!"). No matter, what was of real importance to me was that the governor paid attention to the efficient operation of the courts, and the criminal case against Francisco Rubio was finally resumed.

All of the irregularities were mulled over again and again, and the defects were ordered to be corrected. But then more objections arose, with Ensign Mariano Vallejo swearing with his hand on his sword that the mistakes in procedure were veritable monstrosities. Doña Josefa Soto, who was one of the matrons called in to observe the medical examination of the cadavers conducted by Guillermo Richardson, testified that she only found out about the murders because it was a matter of public knowledge. "It is true I went to see the bodies," she said, "but I did it as a matter of curiosity and I never did it because I was told that Lieutenant Martínez called me. I did not authorize the oath, nor did they read it to me, and if one of the two crosses on the document is said to have been formed by my hand, it is a lie."

Besides, she declared that somebody else had done the crimes! When her husband was questioned, he said it was Artilleryman Ignacio Higuera! Indeed, this Higuera was facing charges of the rape and death of yet another little girl, the daughter of Antonio Valenzia, the niece of Higuera. Her husband said that he believed that Higuera was the true aggressor because Higuera was even capable of consummating his ugliness against his own blood cousin whose death he caused. It was also known that he had attempted to force himself on the three daughters of Señora Teresa Vejola at their house—and they too were his blood nieces!

The court pressed charges against this artilleryman, but the accusation did not exonerate Rubio, since those crimes were perpetrated elsewhere. But why suddenly were there all these manuevers to lift the guilt from Rubio's shoulders? It seemed that Rubio's years of monklike behavior convinced many that he was not the guilty one! In fact, Rubio appealed to the court that his good conduct served as proof of his innocence. "I would work with a garbage cart," he explained. "I hauled it all the way out to the canyon, and never once did I attempt to escape because I had the hope that someday I would be completely shown to be innocent. I would not have worked as such if I had really, truly been guilty!"

Then José María Padrés (not yet exiled!) reviewed all the evidence of the case, concluding that "without reasonable doubt the prisoner was the perpetrator of the rape. Besides, since the time that it was believed that he did do it, no one else had fallen into even a minimal suspicion." Rodrigo del Pliego, a friend of the governor, defended Rubio, while Padrés (no friend of the governor at all!) did not even argue against Rubio's guilt, only that the irregularities would deem a punishment other than the death penalty.

Governor Victoria took in all the arguments and swiftly made his judgment: Francisco Rubio would go to the chapel to receive his last rites, then the prisoner would be brought before arms behind the house of Ignacio Olivas, and there—against the wall of the very house where he committed the crime—*El Coyote* would be shot!

Despite some last-minute attempts to make appeals to México, the sentence was carried out on the first of August 1831. Francisco Rubio was marched by a company of soldiers to the back of our house, and I watched as they blindfolded him. "You are going to kill an innocent man!" he cried out, and the priest exhorted him to confess and die in conformity with the will of God. "God will reward you for doing this," he said, but Rubio knelt on his knees, ready for the bullets, replying only that the priest should "do that which is holy," and he did not confess. Even I felt sorry for the evil man as the bullets split the morning air and dug into the wall, the same wall that was stained with my sister's blood. Rubio slumped back, his face uplifted and seemingly serene.

Oh, how the *dons* denounced the execution! This was the final outrage against the rights of the Californians—after not calling the deputies, then exiling the republicans. The *dons* were also outraged about another criminal case, denouncing the execution of an Indian in Monterey who, they said, was caught simply stealing buttons. (Yet how they saw only what they wished! The Indian, in fact, had stolen a mountain of goods from the Presidio warehouse. He was found out only because he gambled with some gold buttons—a somewhat different story!) Old Don Juan Bautista Alvarado proclaimed that "Victoria treated us as though we were slaves and not free men with the right to complete enjoyment of all the guarantees which the constitution assured all Mexicans, irrespective of race or residence." And to me he said, "I am sorry, my poor child, for the crime against your brother and sister. But the shooting of Rubio was looked upon as a great horror, for an innocent man was dragged to the wall to be shot!"

Yes, indeed, the execution elicited horror, but Don Juan Bautista, in his inestimable frankness, explained that it was the great task of stealing the missions away from the friars which truly excited the rebels. Señor Alvarado explained how secularization would free the Indians from "the tyrannical tutelage of the Mission fathers." But liberty, equality—all of those grand words imported from France—came down to simple things like soil and sweat. José María Padrés would preach that the Indians' "greatest source of delight consisted in becoming servants of white people. And when they would enter the service of settlers and colonists," he declared, "this would naturally spare the white women a great deal of toil, since the Indian women could, with the greatest of ease, be converted into domestics, laundresses, and cooks," while the Indians' land just as naturally would be taken from their emancipated hands. Am I right, *vaqueros*? Yes, you know the true glory of such grand phrases. On whose *ranchos* do you now herd the cattle? The *ranchos* of Indians? No matter, the execution of Rubio served as the spark, and rebellion took hold of Alta California because of such beautiful words.

Forthwith the manifesto of San Diego was pronounced, the rebels defeated General Victoria at the battle of Cahuenga Pass, and José María Echeandía was once again installed as the enlightened governor. How fitting that the victors shipped the defeated "black governor" back to México on an American bark named the *Pocahontas*, for their victory meant the "liberation" of all of that maiden's race.

"Divine justice was more powerful than the friars," Don Juan Bautista told me. "And what wonderful justice it was. Almost at the same time that Victoria was overthrown, Commandant Ignacio Martínez, the ally of Victoria, was hastily relieved of his command of the Presidio at San Francisco. What a coincidence! The men who had assassinated poor Rubio under the mask of law had to lose their jobs—and soon after Victoria even lost his fortune! Truly, God does not forget rogues!"

All of this was lost to the mind of a small boy. Only years later, talking with Don Juan Bautista Alvarado and with others, did I learn of all this. It was the wall that kept my attention, and soon after the execution I once again placed my ear to its surface. This time the roaring was even louder. The blackness was titanic, and I felt crushed beneath the Sierras of sound that filled my skull. Yet amidst this roaring pandemonium I could still discern my sister's small voice faintly appealing to me—but now I heard yet another voice, a man's voice, and I could not help but realize in an instant that now Rubio had been trapped within the wall. Were my sister's shouts even louder because now she was pursued by her rapist even within the purgatory of the two surfaces? Was Rubio's voice the scream of a man fleeing in terror or the howl of one driven mad by blood lust?

As I listened, I began more and more to be tortured by doubts, by questions that seemed only to become more imponderable as time went on. Did they sentence to death an innocent man? Was Ignacio Higuera really the guilty one? And what of the coyote? Was there really some kind of animal the memory of whose hidden presence remains forever as a fresh wound in my soul?

Then, two years later, an Indian was arrested as a thief and a killer, and at his execution he supposedly confessed to the murders of María Antonia and Blas de Jesús, asking pardon from the priest for allowing an innocent man to be killed. I did not see this execution, and to this day I am not sure that it even occurred. Yet everyone began to believe the rumors that an Indian was the killer of the Olivas children and that Francisco Rubio had indeed been innocent, although no one could ever remember the name of the Indian, or if they did remember, his name was never the same twice. Perhaps the coyote whose presence I felt that night was really the savage grunts of an Indian? What really happened? Was my sister raped? Or did she simply see a hideous blackness and strangle on her own screams? I could answer such questions less and less the more I listened to the wall, for the wall kept on speaking to me of mysteries that wanted to be told and terrors that begged to be released, whether they were the torments of my sister or those of the executed soldier.

Days at a time I could keep my ears away from the wall, but

eventually I would be forced back to the smooth surface with an inevitability that I began to associate with God's will. I had no choice, and I had no right to resist. The wall was the mystery that God gave to me, and I had to give myself to the mystery utterly, or else all of my little world would have been swallowed by the roaring animal trapped within the wall, and my mother, my father, everyone would have become nothing but tiny voices screaming for me to save them when I could do nothing but listen again and again.

Eventually, we moved to San José, leaving the house, like the rest of the Presidio, to ruin. But my heart was never at peace—although when I pressed my ear to the wall of our new home there was a silence that brought tears of relief to my eyes. I knew that the wall still stood and that my sister and Francisco Rubio were still trapped with the monster inside, and I knew that I would have to listen, one way or another, again. I knew that if I listened once again, even to a moldering ruin, I would hear the screams. I knew that they waited for me.

But now I am a young man, able to understand and to control myself, and I am certain that it is not God's will that I must helplessly listen. I must release the poor souls within the wall, and thereby release myself from the wall's curse, and the only way to accomplish this is to tear it down completely and to scatter its dust to the wind. And if their howls are to survive, let them be heard by everyone who passes through the dust of the Presidio, for I should not be the only one who must witness their torment.

This, you see, is why I have asked you to help me. Certainly, I am young and have the strength to tear down this house myself—but I will not have the will! As soon as I approach the wall I know that I will lose control of myself. I will not be able to keep from throwing myself against it to listen, and this time I am afraid I would never be able to pull myself away, that I would die with my ear against the wall. Do you understand? My soul would be sucked into its spaces, and I would want to die as soon as possible, if I were to cling to the adobe! Then I would be able to rescue my sister, or so I would think when under the power of the wall's sorcery, and I would not be able to resist. I feel this would happen with absolute certainty. Even now I must resist running to the Presidio by myself, for no amount of *aguardiente* has lessened the power of the wall.

That is why you must help me. I must be there when you tear down that wall, or else I will not be truly released—but you must tie me by a strong rope to a nearby tree as you do it. No matter how I writhe, no matter how I kick like a mule, no matter how I scream and plead to have my bonds loosened, you must not free me! Not until you have pulled down all of it and scattered its dust! Perhaps you do not believe my tale, but you must promise me you will do exactly as I say!

Cannibal in California

This manuscript, entitled "Sam Brannan's Law" and, parenthetically, "or, Sam Brannan's Crime?" was written by William "Cannibal" Eliot on board the *George Washington* while sailing from San Francisco to Panama between July and August 1851. This fragment of a projected larger work, entitled *Cannibal in California*, was discovered only in 1989 and is published here for the first time with only minor editorial changes. Additional details on the recovery of the manuscript are presented at the conclusion of the narrative.

Sam Brannan's Law
(or, Sam Brannan's Crime?)

The *Brooklyn* Mormons

When the *Brooklyn*, with Samuel Brannan and his tribe of 240 Mormons, arrived at Oahu on June 20, 1846, all the white people assembled at the dock to see the young "Elder" lead his flock down the gangplank. The visitors received garlands of leis around their necks from pretty Kanaka girls, and the guests were surprised and delighted. The Mormons were merrily welcomed to the Sandwich Islands by its white citizens, who, unfamiliar with the sect, were happy to see so many Americans, particularly of the fair sex, and the visitors were driven off to homes of missionaries, whalers, and merchants in landaus and phaetons to be plied with luaus, excursions to Pali, walks to Waikiki, etc.

I was introduced to Samuel Brannan at one luau. He was, naturally, taken aback at my countenance, and I had to explain how it came to pass that I had tattoos crossing my eyes like some barbaric mask. I told him my tale: Harvard College, reading philosophy, law . . . Shipped out on the whaler *Rachel* to seek adventure, to chase a blubbery Leviathan instead of contemplating Hobbes' oily beast . . . Captured on Hatutu by natives when *Rachel* watered, confined by them for two years . . . Tattooed, despite my protestations and vain resistance, when adopted by natives, "married" . . . Finally, I escaped aboard the whaler *Harriet* and was brought to the Sandwich Islands, emaciated, ill. Now recovering, I told Mr. Brannan that I desired to leave, to go home to the United States, and that money from my parents having arrived, I hoped to depart soon. "In any case, sir, this accounts for my strange appearance. I am a Christian and a white man tattooed like a savage. And in this way I must live the rest of my life."

Mr. Brannan's eyes grew wide at my tale, then they flashed over with that typical film of horror and revulsion I had long come to recognize. "No," I answered those eyes, "I did not eat the flesh of humans. I was spared that abomination."

Sam Brannan was a young man, in his late twenties I reckoned, who had dark eyes, a booming voice, and a flashing Irish personality, although I learned he actually hailed from the coast of Maine, a fellow New Englander. He commanded respect, wielded power. People were attracted to him like moths to flame. Visionary, crude, bold, arrogant, egotistical, driven, compassionate, bombastic, quick tempered, sentimental, kind—he was immensely attractive, yet I was frightened to get too close to such a cocked revolver.

Mormons? People on the Sandwich Islands had heard little of the sect. When asked about Mormonism, Brannan kept tight lipped, only saying, "Our faith is to mind our own business." I had heard about the practice of plural wives—but it seemed only a salacious rumor, since the ladies appeared modest, unpromiscuous, for the most part. Besides, given my own experience, I did not feel so shocked, nor could I afford to be. Some of the whalers said the Latter-Day Saints had yet another Testament written, which was added to the Old and New ones. As I was having trouble digesting the first two, I had no desire to dine on yet a third.

I was introduced to Captain A. Richardson of the *Brooklyn*, who, upon hearing my tale, signed me up as part of the crew to work my way to California, where they were bound to deliver their colonists. The Mormons were going to build their own colony, a New Jerusalem, fleeing their persecutors in the United States. As I learned later, it was a kind of filibuster scheme, Brannan figuring he could grab a portion of California from Mexico to establish his Kingdom. Brannan was to "prepare a place" for the rest of the sect, who left from Nauvoo, Illinois, to cross overland to the New Zion. When Brannan left New York, war with Mexico had not yet begun. Now it looked like the Mormons might have some competition.

On board the *Brooklyn*, I watched this compact colony of Saints thrive—two children born on board, a boy named Atlantic and a girl named Pacific to honor the two oceans on which they were respectively born—and I also watched this compact colony come apart at the seams.

At first, Brannan had the women sew up uniforms and a corps of seventy men would drill on deck, taught by a deserter from the U.S. Army. This became most worrisome to Captain Richardson, who feared some kind of mutiny, and he soon padlocked the arms and forbade shipboard drill. It seems Brannan had stowed arms on board secretly.

Immediately, there was scandal over the fair sex. One Lucy Eagar garnered much attention, and with reason. I noticed some trysts, passionate embraces, and such like, which were hard to hide on a crowded ship. More importantly, I overheard heated talk about plurality, lust, sin. Apparently, the sect debated the wisdom of polygamy, perhaps something interpreted from their new scripture. Brannan seemed to be opposed to the practice. Some of the sect grumbled over his despotic hand and the privileges he took for himself—particularly the fact that he ate at the Captain's table, that his family was provided with far roomier accommodations than the cramped, fetid quarters of his flock. Brannan spoke about "backbiters and evildoers." Good thing the Captain locked up the rifles.

The Captain did not like Lucy Eagar boldly seducing the men and arousing the ire of the women, so he got several sailors to spy on her. They reported goings-on between her and Elders Moses and Pell. Sam Brannan ordered a trial. Captain Richardson acted as judge, and Sam as prosecutor. Henry Harris, who had studied some law in Honolulu, acted as attorney for the defense. (Harris had become enamored of a pretty *Brooklyn* girl in Honolulu, and, after influential members of the expedition pressed Mr. Brannan to allow him to join the association, he paid his fifty dollars for passage, although he was not a Mormon.) The sailors told their eyewitness tales of Lucy Eagar and her conquests. Verdict: Guilty. The young Elder excommunicated Lucy, Moses, and Pell for "wicked and licentious conduct of the most disgusting nature." Open dissension, with Harris stirring up discord, and about a third of the passengers fumed against Sam Brannan. (I suppose the Captain, as absolute monarch on the seas, can judge a dispute in an ecclesiastical corporation. But what was the crime? Seduction or plural wives?)

"Damn that flag!"

End of July, we sight shore. Captain Richardson orders the Mormons down the hatches as we pass the Mexican fort, fearful of bombardment. We round a nub of land, heading for Yerba Buena cove. A sloop of war rides at anchor, with a village of about a dozen structures emerging from the mist.

A squat adobe house—the Mexican Customhouse—is prominent.

What, ho! On the Customhouse flies the American flag! "Damn that flag!" Brannan explodes when he sees Old Glory through his glass. Somebody else took California ahead of him. I did not hear him say it myself, but the Captain told me afterward. Apparently, either Mr. Brannan wanted to plant the Mormon flag for his independent theocracy or he had worked up some secret arrangement with Commodore Stockton in Oahu to be the first to seize Yerba Buena for America. Instead, the Navy beat him by about three weeks.

Lieutenant Misroon from the *Portsmouth* boards the *Brooklyn* and welcomes us to the United States of America! I had thought that once I disembarked at Yerba Buena I would have to travel far from California to get to my own country. It was an illusion. My country had traveled to me.

Captain John B. Montgomery, master of the *Portsmouth*, probably felt some nervousness in granting permission for the *Brooklyn* to port because of the rumors of the Mormons as a wild, desperate people, unreliable and troublesome. While Captain Montgomery reviewed Brannan's papers, he invited the Mormons to a Sunday Sabbath on board the *Portsmouth*. I joined Captain Richardson and huddled with the sailors and Marines during the socializing after the brief service. "Damn, they look just like other women!" the crew muttered. Legend had it that Mormon women had abnormally elongated teats and that, as one of the Marines said, "Reckon the wives on the outside of the bed clutch for dear life, as they are liable to fall to the cold floor, while the ones on the inside git all the warmth."

The sailors and Marines, overall, were disappointed with the normal-looking Mormon females, although they were pleased to see white women from home instead of Indian harlots. (There were only two white women in Yerba Buena at the time!) The *Portsmouth*'s crew, however, was mighty amazed at my face. Of course, I heard the inevitable question, and I began to reply that "the natives only ate the flesh of their enemies to gain their magic power. It was not their daily diet . . ." I had intended to say more, to declare my good fortune in not being forced to partake of their sacred feasts (as well as not becoming the main course for any of them), but instead I grew suddenly reticent, reluctant to explain anything, although I had no rational reason for halting, and so, there was nothing but awkward silence. "Mate," one old salt finally broke the spell, "if you do happen to have et long pork, just remember you got no cause to hanker me as your enemy." The crew broke into laughter at that, and I smiled with them, although I still kept from actually confirming or denying what it was I did "happen to have et."

As a result of this encounter, my reputation as a flesh-eater was established, along with my nickname. I became a man people desired as a friend—and not just in order to practice Christian charity to a forever-scarred survivor rescued from heathens—for to be my enemy held out the possibility of getting "chawed to the bone" in the middle of the night. Murdering me would solve nothing, because the superstition had it that I would return somehow to partake of my meal. Sam Brannan, of course, knew better, but even the other Mormons eventually began to believe the legend of "Cannibal," and I began to be treated with a combination of pity, incomprehension, abomination, attraction, fascination, disgust, awe, fear, respect. The less I spoke, the more deference with which I was treated, so much so that I spoke less and less, until I attained a profound reticence, almost the hush of a monk, which, of course, only served to make me even more of a spectral figure, my eyes peering silently from behind tattoos, and, as a result, I gained a solemn distinction amongst the hide merchants, sailors, Indians, and Mexicans of Yerba Buena—for, very shortly, no man of the small village considered it worthwhile to count himself my enemy, and "Cannibal" was treated with careful kindness wherever I went.

On Monday, Captain Montgomery gave the *Brooklyn* its landing permits, and the pilgrims unloaded chests, bags, trunks, children's toys, bird cages, cats, dogs, a pet monkey, chickens, geese, pigs, a hundred tents, two flour mills, dozens of plows, scores of picks and shovels, hundreds of cooking utensils, barrels of wine, a printing press with boxes of type and cans of printing ink, along with more than a hundred rifles, with bars of lead and powder kegs—and three cannons. In short, all the tools needed to establish their New Zion were spread before the amazed villagers, and soon the Mormons were camped in their tents arrayed in military fashion on the sand hills by the beach, while Brannan and his family took rooms in the only grand edifice in the village, the *casa grande* of William Richardson (no relation of the *Brooklyn's* captain), the Englishman Master of the Port who had come to Yerba Buena ten years earlier.

Trial by Jury

However, dissension did not cease. Lucy Eagar, joined by Mary Addison, approached Captain Montgomery to complain of Brannan's tyranny, and the representative of the United States insisted on reviewing the notes of the trial kept by Elder Brannan. After careful perusal of these notes, and interviews with Captain Richardson and Mr. Brannan—and after hearing two days of witnesses for both sides!—Captain Montgomery gave his approval to the proceedings and the judgment. (Is it the purview of the United States government to approve excommunication?) The next day Brannan struck back, calling together the leaders of his band to excommunicate Elisha Hyatt, James Scott, and Isaac Addison for fomenting rebellion and bearing false witness! Drilling his seventy soldiers in the village square (the Mormon militia was quickly drafted to defend against the feared Mexican counterattack), Sam Brannan held the reins tightly over the majority of his followers.

Within a short time, Mr. Brannan had the flour mill and the printing press operating, embarked on a farm at the junction of the San Joaquin and Stanislaus rivers, which he called "New Hope," and was preparing to start up a newspaper. Trade was increasing. There were perhaps four or five battered hulks in the harbor when we first arrived, but two months later there were thirty ships. The Mormon colonists included a saddler and an apothecary, bakers, coopers, surveyors, gunsmiths, carpenters, masons, cobblers, tanners, a weaver, a silversmith, a watchmaker, a cigarmaker, and a brewer—and several attorneys-at-law. The sleepy village at the end of the world was quickly changed into a small town bustling with commerce and construction.

I took board at the Portsmouth House (John H. Brown, proprietor) and soon lapsed into fevers, nausea, and other symptoms of the tropical malaise from which I had, evidently, not yet fully recovered. Captain Richardson found a new sailor at one of the grog shops to take my place on the *Brooklyn*. "Go home to yer kin, my boy, after you heal up," he told me. "Go back to Boston for the tender stroke of yer dear mother's hand."

I began to recover and, though still in a weakened state, I started to move about, to watch the city bloom like a field of flowers, with Sam Brannan either as the most beautiful and grandest blossom of the valley or the most vile and pernicious weed. His enemies still ranged against him, and even new rivalries were formed.

Washington A. Bartlett, as a lieutenant on the *Portsmouth*, was appointed alcalde, which is the mayor under the Mexican system that the military still observed. Alcalde Bartlett insisted on Brannan's, getting the customary Yerba Buena initiation after the Elder officiated at the first wedding of white people in the village (a Mormon contract between an old trader from the West and the girl child of a widow). The initiation consisted of the new resident crossing the plaza to touch the flagpole while blindfolded. That day (as, in fact, every day) the plaza was filled with an oozy mud pool, several feet deep, and Sam Brannan, resolutely drunk, his eyes securely covered, was twirled about and set on his way. Of course, he stumbled into the mud pool and wallowed in the muck amidst howls of laughter. But then Brannan crawled up, daintily smoothed the ooze off his clothes, and continued to search for the shaft. Still blindfolded, he grabbed the pole. "Drinks on me!" Brannan bellowed out as he tore the blindfold off of his eyes and headed for the saloon. Sam thoroughly enjoyed the rough horseplay, although Bartlett was chagrined that the Elder had bettered him.

Soon afterwards, Mr. Henry Harris—who my Reader may recall had been the defense attorney in the Lucy Eagar excommunication trial—approached Mr. Brannan and declared that, due to lack of cash, he and his bride had decided to return East to work at his father-in-law's store in Boston. Harris asked permission to draw out of the colony, which was granted, but then asked Brannan to pay him the share of the common stock to which he was entitled. Mr. Brannan refused, as there were no community funds to divide after the association had payed its debts, adding, "Harris, you've been supported out of the community stock of provisions, and you've received thereby a great deal more than your services have been worth. I wouldn't pay a nickel even if I did have it." Sharp words were exchanged between the two, and the next day Mr. Harris went to Alcalde Bartlett to summon Mr. Brannan to court. The action was not raised against the association but against Brannan as an individual who had usurped all power.

Disregarding all Mexican forms, Washington Bartlett, a pompous naval officer who knew almost nothing of law, called for an American jury trial, the first to be held in our newly seized territory. This first jury trial was even more of a sensation than the first wedding, and the little, stuffy mud-floored courtroom was packed, while Indians, Kanakas, and even the town's only Chinaman pushed through the windows and doorway to catch a glimpse of the exotic ceremony held before Alcalde Bartlett as judge. Lawyer George Hyde presented the case for the plaintiff with some eloquence, Colonel C. W. Russell served as counsel for the defendant, and a jury was quickly empaneled.

The articles of agreement, George Hyde explained to the half-drunk jury, included stipulations that the association would, as a group, pay the debt of transportation to the colony and that, in exchange, members would give the proceeds of their labor for three years to a common fund from which all were to have a living—all of which seemed acceptable, even admirable. However, common sense would have it that if a member were to freely withdraw from the association, he would be assigned an equitable portion of the fund upon the dissolution of the bond. "Yet Mr. Samuel Brannan refuses this common justice, this standard act of fair play, holding all funds under his imperious control." And to revile him more, the plaintiff then presented other articles to illustrate the self-serving nature of Mr. Brannan's interest in the contract, which also stipulated that if the "Saints" were to depart from the covenants, the common property was to rest with the Elders, and if the Elders themselves were to fall from grace, the common fund of "Sam Brannan and Company" was to pass to the First Elder, Mr. Brannan. (The corporation was called "Sam

Brannan and Company," indicating the degree to which Mr. Harris was not far afield, morally, if not legally, in challenging the Elder as an individual, as Mr. Brannan identified so intimately the public weal with his own private desires.)

Mr. Brannan led his defense, speaking with great eloquence on his own behalf, as he launched salvo after salvo: Figures were presented to show that all passage money, tithes, and other income had been absorbed by expenses of the journey, leaving nothing to be divided; the agreement was for the term of three years and therefore "could not be broken"; besides which, the plaintiff could not produce a written contract, so there was, in fact, no binding agreement to dispute; in addition to which, Mr. Harris was neither a Mormon nor a member of the communal organization, and therefore had no basis to sue even if he could produce a contract. The jury—ignorant, confused, crowded uncomfortably, boozy and bleary, and unable to leave their seats because of the press of attendance—huddled together quickly to reach their verdict: Not guilty. "The truth was mighty and prevailed!" Sam Brannan pronounced, and the crowd cheered the climax of the drama. "I invite you all—judge, jury, even you, Mr. Harris, everyone—to join me for drinks, on me!" All retired to the saloon, with the exception of Henry Harris, who preferred to nurse his wounds in private.

As my old professor, Theophilus Parsons, would intone, "Almost the whole procedure of human life implies—or, rather, is—the continual fulfillment of contracts." Indeed, this first but highly irregular jury trial in California hammered this "procedure of human life" into the foundations of the new territory's law, with Sam Brannan convincing the new polity of the reality, adherence, absence, transcendence, or violation of all covenants. He was either God, Moses, Jesus, or Satan—or all of them combined!

However, I was not the only one suspicious of the Elder.

While Mr. Brannan won the trial, he did not win the confidence of his opponents, who reviled him with even greater vigor. By the end of 1846, twenty "went astray after strange gods, serving their bellies and lusts," as the Elder expressed it, which meant they settled on their own, caring for their business and their faith apart from his instructions, although Brannan still commanded the allegiance of the bulk of the settlers.

Yerba Buena

Meanwhile, the village grew, and Alcalde Bartlett ordered an extension of the existing survey of the town, which was undertaken by Mr. Jasper O'Farrell, an Irish surveyor. The survey was completed in 1847, and the new map conferred on the streets the names of those men prominent before and after the American conquest. Montgomery, Kearny, Stockton, and other officers of the Army and Navy were honored, as were landed notables such as Sutter and Vallejo. Streets were also named after the merchants, such as Howard, Leavenworth, Hyde—and Brannan. Without the discomfit of being dead, Brannan could enjoy the prospect of a future street (as yet a dirt path) emblazoned with his own name. All the leading citizens were accorded such an honor, which had the effect of crowding events that had just entered into history into the first flush of the future. I could feel the distinction blur between Mr. Brannan as the private man and the public locus.

Indeed, the merchants, with Samuel Brannan preeminent, held the destiny of the little port in their hands. When the name of the village was changed to San Francisco (in order to prevent the name's appropriation by a competing village from across the bay), the first laws for the new American city were adopted. Appropriately, the very first law was designed "to prevent the desertion of seamen," enacting fines for "any person within the limits of this Town" who enticed sailors from their ships and for those persons who "shall feed, harbor, or employ" runaway sailors without permission of the alcalde, while those sailors who deserted their ships would face up to six months of hard labor. As Kearny explained, San Francisco was "destined to become the commercial emporium of the western side of the American continent," and the merchants, well aware of the need to attract whalers, traders, and other ships, sought to reassure all captains that theirs was the port of preference over Honolulu. If sailors freely deserted, this "commercial emporium" would wither and die. In this way, life was breathed into law from the lungs of the marketplace.

Sam Brannan, opposed to the restrictions of military rule, campaigned to remove Lieutenant Bartlett as alcalde, and George Hyde was elected in his place. Early in 1847 General Kearny decreed that the considerable area of land fronting on the cove that had been reserved for use by the federal government would be sold in order to raise finances for the new town. Alcalde Hyde carried out the order by selling lots directly at first, then later by conducting public auctions. The merchants quickly divided into factions over land speculation. One faction, spurred on by Brannan's *California Star*, favored development at the beach and mudflats of the "old town" fronting on Montgomery Street; the other, led by the town's second newspaper, the *Californian*, supported Hyde in favoring development at Clark's Point. Brannan accused Hyde of being part of a clique trying to take over all the beach and water lots for speculation, while Brannan himself was busy buying plots for his own schemes. The *Star* beat the drum loudly, trumpeting accusations that San Francisco was beset by crime, that our town was "becoming a Sunday resort of noisy drunken and profane Indians and Kanakas" because of Hyde's misrule.

Meanwhile, in March, the *Thomas H. Perkins* arrived from New York with Colonel Stevenson and the first detachment of the New York Volunteers. The New Yorkers, mostly mechanics and single men, had enlisted to serve during the war and, when peace would come, to be disbanded in California to remain as permanent settlers. With the runaway sailors in the grogshops by the beach, the regiment added hundreds of young men to the population, and unchecked rowdiness flourished—but, as yet, there were very few crimes, despite the outraged editorials in the *Star*. Still, Mr. Brannan would never forget who sided against him, and George Hyde (lawyer for the plaintiff in the Henry Harris lawsuit) remained a constant target for being responsible for the "lawlessness" of drunken Indians and runaway sailors.

When Councilman Leidesdorff, a mulatto from the West Indies, got in a fight with a gambler in the City Hotel over a horse race, both combatants were brought to Alcalde Hyde, who bound both parties to keep the peace. Leidesdorff became so enraged at Hyde's evenhandedness he proclaimed that "there is no law here but club law, and I mean to go armed and shoot anyone that offers to insult me." Eventually, Governor Mason ordered Alcalde Hyde investigated, after continual complaints of misconduct lodged by Sam Brannan's faction, but no wrongdoing was ever discovered, although Hyde, disgusted with the political bickering, resigned later that year. Leidesdorff's cry for "popular justice," however, would continue to echo, with official and unofficial notions of justice jockeying for legitimacy in the public mind.

When word came of the Donner party's disaster, Mr. Brannan called a mass meeting at Portsmouth Square and made an impassioned speech. The citizens were horrified at the plight of the immigrants, their tale now known throughout the world. Grown men shed tears and gasped in revulsion when they heard of the pitiful cannibalism of the survivors, who ate the flesh of children, fathers, and mothers in order to survive. I walked up to Sam Brannan and, without saying a word, thrust some money into his extended hat, while the crowd in tearful silence watched "Cannibal" show kindness for his cursed kin. Brannan quickly raised fifteen hundred dollars to give to the stranded unfortunates upon their rescue. We were all agitated by the horrible stories of the doomed immigrants, but I stood in that crowd once again amazed at Sam Brannan, how he would always place himself in the center of any activity, define it, appropriate it. Was he propelled by civic responsibility or by an obsession to lead? And, as a consequence, did he expect to reap the rewards of leadership? In this regard, he was no different than any of the other "leading lights" in San Francisco, but he seemed to seize opportunities with such gusto, tenacity, and ubiquity that he outstripped all others.

I observed all of this—the quick growth of the town, the speculation and bickering, the hasty engineering of streets and social preeminence, etc.—with aloofness, protected somewhat from any show of factionalism by my weak health, my disfigured face, and my reputation. I could float, like some ghostly Ancient Mariner, amongst grogshops, council meetings, wharfs, soldiers' tents, or Mormon prayers, always noticed but unhindered, hardly speaking a word but listening to all.

A Daintier Meal

Then Mr. Brannan approached me in April. He explained that there were problems with "New Hope," the farm he had established, and that he was going to travel there to resolve them, then go on to rendezvous with Brigham Young, the President of his sect, who had set out for and was fast approaching the basin of the Great Salt Lake in his quest for a New Zion.

"Cannibal," he said. "I want you to help with letters and accounts at the grist mill and the newspaper while I'm gone. I've seen your hand, and I am well aware that you are an educated and accomplished man, notwithstanding your 'conversion' by savages, and I know that, despite your family's stipend, you can stand for remuneration. You may wonder why I would entrust a portion of my affairs with you, but I have known you and observed you since the Sandwich Islands, and I put little stock in the fanciful stories about you. Besides, you don't talk much at all, and I figure you would not divulge my affairs too readily, a virtue which I regard most highly. Well, Cannibal, what do you say?"

I could not think for the moment. "If you prefer," I finally replied, still unaware of having made the decision. Thus began my employment with "Sam Brannan and Company."

New Hope was filled with greed and dissension, which Brannan tried to remedy with an iron hand, then he traveled on to John Sutter's New Helvetia. How much he wanted New Hope to be as prosperous a manor as Sutter's estate, which even had Russian cannons and a hundred Kanakas in uniforms as soldiers to guard the Swiss baron's domain, but New Hope proved hopeless, racked as it was by human frailties.

Then, as Brannan crossed the Sierras through huge drifts of snow, he came upon the miserable shacks and cabins of the Donner party with the unburied remains of the dead scattered in the snow. Nearby remained the last member of the party, the German by the name of Lewis Keseberg, of whom survivors at Sutter's had told awful tales, accusations of murders and lust for human flesh. Previous rescue parties had refused him help, abandoning the feeble wreck of a man to seek his own way out of the mountains. Brannan, however, shared his food with Keseberg, who, eventually, and miraculously, managed to crawl into Sutter's Fort. Only Samuel Brannan reached out a hand of mercy to this pitiable wretch, who was soon regarded as a despised outcast by all Californians. "The man must be cursed enough," Mr. Brannan explained when he told of this encounter. "If anyone required Christian charity,

Lewis Keseberg was the man. Besides, Cannibal, you should be familiar enough with both the power of social opprobrium and the terrors of eating human flesh."

"If you say so," I replied.

"If I say so, indeed!" Brannan exploded. "Just remember, Cannibal, when I am opposed or reviled or, worse yet, plain forgot, remember that I was the only man who showed mercy to that miserable creature. I have shown you at least as much kindness, and I ain't got eaten yet!" He chuckled at his wit. "Besides, I know well enough what it means to be either the eater or the eaten, for commercial life is only a daintier meal than the one Keseberg may have digested—but a meal nonetheless! Others swear they swallow only air, while I can plainly see their mouths are gorged with flesh!"

I was surprised by the vehemence with which Brannan defended the outcast, but perhaps the outburst was explained by the disappointment he felt when he had finally encountered Brigham Young. There, amidst the alkali desert wasteland, the prophet had outstretched his hands and said, "This is the place!" The Great Salt Lake became the "gathering place" for the sect and not California, despite Brannan's remonstrances. Brannan was puzzled and vexed that Mr. Young had chosen such a barren land instead of lush California, but the prophet had purposely chosen a place far from other human habitation, a place that would require hard work, an isolated desert place that would keep away persecutors who would otherwise surround the faithful in fecund California with hatred and temptation. In such a way Brigham Young had chosen to protect the piety of his followers.

No, the Great Salt Lake was not the place for Sam Brannan. Downcast, he left for the trip back to San Francisco, not yet an apostate but an Elder whose faith was seriously shaken. He had believed California held so much promise, more than the New Zion in the desert, so he could not accept the leader's decision, who said the choice was made by the Lord and not by him. "Watch. They will have such sorrow trying to till that alkali soil that they'll be coming to San Francisco within a year," Brannan said upon his return.

"Yes," I said, "I'll watch," and I moved to the window to stare at some New York Volunteers who were putting on an extemporaneous pugilistic display in the street.

Gilded Scrotums

On his way back to San Francisco, he arranged with John Sutter to establish a store at his fort, creating a partnership with another businessman, Charles Smith, and naming the new enterprise "C. C. Smith and Company." With Young and his Saints planted at the Great Salt Lake, he disbanded New Hope and dissolved "Sam Brannan and Company," selling off wheat, pigs, lots, wagons, a library, the launch *Comet*, and other properties, with the loyal brethren receiving a share of the cash. Whatever could not be sold fell into Brannan's hands, which again caused resentments among his followers, although he continued to collect tithes for the Lord. I could see, as I handled certain of his affairs, how Brannan would take these offerings and re-invest them in other enterprises, the distinction between his communal task and his private affairs gone altogether. I said nothing as the tithes continued, for Brannan was still head of the Mormons in San Francisco.

Brannan arranged for unemployed Mormons to work for Sutter, building his mill, and they are the ones who should be credited with discovering gold flakes in their traces in January 1848. Rumors of gold began to circulate, of course, but no one paid much attention to them. "Sutter showed me some flakes," Mr. Brannan told me long after the gold mania began. "He swore me to secrecy, since he was afraid that the discovery would cause hordes to overrun his empire—which, in fact, is exactly what happened. But I made plans. Now you understand why I bought up every pan, pick, shovel, and sundry supply and then hauled them off to the store at Sutter's, although at the time it no doubt seemed a singularly strange business decision. I knew you were perplexed, although, as usual, you said nothing. Then I sent some Mormons up to pan for gold at Mormon Island, and the evidence was overwhelming. This would be a new El Dorado, and it would not be long before the news got out."

Still, Brannan kept his secret, and I remember now how he clucked to himself when Edward Kemble, the editor of his own *California Star*, editorially dismissed the rumors as "a superb take in as ever was got up to guzzle the gullible." By March, Brannan felt the time was ripe. With a small quinine bottle filled with gold dust, he paraded up and down Portsmouth Square, his voice booming, "Gold! Gold! There's gold in the American River!"

"Yes, indeed, I announced the gold even if I didn't discover it," he told me. "But I knew there was gold in the streams, and there would be more gold in the streams of gold hunters heading for the hills as well. I aimed to collect from both veins!"

Within two weeks of Brannan's parade down Montgomery Street, all of San Francisco had cleared out. When the treasure hunters sought equipment and supplies, they learned that Sam Brannan had the only stocks around. I suppose this was no crime, only the shrewd workings of the business mind to corner the market. But to me it felt like a conspiratorial entrapment, a snare he devised to scoop up adventurers from all corners of the globe. He had engineered the world to his command. History was a theatrical performance, and Brannan was its dramaturge.

Soon both newspapers closed, and there were only seven other white men left in town. I too packed up and headed for the hills to seek my fortune. There I stayed, bending over the streams for months (the tale of my toil and many adventures in the gold country to be recounted in a later chapter). The Chileans, who were amongst the first outsiders to arrive, taught us to hold our dust in the stomach of a ram because of the organ's ability to hold every drop of powder. As the hills filled with Argonauts, however, it became fashionable to hold your treasure in yet another seamless container, the scrotum of a dead man. I took up this fashion both for the scrotum's utility as a purse and because it added to my reputation, which proved a kind of gold itself. No one jumped my claim, no one robbed my stash. Cannibal was left alone amongst desperadoes simply because of his awful face and the rumor that, whether he was alive or dead, his enemies would be "chawed to the bone."

Betimes, however, I lapsed again into sickness and had to leave the diggings in a weakened state. And so, I set off for San Francisco once more, there to recover and, this time, to head for my Boston home. In Boston I expected, despite my tattoos, to be afforded comfort and respect, for I would return with my fortune made. It would little matter that Cannibal had the mark of the savage across his face or the scrotums of dead men in his hands. In those little packets rested the fine powdered lust of the world, and Cannibal would be accounted a gentleman and a Christian by simply opening them up and sprinkling their contents before the eyes of civilization.

The Lord's Receipt

When I returned to San Francisco in April 1849, I found a city utterly transformed by the flood of Argonauts come from every corner of the earth. Hindoos, Englishmen, Chileans, Chinamen, Malays, Frenchmen, Americans—the streets were filled with a wild congress of nations, a dazzling circus of costumes, of sombreros, turbans, pigtails, a spectacle almost entirely composed of men—young men, lusty and filled with life, who sought their dreams in gold, along with the gamblers and other attendant sharks who fished for their own fortunes in the turbid, fantastical waters of those dreams.

So many men! Females were so rare that when a fair maiden passed by the waters would part as if before Moses, and a hush would befall the grizzled horde, their caps meekly and expectantly in their hands, even if the damsel were nothing more than a harlot. Some counted no more than two dozen white women in the city, while the male population reached tens of thousands, with each day hundreds more gold seekers streaming off ships that came from all corners of the earth.

Perhaps the revolutions of Europe had shaken the world, but never had so many revolved around the globe in order to shore up the foundations of civilization with the mortar of gold. This was a revolution to match any by Danton or Marat; this was a frenzy that would tear down whole rivers in order to extract the mortar that would build up its possessor into prince, pasha, or plenipotentate; and in the course of this mighty river of men, San Francisco sprouted like some weed on a tropic isle, although the sweet mint, the "yerba buena" of the little village I saw from the deck of the *Brooklyn*, was long gone, stamped out by the tread of countless pilgrims. Shacks were built up overnight; the hills and sand dunes sprawled with tents; hundreds of abandoned hulks rotted in the harbor or were dragged to the shore to serve as stores and saloons, their crews having deserted to the gold country long before; the unpaved streets were so deep with mud that horses would lose their footing and nearly drown in the muck. San Francisco became the city of desires, of hopes, of hungers, of lusts, a city bounded now by ancient glories and modern desperadoes, all etched with bold words—Argonauts, Midas, Mammon, Golden Calf—vibrant legends that stretched across the city like the crazy outline of its tents, saloons, bordellos, and gambling dens. San Francisco had become, overnight, a myth.

Oh, rare is the chance for a man to live a myth; but how much better is a myth lived in the poem than in the flesh . . .

After I took rooms and rested, I walked along the wharves, which were busy with boatmen—uneasy Chileans and glaring Yankees, mainly discharged members of Stevenson's regiment (whose faces I recognized)—unloading passengers and freight as merchants clambered over goods with prices as high as the Sierras, if not the moon. There I spied Samuel Brannan once again, as he stood amongst a crowd, haggling with an auctioneer over bales of tea. The crowd stepped back as I approached, the many newcomers unfamiliar with this strangely tattooed white man.

When Mr. Brannan saw me he broke into a broad grin. "Cannibal! Cannibal!" he shouted. The crowd, confused as to whether to take his booming exclamation as warning or welcome, shrank farther back. Mr. Brannan embraced me warmly, then turned to the curious assemblage. "Friends, this is Mr. Eliot, whom we call Cannibal, Cannibal Eliot, a white man escaped from captivity by the South Pacific cannibals, a true California pioneer and a man who now returns from the American River laden with his just reward. Treat him well, for he is my friend. But if you do not, ask any old-timer the story of what befalls one who becomes his foe. Do not mistreat him; honor him, and you shall do well. Fear him as you would any Christian—and maybe more so!" Brannan was so esteemed in the bustling city that his word of approval served as a voucher of good conduct, and the crowd resumed its hectic business, reassured that this white Cannibal was a minion of the merchant and not an agent of the Devil.

And a minion I became again, for Mr. Brannan took me back into his service, his interests having extended even so far as the China trade, and I began to work on his letters and accounts, as much as my fragile health would allow. I could not leave until I grew strong once more, and I did not wish to squander my bags of rams' guts and gilded scrotums, so employment seemed a way to keep me in food and lodging while I counted the days before I was well enough to board a boat back for Boston.

Samuel Brannan had drifted far from the Latter-Day Saints since I saw him last. In July 1848 Brigham Young called the California Mormons to come to the Great Salt Lake "to build up Zion," the prophet decrying "bondage to gold" by the faithful, warning that it was impossible "to unite Babylon and Zion." Most put down their pans and shovels and harkened to their leader. Incredibly, the Mormons had discovered the gold, had staked out the best claims, had fortune in their grasp, yet they chose to heed the call of their prophet, willingly letting the gold of this world slip from their hands in favor of the promise of God's greater riches. Brannan, however, refused, resenting the choice of the bare desert over the bounty of California as the gathering place of the faithful, although he still headed the remaining community.

In April, just before I returned, three representatives of Brigham Young had arrived to request "the Lord's money" Brannan had collected in tithes from the gold-digging Mormons. "Do you know what I told them, Cannibal?" I just looked at him, as he narrated this tale over drinks. "Why, I said, 'Bring me a receipt, signed by the Lord. Then I'll gladly give you the Lord's money! *Bring me the Lord's receipt!*' Oh, I tell you, they fumed, and raged, and insulted me. But I would not fall prey to their designs, for I was done with Mormonism. From now on I would take no more tithings, they would go their way, and I would go my own. Do you suppose I would hand over what I collected, what I have wisely invested, for that desert of desolation? I never got an Endowment, I got nothing for my troubles from the church. I would not tamper with the Lord's money now!" I did not answer, but looked at him intently. "Oh, I suppose I should have, eh? No, no, let them bring the Lord's receipt!"

Again I said nothing, but I could see him wrestle with agonies of guilt. "If you prefer," I said, after a time. He looked sharply at me, about to burst forth with a flood of invective, but he fell suddenly silent, tilted his glass up to the roof, slammed it to the table, and with great deliberation walked to the door. "I prefer, Cannibal," he said, uttering each word slowly, emphatically, as if taking a holy vow. "Indeed, I do so prefer!" Then he strode through the door to join the parade of humanity on the street.

His empire—the vast expanse of stores he owned in Sacramento, Stockton, San Francisco, which brought in thousands of dollars a day from the gold seekers; his holdings in property throughout the city; his project of building the Central Wharf, for which he joined with other merchants to capitalize on the booming maritime trade, etc., etc.—all of his wealth was built on the church tithings as much as on his wits and luck; and all of it was inseparable, absorbed into the general operation, unaccounted for, compounded as capital, impossible to extract. This gold was lodged forever in the vast river of Samuel Brannan's enterprise, and nothing, not even the quivers of guilt he felt, could pry it loose. In the church's eyes, Brannan was turned over to the buffetings of Satan; in his own, he still husbanded the investments of the Lord, the covenant unbroken.

The Hounds

Then came the terror of the Hounds. Towards the end of 1848, an association of merchants, including several who later joined with Brannan on the Central Wharf development, resolved to do something about the problem of runaway sailors. The lure of gold was irresistible, and sailors would desert in droves to seek their fortunes in the hills; whole ships would go unmanned, and there arose the danger that no captain would dare enter the bay for fear his ship would remain a rotting hulk, its crew gone and impossible to replace. With only Alcalde Leavenworth and one constable to enforce any semblance of law, the merchants sought to remedy this danger to commerce by contracting with a group of young men, mostly veterans of the New York Volunteers, to capture runaway sailors at twenty-five dollars a head. Soon these bounty hunters realized that they could go into business for themselves, and, with no authority to stop them, they set themselves up as self-appointed guardians of public peace, demanding money from citizens in order to ensure their "protection."

Called Hounds, this gang of desperadoes would congregate at the Shades Saloon, and soon established their own headquarters at a nearby tent, which they named, appropriately, Tammany Hall, for they were mostly composed of Bowery Boys, Plug Uglies, and Dead Rabbits from the dens of Five Points and other depraved locations of New York City. They loved to parade, arrayed in the gaudiest military attire, stepping to fife and drum, marching up and down the streets, making fools of themselves. When not on parade they would charge into saloons and restaurants and stores, filling themselves up on drink, food, and merchandise and contemptuously charging their bills to Alcalde Leavenworth; and were the proprietor to object, bottles, chairs, tables, everything would be rendered shambles. Their parades, revelries, and rampages were always conducted with an exaggerated sense of honor, a grotesque burlesque of decorum. Once a Negro brushed against a Hound who, offended at the assumed affront, swiftly drew his bowie knife and sliced off the poor man's ears!

Before their depredations grew too monstrous, Alcalde Leavenworth, it is true, engaged Sam Roberts, the leader of the gang, to flog a sailor convicted of pulling a knife on his captain. Shoulder strikers from New York wards, they were always available for stuffing ballot boxes, serving as jurors, and in other ways offering their services—for a price. Often they would hire themselves out as claim agents and bill collectors for merchants. Leavenworth himself became a target of this gang, which one night sought out the alcalde with the full intention of hanging him, and once broke into his office to destroy the city records. Yet the Hounds reserved their worst offenses for the denizens of "Little Chile."

While en route to California, General Persifor Smith had issued his proclamation that only American citizens could profit from the gold rush. At first the order was ignored, but as the rush brought more and more Argonauts, resentment grew apace that the skilled *chilenos*, familiar with gold mining from their own country and speaking the language of the conquered Mexicans, took advantage of the Americans, and should be driven from the hills. Several times I witnessed mobs attacking the "greasers" with unbridled violence, and more and more *chilenos* swelled the population of Little Chile, as they fled the vicious attacks by the American miners.

The Hounds would regularly invade Little Chile, tearing down some unfortunate's tent and boldly selling off his belongings at cut-rate prices. Few objected to their predatory ways because their victims were greasers—even the merchants, the town leaders who ordinarily declaimed loudly on every concern, kept quiet—even Sam Brannan was strangely silent. Only after the gang was dispersed did I learn of the deeper and darker criminality which had lain beneath the surface of drunken revelries and outlandish uniforms: the Hounds were minions, too, of the merchants, or at least a party of them, for the ruffians did the bidding of their masters, and only when they grew too obstreperous, only when their antics went too far and threatened the general order, did they receive their rebuke!

The Chileans were not only competitors in the gold country, but among them were many able businessmen, merchants from Valparaiso (many of whom were white men of English and American extraction!), who mined their fortunes in the same vein as the Brannans and the Howards. The depredations against Little Chile were actually designed to drive off competitors under the guise of xenophobic hatred!

And yet, how close, oh, how very intimate were the relations between the Chileans and the Hounds, so that this hatred seemed almost between cousins. The leader of the Hounds, Sam Roberts himself, had been a ruffian in Valparaiso and had served on a Chilean man-of-war before deserting to join the New York Volunteers. When Sam Roberts, while working as a boatman, met the Chilean courtesan Felice Alvarez as she disembarked for El Dorado, he appropriated her for himself, establishing her in Washington Hall, a house of ill fame lavished with Chilean beauties. As much as the Hounds would wreak havoc on Little Chile, they felt no reluctance in holding congress with members of the fairer sex from the same Latin clime. In fact, it was rivalry over the possession of harlots that brought the reign of the Hounds to its end.

On June 21 two Hounds entered the tent of a Chilean storekeeper and quarreled about a payment. Apparently frightened, the storekeeper drew a pistol. As one of the men grappled with him, the pistol went off, hitting the other as he ran out of the tent. A crowd gathered around the injured man, Belden Beattie, another veteran of the New York Volunteers, while the Chilean fled. By the time the sheriff arrived with a warrant, the Chilean's tent and goods had been auctioned off to the crowd. The next day Beattie died of his wounds, and the

Hounds, mourning the loss of their fellow veteran at his funeral, vowed to form themselves as a vigilance committee to protect themselves from lawlessness!

On July 13 the Hounds rebaptized themselves as the San Francisco Society of Regulators, drawing up a constitution for a mutual aid society, and electing officers. Cornelius R. V. Lee, veteran of the New York Volunteers and member of the territory's legislative assembly, was elected president, while John C. Pullis, also a member of the assembly and a veteran of the regiment, was elected steward. The fact that J. C. Pullis was also sheriff of San Francisco should give some sense of the enormous danger facing all citizens, for Pullis, Lee, and other officers and stalwarts of the "Regulators" were also those who held "official" power in the city, including members of the city government and even business associates of Sam Brannan. I felt a vertigo, a sense that all of society had turned to powdery sand on which I could find no firm foothold—for both the lawbreakers and those sworn to uphold those selfsame laws were one and the same!

Two days after the Hounds attempted to gain respectability through their new association, the explosion occurred. A merchant, George Frank, held a claim of five hundred dollars with a Chilean named Pedro Cueto against the purchase of a lot on Montgomery Street. Cueto told the sheriff, to whom Frank gave the bill for collection, that he would not pay it; then Sheriff Pullis deputized the Hounds to assist in collecting the bill. On the day assigned for collection, July 15, only two days after the Hounds were reconstituted as the Regulators, the gang went across the bay to Contra Costa on a rowdy marauding expedition. Upon their return, they paraded down the San Francisco streets with drum, fife, banner, and epaulets in uncommonly hot weather, then retired to the saloons.

Sam Roberts sought the company of his woman, Felice Alvarez, and, decked in the full plumage of his lieutenant's uniform, he rode up to Washington Hall, dismounted, and strode into her room. There, to his utter surprise and chagrin, he discovered Leopold Bleckschmidt sitting on the edge of her bed, dressing, the last of three Germans who had been entertained by Señorita Alvarez that day! Roberts dragged Bleckschmidt out of the house, knocked him unconscious with a club, then began to rake the man's face with one of his spurs until blood streamed from his wounds, the scars from which resulted in designs far more intricate than my own tattoos. "For shame! That is not manly!" someone shouted from the crowd that had gathered. "Manly?" Sam Roberts roared back. "If I catch him with my woman again, I'll kill him! I'll rip his balls off and carry my gold dust in 'em!"

Roberts then stormed into Tammany Hall and enlisted his drinking companions in yet another drunken parade with fife and drum, all the time seething at being cuckolded by the Chilean woman. It did not take long before the Hounds began rioting at Sam Roberts' prompting. "We are going to whip and drive out every damn *chileno* in town!" Collection of the bill against Pedro Cueto was soon forgotten, or, rather, the bill against all Chileans took precedence, the blood of the killed Belden Beattie calling out for vengeance especially.

The Hounds, however, followed a certain logic in their depredations and did not, at first, lash out in mad rage. First they set out to the docks to destroy the rowboats of their Chilean competitors in the business of transporting freight and passengers, then they moved on to the tents of Little Chile. Blackening their faces and wearing their gaudy costumes, they divided up into different gangs. Each would stop at a tent door and call out to the inhabitants inside. If the reply was in English they passed on, but if in Spanish, they burst in, upset the furnishings, auctioned off belongings, if valuable, and destroyed everything else. When the Hounds approached the tent of Domingo Alegría, however, he fought back. They fired into his tent, wounding two of his sons, and Rinaldo Alegría died of his wounds a few days later. Chilean saloons were ransacked and shot up, women were raped, including a mother and her daughter, while the Americans of the city took to their beds and hid in fright.

The next morning was overwarm, as if the fires of the night had fed the ovens of the sun. All of Little Chile smoldered in shambles, while the Hounds slept off their night of excess. The rest of the city timidly stirred, whispering consternation to themselves, puzzling how they could free themselves of this horror. I could not believe what I had seen, such wreckage and rapine, but I was yet more startled when I beheld Sam Brannan mount a barrel at Clay and Montgomery streets where he began to harangue a gathering crowd. "Are we cowards? Are we worms? Shall we let a bunch of dirty rascals from the dark corners of New York set their feet on our necks and spit on us?" Soon hundreds assembled, and, the crowd grown too large, the meeting was moved to the plaza. Brannan got on the roof of the alcalde's building and went on with his speech, insisting on justice for the Chileans. "Oh, California, what have you done?" he thundered. "California depends on Chile for flour, we depend on her skilled artisans for laying bricks, on her bakers for bread. How could we have treated these decent people from a neighboring republic in such savage manner?" Tossing a gold coin into his hat, Brannan started up a collection to help the victims of the rampage, and scores of Americans followed suit.

After the hat was filled, Brannan went on with his harangue, demanding that action be taken against the Hounds. "Are you afraid?" he bellowed to the assembled mass. As the crowd roared back its denial of cowardice, I could hear a few scattered voices that did not follow the tide, for there were Hounds also before the alcalde's building. "Best take care! A bullet might stop ye—or yer house burn down!" came the muttered responses. Brannan paused for a moment, then, standing on the roof of the old adobe, he tore open his shirt and bared his breast. "Shoot! Go ahead and shoot!" he taunted, dramatically. "I dare you, cowards all!" He paused a moment as we all awaited the blast of a gunshot. "Listen to that! 'Tis the silence of cowards! They threaten to burn my wife and children, Americans all! With Chileans they are brave men, but what do you think they are when they threaten Americans?" The crowd replied like the boom of a stormy surf, "Cowards! Hang 'em all! Get ropes and hang the bastards!"

Brannan then stretched out his hands to calm the crowd, appealing to them to clean up the city in an orderly manner, in the fashion of "lawful citizens." With the authority of Alcalde Leavenworth, he selected one of his merchant friends, William Howard, to act as chairman of a committee for law and order, then signed up about 230 volunteers, swore them in as they stood around the flagpole of the old adobe Custom-house that we had first spotted when we sailed in on the *Brooklyn* years before. There he enrolled them in nine police companies to hunt down the Hounds, while two judges were elected to serve with the alcalde, attorneys for the defense and prosecution were appointed, and a grand jury of twenty-four men was sworn in. As all the trappings of law were set in place, most of the Hounds began to slip out of town. Still, seventeen were ferreted out shortly and confined on the United States war sloop *Warren* in the bay. Sam Roberts, however, eluded the hunt for several days, until he was found stowed on board a schooner headed for Stockton. Swiftly, the trial was convened.

All along I was baffled by Sam Brannan's sudden appearance on the barrel, for he had absented himself from most municipal affairs for months. Then, as the brief trial commenced, Brannan disappeared once again; seemingly keen on apprehending evildoers, he appeared uninterested in the fine points of the legal process used to convict them. As the trial began, Francis Lippett, one of the prosecutors, warned of "treason on the part of influential men in the community who lean to the side of the prisoners and throw obstacles in the way of justice." Clearly, with Sheriff Pullis and others on the rolls of the Regulators, and with many of the merchants employing their services, it was evident of what Mr. Lippett warned. Brannan was as close to the Hounds as the rest of the merchants, yet why did he suddenly climb to the top of the alcalde's building, bare his chest, defend the honor of Chile, and whip the mass into an instrument of justice?

The trial concluded after a few days with convictions on all counts, although the jury debated the relative merits of hanging, whippings upon the public plaza, banishment, or combinations of the same. Finally, the criminals were sentenced to various terms in jail, with Sam Roberts sentenced to a ten-year term of imprisonment "in some penitentiary, wherever the territorial governor of California should direct." But with few jails, and with no penitentiary anywhere in the territory, the sentences were worthless, mere flourish. After brief jailings, most of the Hounds were set free and told to leave town. Sam Roberts himself was released and told never to return or he would face immediate execution.

Nonetheless, the Hounds were broken up, and the city slept sounder for months afterwards. Yet, after so much uproar, so much bombast and outrage, it seemed strange indeed that the ruffians would be simply discharged with what amounted to a gentle rebuke. No, I believe Sam Brannan stepped in at the behest of his fellow merchants to throttle the Hounds, for their usefulness was over for the "influential men of the community." And Brannan provided me with some insight into his own interest in suppressing the Hounds when he muttered, "'Tis one thing to put a little heat under some competitors, but to pillage customers is going too far." The merchants did everything they could to ease out the Hounds in the smoothest way possible, and in such quiet manner that none of their connections with their hirelings would be exposed.

Sam Brannan was the hero of the hour, and on August 1, elections for the *ayuntamiento*, the city's council, swept Brannan and others of the merchant notables into office. On the eve of the election, a small meeting gathered in Brannan's office. I was collecting receipts next door, yet could hear clearly as Talbot H. Green and Robert Price, who would the next day also be voted into office, conversed with Brannan. The proposition was simple: The city needed improvements, such as a public wharf at the end of California Street; the city also wanted funds; the city would sell lots to raise needed funds, and the soon-to-be-elected members of the *ayuntamiento* would be in a perfect position to know where to buy lots so as to profit handsomely from the improvements that they themselves would select. I gathered my papers and walked outside.

"Cannibal?"

"Yes, Mr. Brannan."

"I didn't know you were still here."

"Not any more, sir. I am departing." And I left with Green and Price raising their eyebrows at my master, who, no doubt, replied, "No need to worry about Cannibal. He keeps a tight lock on his mouth."

After all of this—"the Lord's receipt," the hounding of the Hounds, the convivial plotting to profit from the city they would the next day swear to protect, and all the rest—Sam Brannan took on an even more peculiar stature in my eyes. I continued working for him, a hireling like all the rest; I could not break away, fascinated as I was by this magnetic personality, this double being who could embody good and evil with equal ease, like a man shifting from one foot to another awaiting a drink at a saloon. Sam Brannan, stern judge, rabble-rouser, engineer of a world's mad craving for gold—he contained all the building up and wrecking down of a new world in his soul, like some Hindoo god creating and destroying the cosmos with a belch; and I was an appendage, an abettor, and an aide-de-camp. I felt at the same time exhilarated and distressed; felt as if I were witnessing the convulsions of this Hindoo god, and at a moment's notice I too could be swallowed up into his gargantuan entrails. Indeed, I kept my mouth shut.

Sydney Ducks

Business resumed its regular cycle in the months after the election. The sales of city lots went ahead, and Sam Brannan and his friends managed to look out after their own interests nicely while they husbanded the town's "improvements," although there were squabbles aplenty. The police were reorganized, and Brannan proposed that the town buy an abandoned brigantine, *Euphemia*, as a prison ship, since an adequate jail was lacking. The council bought the hulk for $3,500 from William Heath Davis, also a member of the *ayuntamiento*, instead of simply taking one of the many other abandoned ships in the bay; but the populace, relieved to have a place to hold miscreants, did not look askance at the intimate relations between public good and private opportunity. I suppose Brannan and the council acted in the selfsame manner as our municipal governments in Boston or New York, and the citizens allowed for private gain of public servants as a matter of course. The council knew where a new wharf would go and, therefore, which lots to buy, using the proceeds from the sale of lots to build the "improvement," thereby increasing the value of their newly acquired lots by fantastic proportions. But when the funds for the town again ran low after a few months, the council cut the number of police officers and lowered their salaries; yet when complaints of lawlessness were later loudly voiced by Mr. Brannan and his friends, such "economies" were conveniently forgotten, or at least Mr. Brannan's hand in them. I, however, had seen enough, and I shielded myself by keeping as much distance from Mr. Brannan's business advantages as I could. I wrote ciphers, figures, and script; but to the secrets beneath the ink, I shut my eyes as much as possible.

Meanwhile, a new criminal element clustered around the waterfront and up along the slopes of Telegraph Hill near Little Chile. Boat after boat brought escaped convicts and ticket-of-leave men from the British penal colonies at Sydney and Van Diemen's Land, along with rough larrikins from Australia's frontier, all of whom congregated in what became known as "Sydney Town." No doubt there were honest men from Australia, but the bulk of these fortune seekers were villainous scum, vile and violent men skilled in every crime. They were called "Sydney Ducks," and when some hideous murder or flagrant robbery was committed, the Americans would simply say, "The Sydney Ducks are cackling in the pond."

Sydney Town abounded in lodging houses, dancehalls, saloons, and gambling houses. I would visit the area on occasion—my South Pacific tattoos elicited somewhat less surprise, while my flesh-eating reputation still afforded some protection. The debauches of the Hounds seemed like the games of schoolchildren compared to these grim characters. At one saloon, appropriately named the Fierce Grizzly, a female bear was chained beside the door, upon which a drunken man would often display his sexual prowess; at the Boar's Head, a sexual exhibition was regularly enacted between a woman and a boar; while at other establishments the lurid entertainments were performed by either or both sexes—but of our species only! Although I witnessed these displays with the same reticence and impassive demeanor that I exercised over Mr. Brannan's account books, I was silently buffeted by storms of nausea, horror, and disgust amidst the hellish howls of the Sydney Ducks; yet I must also admit that I felt a certain fascination with watching depravity; and I noted, almost as if I were a scientist peeping through a microscope at my own soul, that the boundaries of pain and pleasure, like the borders of good and evil, were as porous for me as they were for everyone else in this gold rush.

San Francisco, built with canvas tents and shacks, suffered fires regularly, and in the early hours of December 24, 1849, fire once again took the town. Flames leapt out from the second floor of Dennison's Exchange Saloon at the corner of Kearny and Washington streets; and, although there was no wind, there was also no fire department as yet, so the flames raced through the canvas walls and ceilings until fifty buildings were left in smoking ruins. In the confusion that attended the fire, Sydney Ducks looted whatever they could.

Rumors abounded that the Australians would deliberately set such fires in order to create the proper conditions of confusion and dismay to allow for their unimpeded plundering. While the plundering was clearly evident, the Sydney Ducks were not the only ones who profited from the fires; for the merchants also benefited, as strange as it might seem that those who so depended on property could also cause it to be destroyed.

Let me explain. Much of the business in San Francisco operated on a commission basis, whereby merchants in the East, who sought profits from the boom in San Francisco, would dispatch merchandise "blind" to the merchants in San Francisco. The Eastern shippers had little or no knowledge of demand; and even if they perceived a demand, by the time the ship sailed around the Horn, conditions, which always fluctuated wildly, might have changed drastically, so that, by the time the ship entered the bay, the scarcity might have turned into a glut, thus rendering the merchandise virtually worthless. The merchants in San Francisco acted as agents for the Eastern shippers for a percentage commission on the profits. If the merchandise sold above cost, both the Eastern shipper and the San Francisco merchant did well; but if the goods were lost at sea or sold below cost, the Eastern shipper took the loss—while the San Francisco merchant suffered no loss himself!

If a glut could be reduced by a fire, remaining goods would suddenly become scarce, their prices would shoot up, and huge profits could be gained. Even the lowest-priced items could be given scarcity value by arranging for a convenient fire; and day after day small fires would break out in warehouses or on the docks, posing the danger of general conflagrations, while the merchant that "suffered" the loss from the flames might suddenly find himself counting mammoth gains. "Hang the incendiaries!" the commission merchants would yell—while they themselves may have secretly arranged for the fire to be set!

As I learned, this December 24th fire was set by neither Sydney Duck nor commission merchant; rather, a Negro torched the place to exact revenge against a bartender at Dennison's Exchange Saloon who had beaten him senseless after he had asked for a drink. (The unwritten law allowed a Negro one drink in a white bar, and then he was expected to leave. However, the bartender at Dennison's was a recent arrival, a Southerner unfamiliar with our peculiar, liberal customs. When the Negro had the apparent temerity to ask for a drink, the barkeep felt compelled to "teach the nigger a lesson.") It little mattered what the truth of the matter was, however, for it soon became iron-clad truth that this devastating fire, as well as the others that would follow in the months to come, was deliberately set by the Sydney Ducks.

Events began to blur for me; fires were constantly set and extinguished; robberies and murders mounted; invariably someone would enter a saloon and announce he could "whup anybody here," occasioning an inevitable drunken and fatal melee; life was volatile, like the goods piled up on the docks, and I could hardly keep track of the killings. Only certain incidents would lodge in my memory, such as the time a French newcomer was dancing and inadvertently brushed a particularly brutal character, who quickly corrected his manners by gunning the Frenchman down, then continued swirling his partner about.

Several times the city burned to the ground, although by now there was a fire department and a loud bell; still the rumors had it that the Sydney Ducks endlessly plotted to torch the city for the loot, rumors substantiated by the quite visible evidence of criminals hauling off ill-gotten goods whenever there was a fire.

Through all of this, Sam Brannan kept astride of every development, inevitably profiting no matter what the circumstances. When the *ayuntamiento*'s sales of city lots finally provoked a public scandal—with Talbot Green accusing Brannan of shenanigans in order to cover up his own dealings—Brannan executed a deft political manuever. Voted down on an austerity budget he proposed in favor of Green's motion for additional sales of city lots, Brannan unexpectedly resigned from the council. He returned to his private affairs, departing the next day for Sacramento, leaving the scandal over the sale of city lots in Green's lap. When he returned a few months later, Brannan was welcomed back as a strong civic leader, apparently immune from scandal, in a city that more and more invoked the spirit of Judge Lynch. With the official forces of order unable to stop the criminal element, the newspapers trumpeted the wave of crime that threatened to flood San Francisco, pleading for good citizens to step forward when government failed; naturally, Sam Brannan would heed the call, which was soon to come.

"Fie upon your laws!"

On the evening of February 19, 1851, a man entered the store of Charles Jansen and Co., which was located on the corner of Montgomery and Washington streets, just a block from Portsmouth Square. Although it was closing time, the man asked Jansen for a dozen blankets. When Jansen started to count out the blankets, he noticed yet another man enter the store. The first then stopped him from counting the colored ones and told him he wanted white blankets. When Jansen bent down to get them from a lower shelf, he was struck on the head with a slungshot and beaten senseless by the two assailants. Upon recovering consciousness, he crawled to the door to shout for help, to which Theodore Payne, an auctioneer from across the street who was planning to have dinner with Jansen, responded, soon finding the severely injured merchant on the floor and two thousand dollars missing from Jansen's desk. Payne called for the police, to whom Jansen described his two assailants.

San Francisco was in an uproar, with the *Alta* proclaiming that the crime was "one of the most barefaced, cool, and audacious robberies which the annals in any country give a history." The *Courier* lamented the leniency of the courts, posing the question on everyone's lips: "Is it worthwhile, if caught, to offer them a trial in our courts? Is it not better to make examples of them, if found, by hanging them at once?" The crime was really no more heinous than many others that passed with little notice; but Charles Jansen was a well-known and popular merchant, so indignation galvanized his fellow merchants with a passion for *lex talionis*, the law of revenge.

Soon two Australians were arrested, Robert Windred and a man identified as the notorious James Stuart, a Sydney convict responsible for numerous robberies in California as well as the murder of a sheriff in Yuba County. When the Australians were brought to Jansen's bedside, the injured merchant identified both as his assailants, although he felt uncertain enough that he would not swear absolutely that the two were the culprits.

The man identified as James Stuart vigorously protested his innocence, maintaining that he was not Stuart at all, but Thomas Berdue, a respectable British subject constantly hounded by the law because of his resemblance to the infamous Stuart. James Stuart had escaped from prison, and officers who had guarded him as well as judges who had tried him identified the man as their former charge. There seemed no question: In weight, height, color of eyes and hair, features, and in every other general characteristic, he answered for Stuart. But even more telling, this "Thomas Berdue" had a slit cut in his left ear, a scar over his left eye, and his left forefinger was amputated at the first joint—all of which were characteristic marks of James Stuart! There was no doubt that this man's protestations were merely the sly pleadings of a cunning criminal, and that the hated Sydney Duck had been captured at last.

After Windred and Stuart were brought to Jansen's bedside for identification, they were escorted by police guard back to the courthouse, all the time followed by a swelling, angry mob hooting to hang the miscreants. As they crossed Portsmouth Square, the mob rushed to grab the two suspects but was repulsed by the police. The accused were brought before Justice Shepherd for examination while the mob grew to over five thousand outside the courthouse. After hearing Windred's alibis of his whereabouts during the robbery (asleep in bed, etc.) and Stuart's protestations of mistaken identity, the court was adjourned until Monday.

"Now's the time!" someone cried, then the mass rushed

upon the prisoners. Chairs, railings, tables were swept aside by the infuriated mob, which seized Stuart and Windred, but the sheriff and his assistants beat off the assailants, assisted by the Washington Guards, a private guard company with offices next door, who rushed in to rescue the prisoners. "Shame! Shame!" the mob yelled at the Guards, but they were driven out from the courtroom.

Soon the crowd waxed to seven thousand before the court-house. An impromptu meeting was organized, chaired by William Howard, and several of the most respectable civic leaders addressed the angry assembly, the result of which was that a committee was appointed to see that the prisoners were properly guarded during the night and to report to a meeting to be held the following morning, at which time action was to be proposed. The mass meeting adjourned, as Sam Brannan, naturally appointed to the committee, shouted his displeasure: "Why should we speak of juries, judges, or mayors? These men are murderers, I say, as well as thieves. I know it, and I will die or see them hung by the neck!"

The next morning circulars appeared addressed to the "Citizens of San Francisco!" calling for a meeting the following day for "all those who will rid our city of its robbers and murderers." I suspected Sam Brannan's hand, my suspicion growing when I read the complaint that "when thieves are left without control to rob and kill, then doth the honest traveler fear each bush a thief. Law, it appears, is but a nonentity, to be scoffed at; redress can be had for aggression but through the never-failing remedy so admirably laid down in the code of Judge Lynch. Not that we should admire this process for redress, but that it seems to be inevitably necessary. Are we to be robbed and assassinated in our domiciles, and the law to let our aggressors perambulate the streets merely because they have furnished straw bail? If so, let each man be his own executioner. Fie upon your laws! They have no force." The prose smacked of Brannan's impetuosity, but he would not reveal his authorship when I looked up from the printed bill to search the eyes of my employer.

Before a crowd numbering perhaps ten thousand, the committee proposed—with Brannan's objection—that the citizenry keenly witness the official proceedings. This was met with dissatisfaction by the distraught mob, which considered anything less than a hanging insufficient. William T. Coleman, another respected merchant, then addressed the roiling assembly: "I propose that the people here present form themselves into a court, to be organized within this building immediately; that the prisoners be brought before it; that the testimony be taken, counsel on each side allotted; that the trial be begun by twelve o'clock, and conducted fairly, dispassionately, resolutely; and if the prisoners be found innocent, let them be discharged; but if guilty, let them be hanged as high as Haman, and that before the sun goes down!" This proposal was met with a roar of approval, and the multitude pressed into the building to watch the impromptu court proceed under "the color of law."

At nine o'clock that night the jury retired—although not before the proceedings were interrupted several times by mob attempts to seize the prisoners. At midnight the jury finally returned—but they had split nine to three in favor of conviction! Apparently, the reluctance of Jansen to make an absolute identification of Windred and Stuart caused enough doubt among three courageous jurors to prevent the expected verdict.

When the crowd heard that they had been robbed of their hanging, the courtroom went wild. "Who are the scoundrels who voted to release these Sydney Ducks?" Brannan shouted to the enraged mob. "Give us their names—and we'll hang them instead!" But the jury, pistols drawn, backed away into the jury room, where they remained until the crowd drifted away in the early morning hours. The next day, Stuart and Windred were spirited away by the authorities, the fever of the crowd suddenly cooled, and the regular legal proceedings went ahead, ending with convictions for the two the following month. Windred was sentenced to ten years' imprisonment —although by April he had escaped, never to be heard from since—while Stuart was given fourteen years for the robbery and was delivered to Marysville to stand trial for murder.

I Provide

Intoxication with Judge Lynch seemed to end for the time being, although the outbreaks of crime, fire, and depravity continued unabated. The disastrous business conditions, slumped since the easy placer mines had run out months before, also continued. I watched Mr. Brannan fret, as I scratched out figures in my employer's books. The value of real estate began to plummet, while the glut soared like some aerial balloon. "We can see no chance for improvement until the markets are materially relieved of the surplus on hand," wrote the *Alta*. "We want a general clearing of the market." I scratched silently as Mr. Brannan paced, muttering to himself.

"Oh, if there be a time for some Sydney Duck to torch the warehouses and the docks, God knows that time has come," Brannan moaned out loud.

"If you prefer," I replied.

He looked at me abruptly, sharply. Consumed by his thoughts, he was unaware that I was even in the room with him, and he stared at me in utter surprise. "Cannibal—" he began, but suddenly stopped, glaring at me. His stare continued, it seemed, for ages, until he just as suddenly laughed. "Cannibal, you are quite a fellow, indeed!" he remarked as he strode out the door, chuckling to himself.

Crossing Portsmouth Square as the sun set that day, I felt feverish again, and the outlines of the buildings appeared in heightened relief against the reddish twilight. Ralph Waldo Emerson suddenly came to mind, I know not why. I recalled how Emerson crossed Concord Common at twilight and was "glad to the brink of fear," how he became a "transparent eyeball," while "the currents of the Universal Being" coursed through him. I stared across Portsmouth Square, San Francisco's "Common," and I gasped with a different revelation. Rather than a "transparent eyeball," I felt clogged, dirty, opaque, cluttered, turbid, like the muddied streams of the gold country. I felt more like a gilded scrotum than any eyeball. I could feel no currents of the Absolute, no occult relation between man and vegetable; I could not see through anything; only the surface of things stared back at me, sharp surfaces, impenetrable surfaces—all glaring the way Sam Brannan's eyes burned at me from across my desk.

"Yes! Yes!" I shouted. A few turned their heads, then I hushed. "I shall make the surface of things change and thereby change the course of the Absolute," I concluded to myself. "I will write events just as Sam Brannan does; I will clog the veins of the world, and I will be afraid to the giddy brink of gladness. Yes! Yes!" I was possessed by some sort of feverish daemon; and, though I felt possessed, knew I was possessed, I was nonetheless compelled to carry out the plan which had sprung fully to life like some revivified Frankenstein's monster in my brain. "I will do the bidding of my employer," I thought in the red glow of dusk. "He has asked for salvation, and he has come to me. I shall be his savior!"

Rumors abounded that the Sydney Ducks would set the city ablaze on May 4th, the anniversary of the huge fire a year before. As midnight approached on the eve of the anniversary, I stole into one of Mr. Brannan's warehouses. Crates, bales, boxes of goods were stacked to the ceiling in the dark cavern. I took some rolls of canvas and spread them before me; threw crumpled newspapers all about; splattered turpentine over bales, canvas, papers; then I pulled out my box of lucifers. I stopped for a moment to survey my handiwork, realizing that as soon as I struck the match, all would burst suddenly into a blessed inferno, a conflagration that would soon spread to all the adjoining warehouses, consuming excess shovels, canvas, tea, lumber—everything that restrained the pressures of value; out of these ashes, riches would grow, a phoenix fatter than before; and I would have been the instrument of resurrection.

My meditation done, I lifted the match—when suddenly I heard the bells of the fire company and shouts of alarm in the street! "Fire!" they yelled, and I swung open the door of the warehouse to witness sheets of flame rising from Clay Street and men running in all directions. This was the beginning of a stupendous conflagration, a mighty sea of flame that swept across the city, destroying block after block. I had no need even to strike my match—for my thought alone had ignited the city!

My memory is confused with the recollections of the shouts of the excited populace—the crash of falling buildings—the howls of the burnt and injured—the maddened horses plunging through the streets—the crowd trampling all before it—the explosions of houses blown up to stay the course of the fire. Several of the newer buildings were supposed to have been fireproof, and some of the merchants barricaded themselves inside with their employees, frantically attempting to douse the sparks and protect their receipts—twelve men shut up in Neglee's building succeeded, while six in the store of Taafee, McCahill and Company perished. With a shortage of water, DeWitt & Harrison's building was saved by repeated dousings of eighty thousand gallons of vinegar! And amidst the chaos and screams, the Sydney Ducks went about their plundering, reaping a rich harvest that they carted off to Sydney Town, which, because of the direction of the high wind, suffered no destruction at all! Looters were shot by enraged citizens who were driven to excesses of fury; a French sailor, innocently picking up a burning brand to light his pipe, was shot dead as an incendiary. When the fire finally burned itself out, three-fourths of the city, including Mr. Brannan's warehouse in which I had stood with my match poised, lay in ruins.

Oh, what feverish rebuilding commenced! With joy the merchants set about selling their remaining stocks of lumber, canvas, nails, and other goods! Within a few weeks hundreds of buildings went up again. How invigorating were the flames, how healthful a purification—although the populace seethed with rage at the Sydney Ducks—for the city thrived with rejuvenation; and Mr. Brannan's disposition became buoyant with buying and selling, after the "general clearing of the market" had been so well effected.

What my employer prayed for, I had well provided.

Vigilance

Although no dramatic or especially vicious crime had been committed that day, two businessmen, James Neall and George Oakes, called on Mr. Brannan on June 8th to discuss "the insecurity of affairs, and the need for active measures." I excused myself, while Mr. Brannan and his principal clerk, Mr. Wardwell, met with the two gentlemen. In short, the four decided to call a select group of those "in sympathy with good order" to a meeting the next day at the California Engine House just opposite the Oriental Hotel. The meeting was held, the men agreed to take action, and they appointed a smaller group to draft a constitution; that night, yet a larger assembly met at Mr. Brannan's office to found the Committee of Vigilance, formally adopting a constitution on Tuesday night and electing Samuel Brannan president of the new organization's executive committee. Well satisfied with their work, the meeting adjourned; but even before all the members could disperse, the Committee of Vigilance was called to action.

That evening, George Virgin, a shipping agent, had left his upstairs office on Central Wharf to attend to a ship's departure. Since he was to be gone only a few moments, he left his door unlocked and his strongbox in his desk. An Australian who called himself John Jenkins saw his opportunity, slipped into Virgin's office, thrust the strongbox in a sack, heaved it over his shoulder, and made his way down the stairs to a waiting boat at the end of the wharf. Virgin, who was returning to his office, caught sight of Jenkins with the sack slung over his shoulder, realized that he had been burglarized, and began raising alarms. Jenkins pulled the oars of his boat mightily towards Sydney Town across the cove, but boatmen and others around the wharf heard the alarm and gave chase. Seeing that his pursuers were gaining on him, Jenkins dumped the sack overboard, but to no avail. Within moments he was surrounded by dozens of boats and pointed revolvers. John Sullivan, a boatman, subdued the rascal, took him to the shore, beat him, and escorted him to the station house. But, en route, the party met one of the newly inducted members of the Committee of Vigilance, who suggested that the prisoner be taken to Brannan's building instead.

I learned of all these activities, as did other citizens of San Francisco, when, around ten o'clock that night, I heard a peculiar double tolling of the fire bells. Curious, I followed others to Brannan's building, where the Committee members congregated according to their prearranged signal to deliberate what to do with their catch. William A. Howard, a shipmaster, settled the discussion by slapping his pistol on the table and solemnly proclaiming, "Gentlemen, as I understand it, we are here to hang someone." As I had no interest in hanging anyone, I slipped outside to mingle with the growing crowd in the vacant lot across the street, where everyone was awaiting the outcome of these deliberations.

The police were also kept outside while the "trial" of Jenkins proceeded. At its conclusion, Mr. Brannan appeared before the building to address the crowd. Denouncing the regular courts and the impudence of the criminals, he related the events of that night, how Jenkins was taken, tried, convicted, and, by unanimous vote, sentenced to hang in an hour in Portsmouth Square. A clergyman having been sent for, to meet with the solemnity of the occasion, Mr. Brannan assured his audience that the Committee would endeavor to conduct the execution "to your satisfaction." Then he asked, "Does the action of the Committee meet with your approval?" His question was answered with a chorus of ayes, although there were also scattered nays in the crowd.

As the hour approached two in the morning, Jenkins was taken out, surrounded by four columns of men, twenty ranks deep, with a rope lashed around the entire entourage to prevent anyone breaking in to free the prisoner. Jenkins, his arms tied behind him, puffed jauntily on a cigar, apparently confident that he would be rescued by Sydney Ducks or police. Once, the police did attempt to seize Jenkins but were turned back, and, as the hanging party entered the Square, State Senator David Broderick mounted a wagon, exhorting the crowd to rescue the prisoner for the law. Some people rushed in to do so, but they were turned back at gunpoint. The noose was hastily placed over Jenkins' neck, while the other end was thrown over the beam of the old adobe Customhouse amidst shoving, shouting, and flying fists. His rescuers tried to hold on to Jenkins' legs, while his executors dragged the rope back over a hundred feet, the riotous crowds of both factions pulling the man in opposite directions. Jenkins was soon aloft from the Customhouse beam, with Samuel Brannan crying out in his booming voice, "Let every lover of liberty and good order lay hold of the rope!"

I left the scene almost giddy. A tremendous spectacle, this lynching, with Mr. Brannan bellowing out a fine Tom Paine eloquence, as he launched the Sydney Duck towards the heavens. How apt that it should be done at the Customhouse, the looming structure we first sighted from the deck of the *Brooklyn* five years before. Then I felt the old adobe was the center of the village; now I know its hanging beam is the city's core, its heart of hearts!

The actions of that night and the subsequent reign of the Committee of Vigilance have already drawn the attention of the entire world, and I am sure my Reader has become well aware of these monumental events. Senator Broderick and others attempted to put the law in command, but Broderick was threatened with hanging himself. When a grand jury attempted to hold nine individuals responsible for the hanging, nearly two hundred signed as "accomplices" to the illegal execution, and within days hundreds more joined the ranks. No matter what the official agents of government did, it was the Committee that ruled San Francisco; and this new dictatorship hunted down every miscreant who appeared on its secret list, warning them to leave town or face the San Francisco equivalent of the guillotine.

I felt my fevers return, and I kept to my quarters during the rest of the tumult of June, although I was forced to flee into the streets with the rest of the populace on June 22 when yet another fire devoured the city. The Committee of Vigilance had vowed to rid the city of incendiaries, but the city was still laid low, despite the decrees of our new Robespierres. Soon after the last embers of this conflagration cooled, there occurred yet one more incident which served to drive me, finally, to the margins of sanity.

Leviathan

On July 2, a house at the Mission was burglarized, along with a tent on the California Street hill, and several men went searching for the thieves amidst the chaparral of the hillside. They came upon a well-armed man wearing an English-cut coat who said his name was James Stephens and that he was on his way from the Mission to North Beach. As the path over the hill was the long way to North Beach and avoided the populated districts, the pursuers became suspicious. The stranger denied knowing anything of the robberies, explaining that he had recently arrived in the city, having walked from Sonora in the southern mines, and that he had yet to find lodgings. But, because his linen was clean and his boots not sufficiently travel stained, his interrogators remained suspicious, taking "James Stephens" to the offices of the Vigilance Committee for further questioning.

When he entered the Committee's rooms, everyone present immediately noted the strange likeness he bore to the condemned James Stuart, but the prisoner sat quietly and without complaint in his cell. At the change of guard, John Sullivan, the boatman who had captured Jenkins, walked in, looked twice, then hallooed the prisoner, who acted as if he had never seen the boatman before. But Sullivan related that "this here is no other than English Jim—Jim Stuart!—who murdered the sheriff. I was there when they tried to hang him at Marysville, but the rope broke and he escaped." The Committee was stunned. Other witnesses were called forth who knew Jim Stuart, and each testified that the miscreant now stood before them.

Yet how could this be? The same telltale marks were there that identified "Thomas Berdue" as James Stuart: the slit cut in his left ear, the scar over his left eye, his left forefinger amputated at the first joint—in addition to all the other characteristics. The interrogation continued for several days when, finally convinced that all avenues were closed, "James Stephens" confessed that he was, indeed, the real Jim Stuart—English Jim—and would confess to all his crimes in exchange for a promise from the Committee that he would be turned over to the authorities in Yuba County.

Communication was hastily made with Marysville, where "James Stuart" awaited execution, the Committee explaining that the real James Stuart was captured and that "Thomas Berdue" was, in fact, an innocent man! Oh, such remorse filled the Committee despite remonstrances that the two looked so very much alike that the mishap was understandable. Why, they had condemned an innocent man! They tore at their breasts, wept hugely, and vowed to turn over bags of gold dust to the wrongly accused man as restitution.

My mind reeled, my soul split into splinters like a whaleboat stove in by a monster of the deep! The marks were there to read the man as to be something he was not! His essence mattered nothing at all, for the indicating marks were the same; his identity was mistaken, but for all who scanned the page, the tale read the same. Only when the "real" Stuart, by pure coincidence, by utter chance, appeared, was the meaning of Thomas Berdue's face and amputated finger revealed. The mob was going to hang a representation of evil, and they would have been contented with their work, for if the signs and symbols read true, then was not truth seen through the transparency, like a fish beneath the shimmering clarity of Lake Tahoe?

I resolved to quit this city at my first opportunity no matter what my state of health; and, having booked passage on the *George Washington* for Panama, I had only to bid my Mr. Brannan farewell before boarding. I waited until dusk, that vibrant hour of impenetrable surfaces, waiting for his rooms to be cleared of business associates and Committee members before I approached.

"Mr. Brannan, may I speak with you?"

"Of course, Cannibal, although I do have an engagement shortly. Would you like to come another time?"

"No, Mr. Brannan, my time is brief, for I am boarding the *George Washington* to return to Boston, and I wish to say farewell."

"Leaving at last—eh, Cannibal?" he looked at me as if to drink me up with his eyes one last time. "Well, it's been—been since '46, that long!—that we've worked together. I'll be sorry to see you go, my friend. I know it's been your mind to leave almost since you first got here, so I can only wish you God-speed, although I must say you're leaving in the midst of some heady times."

"Heady times, indeed, Mr. Brannan—that is, if one does not lose one's head."

"Ha!—quite a quip, Cannibal. I have never heard you so loquacious in years."

"Then listen to me now, Mr. Brannan, for I have come to express my gratitude for your kind solicitude."

"Think nothing of it. I have always regarded you fondly, since the moment I saw your printed face in Oahu."

"Thank you. But I also seek to speak with you of something troubling."

"Go ahead, Cannibal."

"Are you sure that you will hang the real James Stuart this time?"

"As certain as the ground I stand on. The man confessed."

"But cannot the confession be a mistake?"

"I think it hardly likely that a man with as long and sordid a history as English Jim would seek to narrate such a tale unless he were truly the scoundrel. Yes, it was unfortunate that we abused poor Berdue, but such things happen from time to time. We are all frail creatures of the Lord, and mistakes are as common to us as December mud in San Francisco. But this confession rings true."

"Well, then, Mr. Brannan, I must also confess."

He looked at me quizzically. "Confess?"

"Yes, you see, I was the one who set the fire of May 4th. I am the incendiary. I scattered rags and papers throughout your warehouse, then I ignited the conflagration. I confess that I am the one who consumed the city in flames!"

"Don't be ridiculous, Cannibal. It's as plain as day that Sydney Ducks torched the town, not you. Besides, the first flames were not sighted at any of my buildings."

"Mr. Brannan," I continued, "you don't seem to understand. I am confessing to setting the city on fire. Go ahead and call your Committee! I am the culprit, I am the one to hang! But I must also confess that I did not act alone, for I acted in concert. I was ordered to burn down the city!"

"What? Who ordered you to do such a thing?"

"You did, Mr. Brannan! 'Oh, if there be a time for someone to torch the warehouses and the docks, God knows that time has come.' Don't you remember, Mr. Brannan? You asked for the fire to clear your stocks, to liquidate the glut; I executed the task. Go ahead, Mr. Brannan, call the hanging party!"

"You must be mad, Cannibal. I never asked you to do any such thing! Just because I muttered some damn foolishness I cannot even now remember does not mean that I ordered you to burn the city down—something which I am convinced you had no hand in doing in any case!"

"But, Mr. Brannan, I am confessing to the crime!"

"You can confess until the end of time; you did not do it—and I did not order you to do what you did not do! This is absurd, Cannibal."

"Perhaps, Mr. Brannan. But I am accusing you nonetheless and I am the witness to your guilt—not just of this fire, but of all of it—your bilking of the Mormon tithes, your confederation with the Hounds—until they went beyond business bounds—your schemes to buy city lots and build wharves, your engineering of the gold rush—all of it, Mr. Brannan. You are the Manichaean beast—both the dispenser of all justice and the originator of all crime! Magnanimous man! Malignant man! You are both! And I have done your bidding! I am confessing to the arson—and you are complicitous! Call in the hanging party!"

"Don't you dare call in anyone, Cannibal, for you'll only end up in the asylum for the insane. Stop this nonsense right this minute!"

"Leviathan, I have harpooned thee! You believe you know the truth—you conduct the affairs of the city with such kingly impudence—but you can only read the scratchings on the surface; you know hardly a thing. You saw the scar, the slit in the eye, the amputated finger—everything fit in place, all the correspondences, as if you were reading the Sermon on the Mount word for word! Here was James Stuart—despite his protestations of innocence. What did he know? You dismissed his denials—yet you accept this 'James Stuart's' confession? No, Mr. Brannan, you do not yet know how to read. Everyone believes that my tattoos signify that I have eaten the flesh of humans, and these Christians read my face and shrink in horror. But you, Elder Brannan, you read my face and detect a false interpretation made of a false imprint. No, you say I have been much maligned; that I have been accused falsely because of my face. But now, Mr. Brannan, what if I tell you that you were the one who was deceived? That the people read my face correctly, like schoolchildren tracing their letters—for I have eaten the flesh of humans! I am the monster!

"But you, Mr. Brannan, you have a smooth face, a clear face, a lustrous countenance, and the people read in it an impetuous but noble man; they search the depths of your soul and extract nuggets of human excellence, of moral rectitude, fervor; they see in you the charitable benefactor of the Donner party abomination, the comforter of Chileans torn by Hounds.

"But I say I read thy face aright: I say thou art Cannibal—you are the eater of human flesh, and you have swallowed more even than I! They know nothing of this Leviathan! I can penetrate your mask! I can read your soul—and I tell thee now that thou art the foul eater of flesh, blood dripping from thy maw! You are the criminal who will rid the city of its criminals. They will hang, these men, one upon another, like pieces of beefsteak threaded into your gullet! Mr. Brannan, you are one of them—and you must swallow yourself! You ordered me to burn the city down; I was but thy minion! You too are the guilty one—you are the one to hang!—and we shall hang side by side, like lovers! Together we shall account for the evil of the city! No, wait—a better plan comes to my mind. When the Committee arrives we can subdue them, and together we can enjoy a feast! We can chaw them to their bones! Yes, yes! Call in thy henchmen now—I am hungry!"

"My God, Cannibal, have you gone stark raving mad?"

"I am awaiting the arrival of the Committee of Vigilance, Mr. Brannan. Will you call them?"

"Listen, my friend, you must have gotten another relapse of your troublesome fever. Why don't you go home now and rest up? I fear for your health."

"If you will not call them in, then I shall depart on the *George Washington* as I planned, a criminal escaping, free of all punishment, a criminal leaving behind his maestro. I must congratulate you on executing such perfect crimes, Mr. Brannan, for you shall go unpunished as you collect shelf after shelf of dead men's scrotums. I only regret that I could not swing from a rope with thee."

"Cannibal, you're actually still planning to leave? In your condition?"

"I am no worse than before, Mr. Brannan. I will survive, and the *George Washington* will have a crew, I am sure, that will whet my appetite."

"Damnation! Cann—Mr. Eliot, William! Will you come to your senses?"

I smiled, and with a slight bow said, "*Mr. Cannibal,* I am leaving thee now, but I fully intend to return." Then I leaned over to whisper in his ear, "But when I do return, I shall be carrying with me the Lord's receipt! When I return, I shall expect to receive payment for this receipt in only one type of currency—your flesh. I intend to eat thee, Mr. Brannan—and I will commence by roasting fatty strips from . . . right here!" And I patted Samuel Brannan's rump, whirled on my heels, and walked out the door.

Editor's Note

William "Cannibal" Eliot died of cholera in August 1851 on board the *George Washington* as it rested at anchor in quarantine off the coast of Panama. This is the only existing chapter from *Cannibal in California,* although his notes indicate that Cannibal intended to write additional chapters, including ones on his life as a whaler, his experiences on Hatutu, his luck in the California gold mines, and his intimate relations with prostitutes. It is unfortunate, for these unwritten chapters, no matter what their literary value, would have been of exceptional historical interest. Little is known of Eliot other than that he was born in Boston on May 22, 1824, of a wealthy Yankee merchant family, left Harvard after an undistinguished career as a student in 1842, and then set upon the adventures briefly related here. Although I anticipate that research will reveal more on Eliot's life, his biography as yet remains mostly shrouded in obscurity.

I am most indebted to the Eliot Family Trust for permitting me to publish this manuscript. While William Eliot requested that this fragment not be published for at least a hundred years, the family, unaware even of its existence, was not intentionally carrying out the wishes of its author. It was only after Thomas Eliot's great-great-granddaughter Rainbow Eliot-Cohen accidentally found the manuscript in a false bottom of Thomas Eliot's strongbox in the attic of her home in Providence, Rhode Island, in 1989 that the document first came to light.

Before succumbing to cholera, Cannibal wrote a short letter, addressed to his brother, Thomas, which explains, at least in part, why the manuscript remained in the strongbox for so long.

August 1851

Off the Panama coast

Dear Tom,

Fever, again. Cholera sweeps the boat. Many die, a great many. I fear that, weakened as I am, I will join these legions of the dead. If I do survive, I shall expand this slender manuscript included here into a larger book, although, as you no doubt can see, what I have scribbled so far must be substantially revised, for it is vulgar, completely unsuited for refined society, particularly for the eyes of ladies. If I do die, dear Tom, I want you to swear to me that you shall keep this locked up. None of this should be published—at least not for a hundred years. By 1951 or 2001, the gold of California and the ashes of Sam Brannan will have all been swept into the same ocean that holds my own. By then, the gold exhausted, San Francisco will have returned to being the isolated outpost of civilization that it was before the gold rush. A hundred years from now it will little matter what I say about the tiny village, for Sam Brannan and all the rest will be nothing but the dim legend of a forgotten place buried in the mists of time.

Tom, I do wish to see you and dear home again. I have been gone nearly ten years, and my heart aches. My journeys have been long and strange—and I do hope my face does not frighten you to death!—but now I wish to rest. Someday I hope to travel again, to the Orient, to Palestine and Egypt. I intend to ask the Sphinx some pointed questions, and I fully expect adequate answers —or I shall never leave that cat head in peace! But for now, I yearn for our jaunts as in the old days, when we would wander the woods and the rocky hills and talk of philosophy and sweethearts! I wish to visit the graves of our parents and to moisten their grass once more with my tears. Oh, Tom, I do so very much wish to come home—but I am afraid that my journeys may have just begun!

Your dear brother,

Will

Belle Cora
and the Vigilantes

·—·▆◆▇—·—·

*"They built the railroad across the isthmus of Panama, my dear, and
now the train has arrived at Fort Gunnybags" (1856)*

The Gentleman Called Himself Smiley

Yes, sir, when Ah Toy first arrived in '49 she caused a mighty
sensation, mighty indeed. Most of us never set eyes on a Chi-
nawoman before, except for some short, ugly specimens that
looked more like squashed-down mules than women, and Ah
Toy's looks were uncommon, comparable even to those stylish
French ladies who came soon after, and her house never did
slack off even with that competition, seeing as how she chose
her girls from among the best pickings in the Celestial
Empire. She stood elegantly tall, her hair coiled up in a
chignon, her eyebrows thin and black, like neat pencil lines
drawn on her white, rice-powdered cheeks, while her feet
were "lily bound," which meant she was a high-born aristocrat
and had to be carried around rather than walk, and each of us
no-name gold diggers should consider it an honor to drop our
drawers in her royal presence.

Everyone hankers to exercise his hydraulics when he comes
back from the Mother Lode. But when he sees Ah Toy he also
harbors the big question, the same one each time. The boys
used to line up for blocks in front of her house—dozens waiting on line—all puzzling over the same thing: Was a China
Polly's equipment the same as a white woman's, or did her
sluice box slant like her eyes? Of course, those of us who knew

·—·▆◆▇—·—·

never let on to the miners just come to town, and we would answer their urgent queries the same way Ah Toy would, *"'Two bittee lookee, flo bittee feelee, six bittee doee.'* So, boys, just two bittee will sufficiently unveil the mystery, unless, of course, you aim to extend your scientific investigation more deeply and your claim ain't played out so's you can afford to, which means pay up your six bittee and find out for yourself!"

Soon as the tenderfoot completed his little experiment in Oriental female physiognomy, he would leave with a grin and get in on the joke, for nobody who did lookee, feelee, or doee would talkee. No, that would just spoil the fun, so any old and highly esteemed customer would only give knowing nods and winks in order to drive any tenderfoot to the lunatic asylum with anticipation, until, that is, he found out for himself and joined the Society of Smug Looks at the saloon counter. Although, away from the uninitiated, the argument would rage between the old Ah Toy hands: Despite their six-bittee doee, some boys still contended that they had to play their hose at an angle, which proved that, slight as it seemed, Ah Toy did slant. I don't know if they worked with their eyes closed or if their members were insensible, but any damn fool should know that Orientals got secrets to make you feel any way they want you to, so Ah Toy just used her mysterious arts to promote yet another mystery and thereby keep curiosity as well as necessity pulling business her way.

But when it comes to doing business in *all* its slants, there is no one more accomplished than Belle Cora. Yes, Belle Cora. And how I grieve greatly for the tragedy that has befallen her, a tragedy laid to the account of Mrs. Richardson humping the Vigilance Committee on Belle's man, Charlie. I aim to do everything I can to help fix her up comfortable when I get back to San Francisco, as a matter of common decency—and I'll do it, too!

I'll tell you about Belle, so you can put it in that book you're writing, like the way you scribbled down what I told you about Ah Toy. I seen you, you can't hide it, the way you scurry off with your marble-covered little notebook. Every other blasted fool is writing a book about California, so you might as well, too. You're probably a journalist for a newspaper back East, and you're in such a hurry to send off your letters you don't even think things through, just vomit up a flood of jumbled-up "impressions." Well, I don't much care, just so long as you get it down right, what happened to Belle Cora. For one thing, I see myself as a little to blame for the bloody mess that eventually happened, so if you are scribbling and scrawling, go ahead, because something other than the sanctimonious cow pies the press has been serving up concerning Belle and Charlie needs to get in print.

I first met Belle when she kept her establishment in an unpainted house on Washington, a building so drab you couldn't even see it, it was so sorry looking from the outside. Yet when you crossed the doorway and entered Belle's domain you were transported into a plush world of wealth and wonder. I like that turn of phrase, "a plush world of wealth and wonder," real melodious, ain't it? I give you permission to use it, although I didn't make it up, that's just the way Lizzie Oliver, my favorite of the ladies at Belle's, says it. Mind you, all of Belle's girls are big book learners, they're all refined, accomplished young ladies, and Lizzie always talks so fine sometimes all I need is to hear her talk and I explode in my pants. Anyways, when you walked into Belle's house, the mud-caked, shabby, grit-encrusted, foul-mouthed, played-out "world" got traded in for that "wealth and wonder" one. What a contrast! French satins lined the walls, with mirrors and paintings on velvets and lace draperies. You floated on velvet carpets that were so heavy that you felt as if you were walking on a cushion of maroon clouds, and the gilt on the chairs and sofas just about blinded you. And, of course, Belle's well-bred girls were so voluptuous, any decent man would quiver like a fiddle string amidst all the finery and polite decorum, waiting for the night to come to its just rewards.

When I came back down from Shasta in the spring of '55, I learned Belle had just moved her parlor house right opposite from Ah Toy's establishment on Waverly Place. She and Charlie and her girls planted themselves behind a neat white picket fence, which I figured was a sign that Belle's "world" would lend a little taste to the city at no charge. Then, soon as she got comfortable, she promenaded the streets, and when she'd nod to her many acquaintances, her little colored servant boy would jump up and hand the gentleman a calling card with just her name and address printed on it. What a sight she made, her skin the delicate tint of the pink-white blossom of the peach, her fiery eyes flashing back and forth between gray and hazel, and her bosom and hips so shapely she looked like a flower opening up to the sun. Yes, indeed, Belle Cora *gave* more to that overgrown mining camp than she received, and she gave much, much more than it deserved!

I was pretty well staked by this time—No, mind you, I won't tell you my business affairs at all, although I reckon they're all well within the law. It's a question of policy, you see: I never let on the whereabouts of my diggings, whether it's of gold or of merchandise. But I can assure you that I had all the goddamn ounces and dollars to make everyone look up when I came down from Shasta. So I bedded myself fancy in the International Hotel, announced my success with a mighty fine suit of clothes, lost some big stakes at the roulette wheel, and invested in a generous tab at the saloon. But I knew I was *in* with the gilded crowd soon as I received an elegantly embossed invitation to attend an exclusive *soiree* at Belle's *salon*. Now, when I say "exclusive," I don't mean small, for she managed to throw her net out mighty far. I reckon she invited every man of substance in San Francisco: the mayor, all the politicians, judges, merchants, gamblers, bankers—why, she even invited the clergy!—and plenty of them showed up.

Yes, indeed, my good fellow, this was a crackling gay party, fabulously gay. With sumptuous food—any delicacy cook or confectioner could come up with was heaped on the tables —while a band sawed away at some high-spirited music to heat up all sorts of whirligig dancing around the carpets. There goes Judge Ned Mcgowan whirling around the room with a sparkling beauty—and there's James McCabe, owner of the El Dorado, sipping champagne with a frail and delicate young thing! All the swells and luminaries were there, and all behaving with the best manners, real dignified, the rooms filled with all that light talk and champagne and tinkling laughter, just like we was in a *salon* of the upper tendom. Yes, it was gay, rollicking gay, and only towards the end of the night did any reveler slip off into one of the upstairs rooms.

Well, that would be the end of it—a mighty pleasurable evening in San Francisco, and nothing more—except for the fact that Mrs. Richardson, wife of the federal marshal, General William Richardson, just happened to be hosting a grand party of her own that very same night. Much as the boys enjoyed Mrs. Richardson's company—and hoped to enlist Marshal Richardson in the sunny side of their own affairs —few of her male admirers showed up. It was just a little conflict in dates, but it was clear which way the wind blew, for only ministers and married men could pass up a ball at Belle's place (and even among these gentlemen there were a few absences due to those types of business and pastoral emergencies that suddenly "come up"). In short, Mrs. Richardson's grand bonanza turned into an even grander bust, although it was mighty mysterious to her why, since no one took pains to inform the lady concerning the parlor-house society calender. But could the real reason of such a humiliation be kept long from a woman? Well, you know the answer: Mrs. Richardson quickly discovered the cause for the skimpy turnout—and uncovering the truth must have ignited a veritable Vesuvius in her heart. From that time on is when I calculate she burned with the rage of a woman scorned.

Anyway, no one—least of all me—knew what kind of explosion was about to happen when they went to the American Theater to see the Ravels perform "Nicodemus; or, The Unfortunate Fisherman." I don't know if you've ever seen the world-famous Ravel family, but this troupe could act out an entire play without so much as uttering a single word. They could convey by their grimaces and gestures a whole stew of emotions, stirring it all up with winks and hands flying off in all directions, so that everyone could follow the conversation with great ease, which I figured was considerate, seeing as how the Ravels were Italian and no one would be able to understand them anyhow. Better yet, the Ravels were to be followed by the famous Martinetti family of acrobats, and spectacular feats were promised.

I had lost a mighty sum playing blackjack the night before and was temporarily short, although I wanted to take in the show, so I camped out in the pit with the boys. From there I looked up to watch all the brilliant, the noted, and the fashionable of the city fill up the boxes ringing all around the first balcony. Have you ever been in the American Theater? Well, it's plush, and those boxes looked mighty fine, the heavy velvet drapes drooping down from beaks of gilded wooden eagles eternally soaring over each of them—a splendid sight, with the chandeliers twinkling like the stars over Happy Camp and with the gentlemen looking prosperous and the few married ladies in the boxes making all the men beneath them think of home and mother, as well as less-delicate associations. To see those ladies would take a man's breath away, since they was so rare that all each of us in the pit could think is that when God made Eve by yanking off a piece of Adam, He must have taken the better part and left the ugliest heap of muscle and bone behind. Such an attitude, needless to say, did not encourage most of the boys to develop a discerning taste in women.

Suddenly, I caught sight of Belle sitting in the back of one box, her arm hooked through Charlie Cora's, and the two of them looking like the glitteringest couple you ever seen. He was like some patent-leather New York Van Vanderoven, and she gleamed like the darling of the entire house! Belle dazzled in that box, a delight to the soul and the senses, like—damn, she was something! For most of the boys, even if a woman looked like a lizard she would get their devoted admiration—but Belle was spectacular, her looks and her fancy Paris gown as stunning a "feat" as anything the Martinettis could pull off. Oh, you can't imagine how she turned to look over the audience like a queen, smiling and nodding benevolence to the many she recognized below, her sea of male subjects who, at one time or other, have knelt at the feet of Her Majesty. She hadn't scouted me out yet, so I waved and winked, nudging the boys beside me, until she got wind of the commotion in the pits and spotted me. She laughed when I saluted and blew me a tiny kiss.

Well, I didn't even bother to look at the couple sitting in front of Belle and Charlie, but after I threw a kiss back to Belle—one a little less delicate than hers, I admit—I noticed that the lady who sat towards the front of the box seemed to think that it was meant for her. This, of course, mangled her sense of propriety, so she turned to her husband for some kind of redress.

Sure enough, the lady's husband whisked out of the box and stood before me. Smelling as drunk as a fiddler's bitch, he introduced himself as United States Marshal William Richardson and demanded to know in deep Southern drawl why I was making indelicate gestures at his wife. Damn, what luck! It was none other than Marshal Richardson coming to the defense of his wife's honor!

Frankly, like I said, I hadn't even seen Mrs. Richardson, really. Would you have spotted her with Belle glittering like Venus in velvets and lace, and Mrs. Richardson looking like . . . like an elephant? I mean no disrespect, and she was only a little overlarge, but I venture to suggest that when folks said that they came to California to "see the elephant," they might have spotted the marshal's wife before coining the remark. No, Mrs. Richardson did not shine, she had no taste in fine clothes, and she weren't about to open like a flower in the sun—more like she would close up into a dark, dusty sack. The fact is, to see Belle sitting behind Mrs. Richardson was like seeing a warm-blooded woman sitting behind a stiff corpse. Isolation from the fair sex hadn't made me forget the difference between gold and pyrite! Still, I hadn't meant no harm to Mrs. Richardson, and it hadn't even occurred to me that Belle and Charlie was out of line, sitting up in the boxes and not in the closed booths in the back of the pit reserved for the ladies of the *demimonde*. But—what the hell?—don't you figure Charlie deserved to sit beneath these gilded eagles just like any one else estimated to be worth over $400,000 did? Well, I resolved that I would unruffle the marshal's feathers with a simple account of the facts.

"Marshal Richardson," I replied, hoping to avoid the idiocy of a duel. "I assure you that there is some grievous misunderstanding, for I did not wish to offend your gracious wife. My little sign of affection, I pray, was not indelicate, nor was it meant for Mrs. Richardson. I was signaling regards to my dear friend, Belle Cora, who sits in the rear of the same box as yours with her companion, Mr. Charles Cora."

"Do you mean, Cora the gambler and Belle the—the—?" he sputtered.

"Yes, Marshal Richardson, Charles Cora is a gambler, a

professional licensed by the State I reckon, and Belle Cora is a woman, which says both the best and the worst of her." I'd be a hog's ass if I would give in one inch concerning Belle's dignity.

I was expecting him to slap my face and set the hour for us to meet at Lake Merced with seconds, but he didn't, and he just shot back, "Thank you, suh!"

Soon as he tore out, I began cussing myself. I figured that no good would come of me calling attention to his boxmates, and certainly no good would come of me waxing a little eloquent in defense of Belle's and Charlie's honor, no good would come at all. Honor—damn those Southerners—honor ain't worth biscuits, but here I went and dug a spur into his ribs, and sure enough Marshal Richardson bucked up to the manager of the theater to demand that the gambler and the lady of ill fame be removed from the premises. The manager wasn't about to get into hauling paying customers out of his theater—especially on the basis of supposed bad character, seeing as how electing who is good and who is bad is business best left to the Lord, especially in San Francisco. The manager respectfully declined to bounce Belle and Charlie from their box seats, although he said he would confide with Mr. Cora afterwards about the values of tradition and the advantages of discretion so as not to cause embarrassment again.

Well, this did not sit too well with the offended marshal. "Balderdash!" he roared. I could see him from below as he burst back into the box and exchanged some heated words with Charlie about soiling the reputation of a respectable lady. Failing to shame Charlie into making his exit, the marshal gathered his wife up and evacuated the American Theater while sporting a noticeable evil-injun look. You should have seen how hot lava erupted from Mrs. Richardson's eyes when she realized that none other than the very same notorious prostitute who wrecked her grand party staked a claim in her very own box!

The next day I caught up to Charlie on the street and told him why Marshal Richardson had dogged after him, and I apologized for the awkward affair. You write that down in your damn marble-covered notebook, write that I apologized to Charlie Cora. I want your readers to know that I acted in a gentlemanly way throughout this whole sorry affair, and that I take my share of blame for how poor Charlie ended up getting hung, although you and I both know that behind it all the real cause was the war Mrs. Richardson launched against Belle that night.

They say Charlie was born in Italy, but I never seen him wave or grimace like the way the Ravels do on stage. He was short, thin, and quiet, never loud mouthing, boasting, or popping off, he was never at a loss for jollification, and he was well known and welcomed in all the saloons. "Never no need for a gambler to be too well known or too flashy," he once told me, "for a gambler needs the quiet of public opinion to steady his nerves—and keep the law out of his pockets." So Charlie listened to me, quietly rubbing his chin, as I repeated the exchange of words with Marshal Richardson of the night before.

"Smiley," he replied, after giving the matter a moment of thought, "there's no need to apologize, since it seems the marshal and his wife feel a bit sullied by me and Belle and not by you." Damn, he cut right through my dilemma like Solomon slicing up babies. "Besides," Charlie continued, "the marshal was so drunk last night I wager that when he woke this morning he could not remember much of anything from last night, much less the best or worst of Mrs. Richardson." He shook my hand and roared a laugh, "But ain't we ones to spoil propriety? Cheer up, boy, and join me for a drink." I accepted, but seeing as how I had some business to attend to, I arranged to meet him the next day.

Well, that was the last I seen Charlie Cora, though I heard from people that was there about what really happened—and you can read the newspapers yourself to get a notion about what really did *not* happen. Later that afternoon Cora was walking down the street with friends when his path crossed Marshal Richardson's. Some heated words passed between them, although I could never find out exactly what was said. I do believe Charlie remarked that drunk federal officers who don't have the faculties to tell the best or the worst of anything, much less a woman, might be a public menace. I ain't entirely sure of this, but I have yet to hear anyone tell me that ain't what Charlie said.

That evening Charlie was in the Cosmopolitan Saloon with Dr. Mills when Marshal Richardson came in for refreshment. Dr. Mills was a friend of both Charlie and the marshal, so the doctor ventured to smooth out the bad feelings between the two by introducing them. Well, they ended up sharing several amiable drinks, and it looked like hostilities had ceased. Dr. Mills tells me they left the saloon together with smiles, but once they stood outside Marshal Richardson let loose his barrage of insults again, threatening to slap Charlie's face. Now you know Charlie did not hanker to draw on a man as drunk as the marshal was, so he kept icy cool, just turned back into the saloon and told Dr. Mills about the challenge. But Marshal Richardson followed Charlie into the saloon, and with a strange, foolish grin he drawled, "I have promised to slap this man's face, and I had better do it now." Well, Dr. Mills and some of the boys wrestled that notion out of the marshal's head by pulling his hands down on to a nearby shot glass. "How about we have Richardson and Cora tip up another drink together, sort of iron 'em out agin?" one of the boys suggested, but it seemed like the best policy was to ease

Charlie back out on the street while the marshal was kept pinned down by rapid volleys of whiskey.

Next afternoon Richardson traveled from bar to bar looking for Charlie, vowing vengeance. He finally met up with his enemy while Charlie was walking with John Stanton, but by then the mercurial marshal was amiable again and invited his old foe for visits to a couple of bars. George Hoskins told me that by this time Richardson was loaded pretty well but that he looked sober enough to defend himself—in fact, sober enough to inflict a mortal blow. In any case, the two parted after their cordial drinks, and Charlie moved over to the Blue Wing on Montgomery Street. After a few minutes a messenger came in the saloon to tell Charlie that a friend was waiting to see him outside. Well, it turned out to be Richardson again. They talk peaceable for a while, walking together down the street—but Richardson recommences arguing, after a piece. Suddenly, the marshal reaches for his weapon, whereupon Charlie outdraws him—shoots him dead with his derringer—as simple as that.

I know some people say one thing or another, that Cora shot the marshal down in cold blood while the man cried, "Don't shoot! I am unarmed!" I know Cora—I know how careful Charlie is, how his policy is—and I know he would wait for the marshal to begin to draw before plugging him. No gambler in his right mind seeks out the opportunity to gun down a federal marshal—it don't make for much business sense.

People also talk that Richardson was so drunk that he couldn't even stand up, much less reach for his revolver, meaning that Charlie took unfair advantage of an inebriated man. But I seen how drunk the marshal was that night at the American Theater—he smelled like he had soaked up half the bay—yet he still walked straight, leveled his eyes at me without a wobble when he drawled out, "Thank you, suh." No, as much as Marshal Richardson was a drunk, he still carried himself with the military bearing befitting the general that he was. Too bad he had to be spurred by an indignant woman into rashness, but I don't see how Charlie could have done different. I hardly reckon you would let yourself be shot, seeing as how you may not be able to write it up afterward. I dare think you ain't too stupid to allow yourself to get shot down, are you? So Charlie only did what he had to do to protect himself—he drew, and he shot.

That gunshot echoed up and down the street, and, quick, all the bars emptied out, with a crowd starting to chant, "Hang him! Hang him!" while Charlie was quickly taken by the law. But the mob that circled around Charlie and the officers took a hasty vote—the ayes for hanging him right then and there, and the nays for letting the judge do it. Well, the nays elected to have Charlie taken by the officers instead of by the lynch mob, which goes to show that plenty of folks knew Cora was a man of policy and felt that it just might be possible that Charlie killed Marshal Richardson to protect his own life. Still, Sam Brannan, not satisfied with the vote, jumped up on a barrel and began haranguing about the virtues of rope until the police finally arrested him too.

Next came the inquest, which is when I decided to swiftly relocate my business affairs to Weaverville, for I could sniff the odor of vigilantes pretty strong, and I figured I'd rather sit out *all* the proceedings, both legal and extra. I won't bother you with the rest, the trial and how the jury came in deadlocked, and how the vigilantes hung poor Charlie from Fort Gunnybags, seeing as how you can get a firsthand recollection from someone who was there. But I highly recommend that you talk with real people and not with editors, otherwise your little notebook will fill up with lies.

But, before I finish up, there's still one more item for me to relate that would, like Lizzie Oliver says, "illuminate" Belle's character. Allow me to tell you something which I have not shared with any other soul. I figure you're the one to write all this up so as to allow the public to know, and for the sake of truth I'll share the secrets of my heart with you.

You see, Belle once confided to me the story of how she "fell." That's right, she told me, told me how she entered into her profession, and how she met her Charlie. When you know Belle's history, you'll regard all the abuse and insults heaped on the lady in a mighty different fashion, I am willing to wager.

One day I was taking a little tea with the girls, when Belle suddenly started to weep. Oh, they was little tears scooped up by her handkerchief quick, but I asked her what the matter was, and how I could help. She thanked me and just said that sometimes the past came over her like a veil, the memories burdening her with sorrows long unspoken. "Sometimes you can unhitch those sorrows by talking," I said. She smiled and real quiet and seriouslike she told me she was born the daughter of a clergyman in Baltimore—yes, Belle's a clergyman's daughter! She wasn't even eighteen years old when a young man captivated her, fired her up, and then abandoned her. When the secret became known to her father—including the child that, alas, she already was carrying—he cast her out and closed his doors forever against her.

Belle went to New Orleans. There the baby was born, and there it soon died. Alone, forsaken, and unable to return to her family, she wandered one day into the market by the Mississippi River to sit and sip her coffee amidst the bustle when a woman bedecked with jewels and dressed in a handsome gown came over to her to comfort her and to offer her help. At this sign of compassion the poor girl broke down and sobbed her story. The woman told her of the ways Belle could help herself, for Belle's newfound friend initiated the forlorn girl into the advantages of the fallen—and fallen she was, for what else could she do? Her father had cast her out—her reputation was already ruined—there was nowhere else to turn —so she laughed recklessly, and together with her friend she boldly walked across the narrow cobbled street to a new life.

Well, this might have been the end of the story—but it so happened that Charlie Cora was then operating out of New Orleans, and he came sauntering through the market with a dealer from one of the casinos. The pair of gamblers spotted the two ladies crossing the street. While the dealer recognized the older lady (and her profession), neither of them ever saw the girl before. Cora took out a twenty-dollar gold piece from his pocket and said, "Here's for the one to learn who the young lady is." Cora won the toss, crossed over, and introduced himself. "Oh, how handsome Charlie looked with a white Panama hat drooping over his big dark eyes and his mustache," Belle told me, aglow in the memory of that meeting. Then her voice got real low and confidential, and she said, "I want you to know, Smiley, that I went to live in the *demi-monde* of New Orleans with that fashionable, kind lady," then she whispered in my ear, "*but I have known no man but Cora!*"

I tell you, I felt myself getting misty eyed, listening to such a tale. Although she went to live with the other girls in that gilded house, Cora saved her from the baser appetites of men who came to devour any of the young radiant creatures. Her loyalty to Charlie became rock hard, grew almost to the point of worship.

When word of the California discovery reached New Orleans, Cora developed a keen interest, particularly when he heard of the excellent business opportunities for someone of his profession, so he decided to leave for the new field. He kissed his devoted Belle good-bye. "Nothing could persuade me to remain behind without him," she told me, "and I insisted on sailing along with him." She was just a young girl of twenty-two, but she was willing to embark on adventures and dangers all because of love.

"When I arrived in San Francisco," she explained to me, "I quickly saw that I could use what I had learned in New Orleans—to become the proprietor of a tasteful establishment that entertained a city starved for the charms of the fair sex. I have no regrets, Smiley, and yet I shed a tear for my poor father who cast me out, and I remember my childhood in Baltimore and the hymns we sang in church . . . You know, it was only Charlie's kindness that saved me from a far harsher fate, only my gallant Charlie."

She began to weep gently, dabbing her eyes, and I was feeling about as low as the Dead Sea—then she broke off all of a sudden and changed the subject, talking about all the champagne she had to order for the *soiree* the next night, and she filled the room with her laughter, although I could still see the mists of sadness clouding up Belle's eyes.

Now, don't you find yourself dabbing your own eyes at a story like that? Don't you wonder at the strength of character of a woman who refuses to leave the side of her man like that, a woman who comes to a strange city inhabited almost entirely by men but keeps loyal despite the temptation to become the mistress of the mayor or any of the other high rollers? Here is a young girl cast out of her home by her father because she fell into the clutches of a smooth and engaging young man, a girl who then gives her heart and holy devotion to the man who saves her, a boon companion who sticks by his side despite calumny and calamity. And yet, this is the woman whose name was dragged through mud, who was spat upon as a dirty harlot, as the evil spoiler of home and family! It burns you up, don't it? Mrs. Richardson don't feel proper sitting in the box with the likes of Belle!

But I'll tell you one thing: The way I do my arithmetic, Mrs. Richardson only has herself to blame for her husband getting killed. Not only did she kill her own husband, and in so doing she widowed Belle too—all because her sense of propriety was injured in a theater! It made no difference if the trial was about Charlie shooting the marshal, people all the way to Oregon was arguing about the real contest that took place in the American Theater: respectable Mrs. Richardson versus that notorious Belle Cora.

Oh, how they threw mud on Belle, and how she stood by her Charlie throughout the whole trial, paying for his lawyer, paying off the jury, doing everything she could to save her man—all while the editors and the preachers and all the other puffed-up "businessmen" and vigilante cowards snickered and hollered insults. It may have been Charlie who was put on trial and hung, but it was Belle who they burnt at the stake in their hearts because she lent herself to the wanton pleasures of men, because she was fallen.

So far as I can tell, every woman is fallen, and every woman attends to her man—or at least ought to—and I seen quite a few married ladies who treat their men considerable less able and less noble than the way Belle treated Charlie. What else can these hypocrites expect? The only crime I can figure Belle is guilty of is the fact that she's a woman! And, to tell you the truth, that crime still ain't common enough around here!

She Said Her Name Was Lizzie Oliver

Smiley is the type of client whose pleasure is enhanced by indulging in sex with the *idea* of a woman. Well, let me say it a little differently: his lust increases in direct proportion to the degree that he believes the woman he happens to be soiling is clean. Consequently, it's a good practice to massage him with a story and paint it up with grandiloquent words, which then gets him as frisky as a dog in heat. He loves to have sex with the accoutrements of culture, as if he were screwing a facade. Better yet, if he can believe that the exercise of his organ can protect womanhood by plundering it, Smiley can become positively beatific, and he comes back again and again, a client to be valued for regular cash. However, as concerns all the recent troubles—Smiley is a fool. Whatever he told you, I would suggest that you weigh it all with a boulder-sized grain of salt.

You look intelligent, so I won't belabor my point. But let me ask you if he told you that Belle was a minister's daughter from Baltimore, that she bore a child who—ah, yes, I see that he has repeated that sorrowful tale. You don't believe it, do you? Belle found that clients like him enjoy the idea of reha-bilitating fallen women with their members, so she elongated truth a little in order to elongate his. Will I tell you the *real* story? Sir, *there is no real story,* and I certainly will not tell you anything that seems realer, except to say that she was chris-tened Clara Belle Ryan, her father was prosperous but no cler-gyman, and she entered the profession after working with her sister for a dressmaker in Baltimore that tailored gowns for an establishment catering to sea captains. After a while, she and her sister decided it would be better to wear the gowns than to sew them, and, of course, in order to wear the gowns, one must be prepared to take them off. Belle was ready for such a contingency—and the rest of the story is boring.

Perhaps you are someone whose titillation comes from hearing the "truth" before you actually grope for Plato's shad-ows between a woman's legs. However, if I understand you rightly, you are only interested in the story and not in sensual pleasure. This is peculiar, and you are perhaps even more per-verse than Smiley, but I will entertain your desire the same as anyone else's, answering your questions with all the delicious, bold, delightful, frank, sensual truth that you desire. Such ser-vice saves on the back and surely saves on the laundry bill. Do you like it if I talk like that? I should warn you, however, that what I tell you may seem vulgar, and I may use terms that are—how shall I put it?—overprecise or too direct. Many men like it when their penises are put in our mouths, but they find it uncomfortable when we mouth the word around which our lips have just formed—although, given all the varieties of taste, there are even those who love it when we speak the filthy talk of men, and they pay like all the rest. So be it.

People regarded Belle as Charlie's mistress, but Belle was actually the one who often bankrolled Charlie when he lost big. Without Belle, Charlie would have been squeezed out from the gaming tables a long time ago. "The more we perform as women," she would say, "the more we become men." This was the motto on her coat of arms, so to speak, for her intention was always to remain as independent as a man, although Belle allowed everyone to think that Charlie payed for her favors. So, when we heard that Charlie had killed Marshal Richardson and was taken by the police with a lynch mob at his heels, she called together some of the girls to comfort her and to consider what course to take.

We're not like those girls who sprawl around all day in cribs, working man after man. We are at the top of our profession. In order to reach such a pinnacle you must have beauty, but you also must have accomplishment, sexual and otherwise. I will not talk to you about bedroom skills—for those are guild secrets—but when I talk about Belle and the troubles she faced, you need to know the depth of her "otherwise" accomplishments.

Each morning, close to noon, after our customers of the night before have departed for the day and we have rested and attended to our toilets, all the ladies of the house would gather for tea and talk. Belle would have one of the girls read the newspapers out loud, and we would discuss the events of the day—for it is required of us to understand the intrigues of politicians and businessmen in order to avoid tricky currents in the flow of money and power. It would be most inappropriate if, for example, two protagonists in a feud ended up glaring at each other across the same divan. We would also indulge in novels and poems during our daily gatherings

—Byron was my favorite, while Belle marveled over Shake-speare—and we would organize little readings and perfor-mances for our own entertainment. I think her favorite play was *The Tempest*, and she even wrote a travesty of it in which she played Prospera, an injured madame who used her magic books to shipwreck some business for her Miranda.

So, when Belle rang the bell that day, it was as if she called us together for a little teatime amusement and edification —but we wept instead when we learned the startling news. After time, though, our tears ceased, for Belle aimed to become a real Prospera raising storms and spirits. We sipped our tea and planned the battles, and reading the newspapers became the focus of our daily strategy sessions. They were shocking, for the papers all blared forth that General Richard-son was assassinated in cold blood "without a single effort at resistance," that Richardson was "of a most kind, generous, and noble nature," while Charlie was merely "a low-life char-acter groomed by harlots," and the such like.

James King of William was especially fulminatory, for it seemed that the killing fed into his latest frenzy against sin and corruption, and in his *Bulletin* he foamed at the mouth like a mad dog—What? Where did he get that "of William" business? I couldn't figure that out either, until I heard the story: He called himself "King of William" because where he grew to manhood in Washington, D.C., there were so many boys named James King that he hitched his father's Christian name to the end of his own like a tail. His brother, Thomas, didn't seem to have any competition, so he goes around with-out the "of William" freight dragging behind. The way I look at it, this James probably dreamt he was a king of some realm called "William," because I'll tell you one thing, he was no king of San Francisco.

Anyway, this King of William lashed out against poor Billy Mulligan, the jailer, simply because Billy was a friend of Charlie's and a friend of the gaming tables. "Hang Billy Mulligan! That's the word!'" Martha read out loud the *Bulletin*'s editorial in her most authoritative voice. "'If Mr. Sheriff Scannell does not remove Billy Mulligan from his present post as keeper of the County Jail, and Mulligan lets Cora escape, hang Billy Mulligan, and if necessary to get rid of the sheriff, hang him—hang the sheriff!'

"Dear me," Martha paused. "I do believe Mr. King of William is anxious to hang someone—anyone!"

"Go on, Martha," Belle urged.

Martha cleared her voice and resumed: "'Strong measures are now required to have justice done in this case of Cora. Citizens of San Francisco! what means this feeling so prevalent in our city that this dastardly assassin will escape the vengeance of the law? Oh heavens! what a mortification to every lover of decency and order, in and out of San Francisco, to think that the sheriff of this county is an ex-keeper of a gambling hall; his deputy, who acts as keeper of the County Jail, is the notorious Billy Mulligan; and a late deputy, Burns, the late capper at a string game table! Merchants of San Francisco, mechanics, bankers, honest men of every calling, hang your heads in very shame of the disgrace now resting on the city you have built!'"

After Martha finished we just sat, stunned. "Well," Belle finally spoke. "Mr. King of William seems to have some problems with those in the gambling business—but I do believe that the *Bulletin*'s editor has no need to fear Charlie's escape. Considering the regular chorus of 'hang him!' coming out of his mouth, I would think the safest place for Charlie right now is in jail. Indeed, the gentleman would be pleased if Charlie did escape, so he could suspend him, along with everyone else, from the rafters—but I don't think we'll give him the satisfaction. No, what we need to do is get a lawyer, the best lawyer money can buy, and we'll wriggle Charlie free through the courts."

So we took up a subscription among the boys—I lent her thousands I was saving to open my own parlor house. Combined with her own money, we had enough to secure the services of the renowned Colonel E. D. Baker—an eloquent, gracious, selfish, cowardly man—for the unheard-of sum of thirty thousand dollars, half of it in advance. When the press got wind that such a distinguished lawyer was retained, they lashed out viciously: "To think that a man who lives in a bawd house and is instigated to a murderous deed by a harlot can cheat the law of its course by a subscription organized by his mistress!"

"Watch," Belle remarked after the Colonel took his money. "He'll be back trying to beg off because the humbug 'lovers of decency' will put the screws to him."

Sure enough, a few days later Colonel E. D. Baker came back, trying to weasel out of the case. Well, at least he returned in the person of his associate, Mr. Foote, in order to hand back the fee. Belle was prepared, however. She coaxed, she pleaded, she wept—all to no avail. However, she called up her reserves and told Mr. Foote to remind the Colonel of his preference for paying certain visits to the ladies whilst wearing women's undergarments. You could imagine when he received that message from Mr. Foote how Colonel Baker was paralyzed, never thinking for a moment that Belle would even consider disclosing such a—uh—private matter. He was impaled like a butterfly on a pin, wriggling between his fear of the vigilantes and the terrors of humiliation. The battle raged in his soul for a few moments—but only a few—until his fear of ridicule triumphed. He continued on the case—much to our good fortune, for the lawyer who enjoyed prancing in garters and silks proved to be worth every penny we paid him.

Belle knew everything about the courts, so she tried to pay for as many witnesses and jurors as she could, naturally. Most important, we needed to make sure that Maria Knight, who happened to be standing in the street during the fracas, would testify that Charlie shot in self-defense. Belle arranged to have two well-known, upstanding gentlemen trick Maria into coming to her house. At first Miss Knight was appalled when she learned in whose parlor she found herself, and she sat stiff as a board next to the side table with its silver tray, decanter, and glasses. She wouldn't drink any wine, though, and she turned down the tea we prepared, thinking probably we were trying to poison her, which, of course, was not our plan. So Belle started to relate one of her life stories, of how she was one of two orphan girls, how Charlie met her when she was a young girl and paid for her education, and all the rest. Oh, this was a prodigiously pathetic story, very moving, and I could see Miss Knight's eyes glisten—the woman was as gullible as Smiley!

Then—bang!—we had Murphy and Bear Tooth knock on the doors, barge in, rage about the miscarriage of justice against their dear friend Charlie Cora, then discover Maria Knight as the one who would lie that Charlie drew first, and at such a revelation the two brutes then roar with indignation. Bear Tooth yanked out his knife and threatened to kill Miss Knight then and there, but Belle threw herself across her, "No! No! You'll do no such thing! She won't lie! She'll tell us what she saw that day." Miss Knight began to spin out her tale laboriously, how she was walking down the street on the way to the milliner, and the sky was—"Yes, yes!" Belle interjected, "But what did Richardson have in his hand?"

"Nothing. Marshal Richardson had nothing in his hand, so far as I could see," she answered, either a naive fool or a cold, calculating operator.

"Woman," Belle shot back, "if you expect to get out of this

house alive you must say that you saw Richardson with a pistol in his hand. That is the only ground we have to save my husband's life! Isn't one husband's death enough?"

Suddenly Bear Tooth lunged at her with the knife, while Murphy struggled to hold him back. "Hold off, my friend," Murphy gasped. "She surely deserves to die, but maybe there's a way she could save herself." Bear Tooth gave him a cross-eyed look, but Murphy offered to give Miss Knight one thousand dollars and spare her life if she agreed to tell the truth —on the witness stand—that Richardson threatened Charlie with a gun before Charlie drew.

Well, she said she would agree out of sympathy for Belle, for the suffering of a "wife" of such a man. Arrangements were made, and all seemed well—except as soon as we turned around, she went right to the district attorney's office to report our little get-together. "A scandal!" the editors exploded, as if coaxing proper testimony was an uncommon thing. Still, it was an embarrassment, and we had to admit that Maria Knight was not so naive—although at the trial she still reeled out Belle's life story as a young orphan with wide-eyed belief—and she was definitely very shrewd.

I tell you it was hard, hard trying to outflank the opposition. Of course, it became clear that it was really Belle who was on trial, that Mrs. Richardson, already having offered up her husband, was angling to get Belle by way of hers. The newspapers formed a Greek chorus chanting, "Harlot! Harlot!" How would you feel? I tell you we felt low, too low to plumb, for it looked so very like that Charlie was going to be sacrificed, nailed to the cross.

"Colonel," Belle addressed the attorney as we conferred at the start of the trial. "This is a war, as you well know. The way I view it, sir, some people want to regulate business so as to control it for their own narrow profit, while others want to keep business risky and loose and easygoing for everybody's benefit. Let us call the first group the upstanding, the upright, the uplifting—let's call them the verticals. The second group, of course, would then be the horizontals—the supine, the low life, the outcasts, the fallen. All of us here are the horizontals, for no one can be more horizontal than a woman—and I am regarded as the chief of the horizontals."

The Colonel peered at her with a puzzled look. "My dear Belle, what is your point?"

"My point, my darling Colonel, is that this is what this trial is all about. You must fight this case not only on the evidence —the fact that the marshal raised his hand to draw forth his derringer—but you must also win it on the battlefield of public opinion, where the weapons of *sentiment* reign supreme."

. She regarded her lawyer for a moment as if judging his intelligence. Could he fathom what she was telling him? "Colonel," she continued with great deliberation, "you must take me, the chief of the horizontals, and you must pull me up straight—you must make me vertical! Do you understand? *Make me vertical!* You are the most eloquent man in California. If anyone can do it, you are the man."

The Colonel thought for a moment, his gaze lost in the folds of the velvet curtain. Then he looked up, his eyes brightening, and he broke into a smile that told us he knew exactly what she meant. Belle beamed back at him, reassured.

"I see that you understand," Belle smiled. "Good. *Now all you've got to do is use your mouth!*"

"Yes, Colonel," said Emily, who entertained the attorney most nights. "Use your mouth, darling."

And that's, of course, just what Colonel Baker did in court. · I mean, he let everything slide, all the slurs on Charlie's character, all the assaults on gamblers, and all the "harlot" ejaculations shot out from the prosecution. Throughout it all the Colonel just sat quiet, somber—and he waited, letting the jury get put to sleep, until he was ready to set off his own cannons.

Meanwhile, Belle stayed away, secluded at home. But even though every day her name was scandalized in court, she quietly went about her business of helping her Charlie. For each meal she would have a delicious dish prepared to be delivered to Charlie's cell; she supplied him with freshly cleaned linen every day; and she outfitted him with a richly figured velvet vest, along with the pleated shirts and kid gloves to which he was accustomed. And, oh, did he look so elegant, so sharp, for every session in court—and how the newspapers did sneer at the soft treatment the gambler received at the hands of the harlot!

The Colonel just looked like he was fading, his face and his hair getting grayer by the minute, his body heaped into his chair like an old sack, as the prosecutors flailed away. Every day the boy would come to the house and report on what happened in court. Very quietly we would listen to his account, compare it to the newspapers, and weigh all the twists and turns.

Then it came time for the defense's final words, and we knew the Colonel had to play his cards.

The Colonel at first droned on, mumbling about how all the witnesses were people of fine character, how sorrowful he was at the unfortunate death of Marshal Richardson, on and on. Hand me the scrapbook there. Thank you. Also my spectacles. I can read to you what he said, and he droned on interminably, so I'll skip that. But after he rocked the jury to sleep, he paused. That's when he set off his first real blast:

"The man who is here struggling for life—who is arraigned for the death of one claimed to be one of the purest of our citizens, is said to have followed degraded and vicious pursuits. It is said of him that he is cared for by a woman of very bad relations in life, whose name, indeed, is a reproach. Against this man at the bar the whole public press—that mighty engine of passion and power—have poured all the concentrated vials of their wrath and indignation . . ."

Pretty good, huh? Well, he was just getting warmed up, for all he ended up asking for in this line of argument was for the jury to extend a little "human sympathy" to Charlie.

But then he spoke about how Marshal Richardson himself was not so fine a fellow after all, about how the marshal was drunk all the time, how he went about blustering and threatening everyone and everywhere. Let's see—ah yes, listen: "I appeal to facts. Whatever the prisoner is, he was peaceful, amiable, kind. Good though the other man was as a husband and a father, he was violent, dangerous, and, in his anger, deadly . . . Richardson was a violent, quarrelsome drunk."

The jury squirmed around a bit when they heard that, because everyone knew it was true, especially the whisky end of it. But the Colonel wasn't done with this, for next he plunged headfirst into the mouth of the real volcano: He began to talk directly about Belle Cora, about how the prosecution sneered that our defense was concocted in "a haunt of sensuality." The boys tell me he paused, just drilled a look at the jury in silence, and when he resumed he defended Belle's attempts to buy off jurors as nothing but an example of womanly devotion!

Listen to what he said: "In plain English, Belle Cora is helping her friend as much as she can. It may appear strange to the prosecution, but I am inclined to admit the plain, naked fact—and in the Lord's name, who else should help him? Who else is there whose duty it is to help him? If it were not for her, he would not have a friend on earth . . . It is a woman of base profession, of more than easy virtue, of malign fame, of a degraded caste—it is one poor, weak, feeble, and, if you like it, wicked woman—to her alone he owes his ability to employ counsel to present his defense. What we want to know is, what have they against that? What we want to know is, why don't they admire it?"

Indeed, the Colonel could use his mouth, and splendidly.

The boys described how the prosecution sat, beginning to kindle, suspecting the drift of his argument, and I can just try to picture how their eyes blazed with holy indignation.

But then the Colonel pounced. This is what he said: "The history of this case is, I suppose, that this man and this woman have formed a mutual attraction, not sanctioned, if you like, by the usages of society—if you like, not sanctioned by the rites of the Church. It is but a trust in each other, a devotion to the last, amid all the dangers of the dungeon and all the terrors of the scaffold." Right here, the Colonel made another significant pause, then rolled on: "They were bound together by a tie which angels might not blush to approve. Remember Magdalene!"

Magnificent! What a speech! *"They were bound together by a tie which angels might not blush to approve."* He said each word deliberately and slowly and with the weight of reason and moral authority! Oh, could the Colonel use his mouth! He was a master orator, a Demosthenes of the Golden Gate! The jurors were startled, moved almost to tears, speechless! To think, Belle was merely a devoted wife, a woman to her man, and here they were scorning her, deriding her efforts, no matter how . . . how irregular, to save her man! I tell you the accusation just stabbed them—and the boys of the audience gasped, shocked; they were horrified like the jurors, for the Colonel had said it all as direct as could be, and the arrows had penetrated all their hearts.

When the boys came back that day to report on the Colonel's speech, Belle's smile reached across the room, and she whirled about, and she sang a mad little song she made up:

Oh, the Colonel set me standing up, standing up, standing up.
The Colonel set me standing up so vertical this morning.

Over and over, again and again, she sang the impromptu ditty, twirling like a dervish, and the rest of us clapping our hands and singing, "*Magdalene! Magdalene!*" like a chorus of colored girls in church. I dare say we were vertical alright—until we fell flat on our backs, exhausted, laughing.

Oh, and how that man's mouth did work miracles! For when the jury came back, they were hopelessly deadlocked. Most voted for a guilty verdict, but at least three of the jurors thought otherwise, and there seemed no question that the Colonel had been the one to plant the seed of doubt in the fertile soil between their ears. And that's how Charlie beat back the court. What a victory! A stunning, beautiful victory!

But, of course, "King James" of William fumed at the outrage. Belle read his pronouncements out loud, employing her most Shakespearean declamatory style—she called it her Hamletta style: "Hung be the heavens with black! The money of the gambler and the prostitute has succeeded, and Cora has another respite. Rejoice, ye gamblers and harlots! Rejoice with exceeding gladness! Your triumph is great—oh, how you have triumphed! Triumphed over everything that is holy and virtuous and good; and triumphed legally—yes, legally!"

A beautiful tirade—and triumph we did, and legally! We celebrated that night royally, for we knew that at the next trial we would smother any chance for conviction and keep on wriggling Charlie through the courts until the public got distracted by something else and the lawyers got too tired and Charlie slips out once a simple deal ends up getting made. Now all it would take would be time.

Charlie waited patiently in jail, and every day we sat on our sofas, and we drank our tea, and we scanned the newspapers; we conducted our affairs quietly and out of the public eye, and we waited for the next trial.

After this, everything went to Hell. You can talk to someone else about how that damn fool "King James" of William started to hound James Casey, ranting and raving that the supervisor was corrupt, that he stuffed the ballot boxes, that he was a subscriber to Charlie Cora's defense—on and on —none of which bothered Casey too much. But when the *Bulletin* started to harp about the time he did back in Sing Sing, he just boiled over. So Casey ends up going to the editor's office, hollering that he didn't want his past raked up, especially the mistakes of his youth, then he shoots down the fool newspaper editor right in the middle of the street!

I'll tell you, if Casey hadn't shot James King of William, Charlie would have been freed instead of getting hung. And Charlie knew it. Soon as they brought Casey into the jail, Charlie looked up at him and said, "Now you've gone and put a noose around both our necks."

I don't want to talk about the Committee of Vigilance. You just go over to Mr. Coleman or any of the others and ask them. It hurts too much to talk about poor Charlie getting swept off into Fort Gunnybags, caught in the fervor against Casey. The vigilantes mustered an army—thousands of troops—rolled out their artillery, and they went to get Charlie and Casey from out of the jail. Belle rushed to his side while the cannons were rolling up to the door, and she stayed with him until Charlie saw it was hopeless, and he agreed to hand himself over after he wrote his will, and Belle hugged him, and she said, "Good-bye, Charlie. I've done all I could to get you clear."

We knew once Judge Lynch had him only the U.S. Army could free him, and the Governor whipped up some banker, William Tecumseh Sherman, who agreed to blast the rebels out of Fort Gunnybags for the sake of the Federal government —even though lots of folks knew very well that Mr. Sherman detested the editor so much—all his sanctimonious, meddling ways—that he hankered to kill James King of William himself, and said so publicly at least on a few occasions. Anyways, Mr. Sherman withdrew once he saw how the Governor wobbled and wavered, so that was the end of the troops. The vigilantes had Charlie, they had him good.

They put Charlie on some kind of trial—not a genuine trial but one they fixed up to make themselves look legitimate, as official as they could—considering that they had, after all, usurped the United States government—they kept records, drummed up a judge, defense, all the fixings—they even hauled out Maria Knight to testify again, while, of course, none of Charlie's witnesses felt comfortable enough to walk into Fort Gunnybags to testify on his behalf—and there was no Colonel Baker this time, of course, for the colonel had to flee town for his life. And right in the middle of it James King of William, who had been lingering for days on his sickbed, finally gets up and expires, and the whole room in Fort Gunnybags fell to a doomsday silence when they heard the tolling of the death knell. Those damn bells ended up so poisoning those court "proceedings" that the rope seemed all but inevitable.

But even in this court, when the vigilantes took their vote they could not get a unanimous verdict. Maybe those who voted against the rope thought Charlie was forced to defend himself, or at least there was enough of a doubt for them. No matter. No, the vigilantes went by their own rules, not by the law's—and they agreed in advance that the verdict would be rendered by *majority vote*! Charlie was *elected* to be hanged fair and square, real democraticlike, although they agreed that after the majority's decision all the "jurors" would change their votes to make the conviction unanimous, just to keep up appearances! They couldn't get their way through the law, so they decided to invent their own!

No, you can talk to them to find out all about it. I'm done. I see what you've wanted from me. You're the type who loves to see a woman weep, to see her heart broke. Well, you can see all you want, for my tears are real enough—but you never did see how low Belle got, how she locked herself up in her room, the curtains all drawn, and she would just sit, listening to the few boys who still dared to stay in town tell which direction the fury of the mob would blow, and how the tears silently flowed down her cheeks. They even arranged for both Charlie and Casey to hang together on the day of James King of William's funeral!

"Charlie is lost," she sighed when she learned that Charlie would die that Thursday. Belle began to speak in snatches and fragments, her voice trailing, her face pale. I sat with her alone, and she held my hand, talking, trying to think, to scheme, but only coming up with more tears—for what stratagem would prevail now?

Yes, I remember what Belle said. She first said something peculiar. She said, "They built the railroad across the isthmus of Panama, my dear, and now the train has arrived at Fort Gunnybags."

I looked at her queerly, just like the way you're looking at me right now, but she went on, and she went on to say all kinds of things, some crazy, but all of it of a piece. She said, "Now the wives will come, for it's a holiday picnic to cross the isthmus because of the railroad and no longer a difficult passage . . . Do you know what the miracle of California is? The miracle is an instant market formed suddenly from diamonds and dung from every corner of the world, an instant market of the world, and now the wives are coming too! Gold's not so easy to find anymore, Lizzie. They need big crews to mine the gold now, using hydraulics and the rest. A lone miner can't make out like he used to; now they need joint stock companies. Business in town is down, except for us . . . Merchants, all of them, waiting for the flush again, and they figure to lay claim to all the diggings, even ours . . . Do you think the shops for fine furnishings, the restaurants, the musicians, the gown makers, do you think they would stay in business without us?

Who would buy? How foolish they are to separate the fallen, to cut the city into two . . . Our enemy is a mob of Know Nothings who have decided to lynch the Pope! Our enemy is a cabal of Yankee peddlers ranged against New York and New Orleans, against Italy and Ireland! Our enemy is—They are a bunch of thieving, murderous hypocrites! Oh Charlie, my poor Charlie, now you are lost . . . now you are lost . . . How pleasant is the railroad across the isthmus! No long, tedious voyage around the Horn and its ferocious storms, no dank trek through the unbearable jungle . . . Yes, the wives are coming . . . from Boston, from Philadelphia . . . Their husbands invent the law from the heights of Fort Gunnybags with their cannons, protecting their women from other women . . . and it's all because the isthmus of Panama has a railroad, and the wives will come to San Francisco, and when they come they will give to these men . . . Give them what, Lizzie? Will they give them civilization? And if that is so, then what do we witness today? The train across the isthmus runs straight to Fort Gunnybags, where the hangman waits on the platform . . . ."

Oh, it was sad, indeed, to see her like that, and I'm glad to say that she regained her composure soon after. I understood her, though, about the changes and the conflict that inevitably flowed as a result, for the families coming was a sign that San Francisco was becoming a real city, and it was good that they were coming, I suppose, for I feel we'll still work for a living no matter what. Unless we fish out a husband from this sea of men, what's the choice? It's still cheaper to pay a Chinaman to do the wash than a girl who's white and free, so we knew one way or another we'd have to manage our own affairs, but it was sad, and I stroked her arm and hugged her, and you can imagine that it was hard, very hard.

Belle stood by Charlie's side right up to the hanging. They were alone, so I couldn't tell you anything, anyhow. Father Accolti came for spiritual comfort, and he married Belle and

Charlie—in holy, official Catholic matrimony, most vertical-like, so her poor Charlie would at least be hers in the eyes of the Church and the world, and maybe that would ease Charlie's way in with God. Amen.

But how that James Casey carried on! He sobbed on the gallows, crying out to his poor mother, pleading that his aged mother not hear him be called a murderer, that he was "brought up to do right, and to resent wrong was his province . . ." like Casey was making a campaign speech, whining on and on, and all the while the funeral bells for James King of William was filling the air.

When it came to Charlie's turn, he said nothing, he just nodded. Yes, Charlie was never more dignified, never cooler, and the pitiful, weeping James Casey seemed a weak, insignificant creature beside the dignified gambler—who was thin and short and dark and never said a word as he stepped to his death.

Belle blackened her house and kept to her room for a month of mourning after the hanging. But there would be no peace for her suffering heart and tortured soul. Two days after the funeral the *Bulletin*, which was now edited by Thomas King, the slain crusader's brother, printed a disgusting, hideous, heartless letter. Listen to this:

> Gentlemen, one thing more must be done: Belle Cora must be requested to leave this city. The women of San Francisco have no bitterness towards her, nor do they ask it on her account, but for the good of those who remain, and as an example to others. Every virtuous woman asks that her influence and example be removed from us.
>
> The truly virtuous of her sex will not feel that the Vigilance Committee have done their *whole* duty till they comply with the request of —"

And this monstrous epistle is signed "MANY WOMEN OF SAN FRANCISCO."

Oh, this was shameful, indeed, but Belle just kept to her sequestered house of mourning. I imagine the vigilantes were too busy with other more pressing matters than to concern themselves with what "many women of San Francisco" might request, for nobody came pounding at our door with a note that had a little eye in a triangle scratched on it. Then, a few days later, someone else sent a letter to the *Bulletin* in reply:

> A woman is always a woman's persecutor. In my humble opinion, I think that Belle Cora has suffered enough to expiate many faults, in having had torn from her a bosom friend, executed by a powerful association. It was just and right that Cora should die, but I contend that by his death the public is avenged. She had shown herself a true-hearted woman to him, and such a heart covers a multitude of sins. This very circumstance of expulsion might be the means of utter desolation of heart. The effects of the tragedy may be the means of improving her moral character and making her socially a good woman.

And this tender appeal carries the signature "Adelia."

After a month of mourning, Belle emerged still dressed in her black weeds, as she went ahead with her customary promenades, undaunted. I don't know who wrote these letters—for all I know they were written by two different gentlemen in the Committee of Vigilance in the name of what they believe ladies must feel—but the attack stung so badly that we really felt "utter desolation of heart," so reading "Adelia's" appeal touched us deeply, although Belle has always known that she was a good woman.

I am done now, absolutely. Although I should tell you one more thing, if you promise not to write it down. We're not ready to spring the trap just yet. Belle went about her ways, and business resumed in a more discreet fashion, but she decided that she would get revenge for Tom King's continuing slanders. We wrote several letters to friends around the country, and we made a very, very interesting discovery. Do you know what? Tom King—brother of the martyred James King of William—has a wife. What is so startling about that, you say? Well, it seems that not only is Mrs. Thomas King divorced, but she is the madam of one of the most expensive parlor houses in Washington, D.C.! When one of the boys went back East he stopped off in Georgetown specifically to verify the fact. He wrote back that Mrs. King was very charming and not in the least bit shy about talking about the husband who had abandoned her. What do you think we could do with that little piece of information? Can you imagine? Oh, I'm sure we'll be able to exact at least a little revenge for Charlie getting lynched, although it hardly eases the heavy sorrow weighing on all of our hearts, most especially Belle Cora's, now that Charlie is dead.

Laura Fair's
Orphan Child

From *Thoughts of a Female Typesetter* by Hattie Fisk

In the wheelhouse Leland Stanford and his railroad cohorts, just returning from Sacramento, escape the damp and chilly November dusk in the company of Captain Bushnell. "Gentlemen," the capitalist intones as he lofts the hot toddy prepared by the captain, "here is all the hair off your heads." Up go all their mugs, after which the Governor blesses the brew, "Mighty fine, Captain! On a night like this, we need a man's liquor, and a man's drink!"

But on the upper deck there walks a woman dressed in black silk, her face hidden behind a dark veil that falls from her broad-brimmed black hat, her waterproof cloak hanging from her shoulders as she stares in almost dreamlike fashion. Mrs. Fair stands in the corner of the saloon, gazing through the glass pane at the deck, looking at A. P. Crittenden as he sits on a bench by the ferry's wheel with his wife and his fourteen-year-old son Tommie arrayed in the full uniform of his military academy. Crittenden does not see his lover watching him to witness if he keeps his promise that this time, after eight long years of manipulation and shabby treatment, he will divorce his wife. "If Mrs. Crittenden returns, one of us will have to die," the distraught woman lets fly. "Have I not assured you that I kissed no other?" he had consoled her.

"The first thing I remember after being on the boat was Mrs. Crittenden's voice," Laura Fair later explains in court. "She had . . . a peculiar voice, and it was disagreeable, the sound of it. I looked to see where it came from or what it was,

---

and I know I must have put my hand on some glass. I think I know I put my hand on something that was cold and wet. I was standing up. I remember seeing—as I turned and put my hand on this glass, or whatever it was, I saw her and him together. I do not know if they were sitting or standing. I cannot remember that, but I know I reached my hands out and I touched something cold. That made me remember, and I thought to myself, 'I never put my gloves on yet, for my hand is wet.' The glass seemed to be wet, and I can remember nothing else after that."

What Laura does not remember is that she leaves the saloon, walks out to the stern deck, sees them sitting arm in arm on the bench by the railing, sheltered by the wheel housing. Then she gracefully crosses the deck, reveals a pistol in her hand, fires once at Crittenden who had half stood, startled at her approach, then drops her weapon, and walks away. "I am shot!" the lawyer cries before collapsing amidst screams and tumult as Laura almost invisibly retires to a bench in the cabin. Parker Crittenden, one of the dying man's older sons, who was about the deck when the shooting occurred, discovers his mortally wounded father, then jostles into the cabin with the police officer and walks up to the veiled woman whom he knows to be his father's mistress to declare loudly, "Captain, this is the woman. I accuse her of the murder of my father. Arrest her!"

Then Laura lifts her veil and answers in a clear voice, "Yes, I did it. I don't deny it, and I meant to kill him. He ruined both myself and my child!"

Governor Stanford, aroused by the shouts, marches to the deck, inspects the scene of the expiring man, the police officer pushing back the crowd, and he offers his sympathies to the man's wife. He knew Crittenden as a prominent lawyer, someone who made his fortune from the endless litigation arising from the conflicting claims to the Comstock Lode, and he looks at the fallen man with consternation. Next he strides to the cabin where Laura Fair is held, pushing in to examine the face of a female killer. Her hands rest in her lap, her eyes are blank, her hair disheveled, but he can see nothing in that face. The police officer tells him of her confession, and the former Governor shakes his head, staring at the woman who has just begun her descent into the vortex of convulsive madness from which she will not emerge for weeks. "I am afraid that this woman will hang," the Governor says, shakes his head, then returns to his private cabin and to a man's liquor.

While on board the *El Capitán*, Laura D. Fair (widow, mother of a daughter) shot and killed Alexander P. Crittenden (respected member of the bar, husband, father of seven) as the ferry crossed from Oakland to San Francisco on November 3, 1870.

That simple statement is, perhaps, the only aspect of the murder case upon which everyone agrees: Mrs. Fair killed Mr. Crittenden, of this there is no doubt. The rest has become a vicious, uneven contest fought in the Bar, Press, Pulpit, and Stock Exchange, in which realms Mrs. Fair is vilified as one of the most vile and depraved of living women. The prosecutor, Mr. Campbell, calls forth the hardest names in denuciatory slang to describe the tormented woman—hyena, liar, human monster, demon in angel form, devil, adulteress, prostitute, robber of home, creature of lust and avarice—Mr. Campbell delivering a continual torrent of suchlike shyster billingsgate throughout the trial. The intense clamor for the blood of this poor, wronged, weak woman, who is pursued and persecuted as the Cuban bloodhounds pursue their victims, is none other than a cry of alarm from the advocates of masculine free-loveism, a cry to "nip this thing in the bud" by those cowardly, curbstone libertines who are apprehensive of a like fate. By their logic, Mrs. Fair must be made a terrible example: "If women are to be allowed to take vengeance in their own hands, right their own wrongs, and execute justice on their betrayers, who then can be saved? If a man cannot seduce, ruin and forsake his victim without the fear of the revolver or the knife, the world is coming to a fearful pass. If he cannot keep or discard his mistress at his own will or pleasure, without the fear of losing his life at the hands of his concubine, it is time some of them were hung to make an example of!"

⚹

"Madam, I do not believe this is the appropriate place for ladies," the bailiff who stands before Emily Pitts Stevens politely advises. The men stand all about us, pressing in, leering, as the five of us, accompanied by Mr. Richard Snow and Mr. Francis Hughes, present ourselves in the door of the courtroom.

"Officer, I have no intention whatsoever of disturbing the sanctity of the court, but no law bars me from entering this courtroom. We are journalists from the *Pioneer*. I am the publisher and editor, Mrs. Emily Pitts Stevens. We have the right of a free press to observe this trial—and we *will* observe this trial. Now, please be so kind as to step aside, for to do otherwise is to trample on our rights and to arouse the ire of the Fourth Estate and the wrath of an injured sex." Aghast at Mrs. Stevens' bold riposte, the officer stumbles back, and we enter the courtroom to take our seats, the first women ever to trespass such a male enclave. How the "gentlemen" make loud, raucous, lewd remarks at the unprecedented violation—but we sit with our heads held high, outwardly impervious, although inwardly in terror at the taunts.

"Women are decidedly out of place in the courtroom," complains one newspaper—it matters little which, since nearly all the San Francisco journals emit the same howl of

⚹

moral outrage. "Attendance by these strong-minded women with their unclean petticoats and dirty stockings is unmodest and unwomanly. We believe in practicing muscular Christianity upon literary Hoodlums, and the 'journalists' of the *Pioneer*, this small coterie of social mischief-makers, should be removed from the sanctified and decorous precincts of the law—by force, if need be."

Our presence seems to be proof alone of how we have unsexed ourselves, and in the eyes of the jackals we are as much on trial as Mrs. Fair, for we represent a remarkable exhibition of depravity. Even our friends need moral sustenance to accept our presence, although I readily can discover support as I read our correspondence. For example, Mrs. R. R. Emery, writing from Stockton, reports that "the fact of the ladies attending court on the occasion of the trial has created quite a furor here, but I think we shall survive it. I am glad that there is real principle embodied in the determination and willingness to witness this most heartless persecution from beginning to end." Mrs. Stevens simply explains that, just as women demand the right to vote, to serve as jurors, and to fulfill all other obligations of citizens, we demand, at the least, the right to witness this masculine travesty of justice.

I set Mrs. Stevens' rejoinder for the next issue of the *Pioneer*, feeling each letter with my fingers as I pull it from the case box. She dismisses the hue and cry for our removal and addresses the heart of the case, the suffocating "masculine sphere" in which Mrs. Fair has been confined. Mrs. Stevens first observes that the one-legged General Dan Sickles, hero of Gettysburg, who had shot and killed Philip Barton Key in Washington, D.C., over his offended sense of honor, was acquitted because the murder was committed while he was in the grip of uncontrollable passion: the General is even now serving as "King Grant's" ambassador to Spain. Is not the case of Mrs. Fair very much the same? Then, letter by letter, I can feel in my fingertips her outrage take the form of other thunderous questions whose answers, should they honestly be provided, will shake the nation:

> May not a woman be allowed the same right to judge of her own wrongs, to avenge them according to her ideas of justice, and to be set free and travel the earth at her own pleasure? Will it not have a cowardly look for a masculine judge to arraign this woman under masculine-made laws, to be tried by a masculine jury, to be confused and bewildered by the conflicting array of masculine authorities, good, bad, foolish, and indifferent, and finally condemned and executed under a legal, judicial, and executive system, in the shaping and directing of which she has had no more voice or influence than had the plantation slaves over the creation of those laws which took from them their personal liberty and property creations?

Yes, there is no question but we are triumphant, sitting straight, well-mannered, determined, unblushing, even as the medical ninnies pronounce their judgments upon Mrs. Fair's tipped womb, or as the most private correspondence between the lovers is read aloud before the masculine throng, or as Mrs. Fair submits to the repeated insults of Mr. Campbell and the other prosecutors as she tells the story of her wrongs. We sit, we listen, and by our presence itself we have determined this to be a part of "woman's sphere," just as my own fingers, reaching for type and lead and block, mixing ink and wiping rollers, demonstrate a new definition of "woman's work."

—•— ≍✦≍ —•—

Sitting in court, I think repeatedly of that pane of glass upon which Mrs. Fair rested her hand. A pane of glass, something that you can see through but which makes a separation, something that turns what is on the other side into illusion simply because of unseen partition. When you peer through a pane of glass you are looking *at* a scene from which you, the viewer, are distinct, separate; you are no longer *in* the scene, although the medium of change is invisible. When you see Niagara Falls cast by the magic lantern, do you see the "glass" or the rushing water? When you read the *Chronicle*, the *Bulletin*, or the *Alta*, do you see the "glass" or the blood of the Paris Communards? Laura Fair put her hands on the cold and wet film that covers life with its sense of realness, of being there, and yet the glass is merely a proscenium or a screen for shadow plays. It transforms the world because you view it through its cold, transparent surface. Put your hand up, as did Mrs. Fair, and you are suddenly made aware that you are on the other side of the stage; then allow yourself to have your mind turn itself invisible, and you shall see how easy it is to step through the glass and onto the stage itself, as easy as entering a dream or madness.

In the courtroom, we can see the maelstrom into which Crittenden has sucked Laura Fair at the same time that the men stare through the film to see the utterly different picture of Crittenden snared in the coils of a monstrous virago. As the trial proceeds, with all of its agonizing moments, its leering, libidinous, brawling men in the spectator section lapping up the private love letters between the lawyer and his victim, I feel as if I walk within a bubble of glass. I look out and through, but I feel I am never quite there, as if I am a comfortable spectator, myself kept apart from tragedy—although I am very much a part of the stage, very much put on trial, like all the women of the *Pioneer*. Still, I put my hands before me, even when the prosecutors vomit hideous insults regarding "strong-minded women," and I feel that pane of cold, wet glass. Listening intently, I peer at the drama before me as if I am watching a dream, vainly attempting to keep myself the dreamer and not the dreamed.

＊＋＝◆＝＋＊

I must admit I was astonished when Mrs. Stevens invited me to join the delegation to the courtroom. Dedicated as she is to

＊＋＝◆＝＋＊

the uplifting of even the lowliest woman, I was still taken aback, and filled with no little trepidation, although, along with her great kindness and the boundless admiration with which I hold Mrs. Stevens, her explanation that a representative of working women should be included as part of our phalanx persuaded me to take my seat on the hard benches of Judge Dwinelle's profane theater. Oh, the distance I traveled, the bounties with which Providence provided me, the redemption bestowed upon my soul by Mrs. Stevens' great generosity, by her penetrating intelligence, and by her great love for all of God's creatures—with all of this at that moment combining, I arrived at a pinnacle. To others, the request would have been tantamount to an invitation to be killed; to me, it was an invitation to be reborn.

When I first met Mrs. Emily Pitts Stevens I was at the edge of a precipice about to plunge into a moral pit. My husband of less than a year, who soon after our nuptials had revealed his true drunken self, had suddenly fled into the night. Vainly I searched for him among his dissolute friends, learning only that he had reappeared briefly in Virginia City, then vanished forever. I did not regret his departure, for I lived in terror of his drunken rages and his brazen sexual debauchery, but I did regret being abandoned, penniless, alone. My parents long deceased, and my only surviving relation, my dear uncle, having just recently passed away, I had no one to turn to. Oh, how I was left to drift until swallowed by evil, but I soon found room in a female boardinghouse and work as a milliner's assistant for pennies. Often, when I walked the streets to my meager employment, I would be accosted by sinister men who sought to recruit me to walk down well-trod paths, and I feared that my life had plunged to such a nadir that, in order to avoid starvation, I would discount my revulsion and take such a dreadful course. All of this is familiar enough to anyone who knows the tribulations of women in San Francisco or in any great city, and many would shed a tear and offer a prayer that I would not fall as had those of my weaker sisters who walk draped on the arms of a peacock fellow or languish locked in a dismal crib—although a tear and a prayer hardly suffice.

But it was at this point that the oft-told tale took a different turn, one of which, just a year or so earlier, I would have heartily disapproved. "Does the native American white female flourish the tomahawk or the chopstick?" I had read the woman suffragists plead, as they petitioned for the vote. "Does she subsist chiefly on roots? Does she dote on rats for a steady diet?" Of course, I was as much a product of civilization as the American male—entrusted even with inculcating its elevating spirit to future generations—but I never felt it seemly to enter saloons or voting booths in order to debase the divine mission entrusted to our sex, nor did I feel anything like a Digger Indian by my exclusion from them. But, working for pennies and warding off the advances of diabolical emissaries, I happened to pass Dashaway Hall, where Mrs. Emily Pitts Stevens was lecturing on "Working Women," and I felt that I suddenly outstretched my hand to touch the unseen glass separating me from the drama of the world. I was abruptly brought from the brink of despair by her words, which seemed to penetrate my heart even as I entered the hall.

"Open to women, we cry, a fair field of industry, let her do anything her hands find to do; then how many women in this town, think you, would be content to debase themselves for dress and ease? How shall we cure or lessen vice in our large cities? There is but one way—leave women free to choose their own employments; make them responsible, self-reliant human beings; give them an earnest interest in life; something to stimulate them. The best medicine for humanity is occupation."

I peered intently at her as she spoke so eloquently, with such force, and yet with splendid dignity. Her curly hair was cropped close to her head, her mouth was large, and her eyes, which seemed strangely of different sizes, were clear pools of perception and intelligence. I was entranced, as if I were hearing the words of a female Jesus who had come to save no one but me.

"It is said there are as many women as men *obliged* to rely on their own efforts for bread; but the whole mass of women must find employment in two or three avenues of labor—teachers, milliners, servants and the like—while all fields, all avenues are open to man. Is this the fault of capitalists? No! It is the fault of our public opinion, which sets its face like flint against woman's work. Look at our public schools! Why is it that woman is paid one half for her work—just as well done as the other sex? Why is she so illy paid? Because hundreds of teachers are waiting for positions; because that avenue of labor is overcrowded. Can they seek other employments? No! they know too well there is but one alternative—to teach, to starve, or do worse. Is it known from what source are the ranks of profligacy recruited?—from the ranks of illy paid, half-starved working women. Trace their history in the old world and the new, and you will find that one-half of the sisterhood who have gone down that great sea of profligacy found their way there through slow stages of starvation.

"What, then, is the great problem for this commonwealth to settle? It is the great question of labor. Shall we make it respectable or degrading? The dainty notions of the present age have made woman a hothouse plant, and one-half the sex from this cause alone are invalids. Woman will never study the great questions that interest and stir so deeply the human mind until she looks at them with responsible eyes. Teach her to choose an honest employment in freedom, responsible as she is to no one but her God. Oh! woman, cease to care for the sneers and innuendos of the weak, the frauds and misstatements of the malicious. Stand out in your individuality;

choose your occupation, and work wisely and well. Show to the world that as women we can and will settle this great problem of woman's work and woman's sphere!"

I repeat her words at length, writing them now as I soon would typeset them for the pages of the *Pioneer*, for they were from that moment engraved in my heart. Mrs. Stevens spoke then not of suffrage but of suffering, which she interlaced with all the great questions of the day, and all, always, returning to the burning necessity of equal rights achieved through suffrage. I was confused and frightened, alarmed that, despite my desperate situation, I would yet unsex myself by falling in with such social misfits. Nonetheless, I went up to her after her lecture, not knowing what I would say, and found myself stammering out my tale to her. Recognizing in my incoherent words the familiar story of woman's plight, she drew me to her bosom and invited me to join the vocational night school for young working women that she had inaugurated.

There I came after work to learn the male trade of typesetter; to practice the skills to run a printing press; to discover my hands blackened with ink, but my heart washed pure with joy. I excelled as a typesetter, and I gained a kind of sensuous pleasure feeling words emerge from my fingertips. I no longer merely read journals or books, but felt them in my flesh instead. "Woman Suffrage" was not a slogan but a combination of hand motions, a series of swift lunges on the job case, a surface of elevations and depressions I could sense with my own hands, and my "individuality" became something I could actually perceive as I gave birth to it day after day.

Soon I was working at the *Mercury*, the literary weekly in which Mrs. Stevens had bought a partner's share, earning a wage equal to any male typesetter. There I worked until that moment in January 1869 when Mrs. Stevens gained full control of the journal, whose name in November she changed to the *Pioneer*. I set the type heralding the new day in our announcement:

> The old name did not please us. It symbolized neither our thought nor our object. Supple as a moral acrobat, unscrupulous as a Wall Street gold manipulator, tricky as a ward politician, enterprising as Vanderbilt, and as plausible as a diplomat, Mercury, the classic divinity, typifies more the character of the modern financier than that of the sincere and earnest reformer of the last half of the nineteenth century. Inspired with the spirit of modern reform, and possessed with an earnest desire to contribute our mite to the cause of woman's elevation and enfranchisement, we saw, some ten months since, an opening in the department of journalism. But this branch of industry and enterprise had not been opened to our sex. Some few women had learned the art of printing, but they were not allowed on this Coast, to follow it as a profession. Women had traveled the path of authorship, but woman as a journalist was considered outre.

How her words danced on my fingertips as Mrs. Stevens railed against the narrowness and bigotry of the typographical associations, "their intolerance and savage cruelty," for "we felt that we had a mission—a work to do—and could not restrain our desire and our determination to enter this new field, though calumny with its thousand tongues should slime our path, and opposition combat us at every step." She outlined the newspaper's aim to give employment to needy female printers, to vindicate woman's capacity to labor, to fill its pages with the words of female journalists.

> In addition to our editorial labors we do our own soliciting. We make our own collections. We assist in mailing each edition of our paper and devote the proceeds to teaching its advancement. The first woman on this Coast to demand the ballot for our sex, we are now surrounded by an army of noble women who are earnest in the work of female elevation, emancipation, and enfranchisement . . .

Pioneer is a word that more nearly covers our thought and fills the measure of our object and ambition. A pioneer signifies one who goes before with pick in hand to prepare the way for others to follow. For our motto we have chosen three words of mighty import. They are *Freedom, Justice,* and *Fraternity.* We employ fraternity, because the paucity of our language, immense in its number of words and rich in synonyms, has no word to express the brotherhood and sisterhood of the race.

Even words that did not yet exist danced on my fingertips; and I felt ever so much like a pioneer, charting new territories for settlement by a female future filled with the "fraternity," the "humanity," the "joint sovereignty," the "mutuality," the "solidity" of both sexes, and not the pathetic "idiocy" that divides us today.

Now I am sitting before Judge Dwinelle, who scowls at our delegation but who, out of a sense of chivalrous propriety, says nothing, allowing the scoffing press to say it for him, while we observe the persecution of Mrs. Fair. Every day I sit, and every day we adjourn to our office, women joined in all tasks intellectual and manual; and there in the offices of the *Pioneer* we gather to cull the daily press, to scrutinize the day's transcripts, to sift our correspondence, to fashion our editorials, to write our new words into existence, which, weekly, I put into type and feel with the tips of my fingers as if I were smoothing the brow of my very own child.

＋－ ⚎◆⚎ －＋

The doctors commence their parade, speaking with the utmost assurance of the female anatomy. Mr. Cook, her lawyer, charts the argument that at the time she fired the fatal shot Mrs. Fair "was not a responsible agent—that reason, for the time, was dethroned. Shoot the man she loved!—the man she adored above all other living beings, when the object of her hatred, if she had any—Mrs. Crittenden—sat by his side,

＋－ ⚎◆⚎ －＋

and she might have blown her brains out!" Her reason was dethroned because of "retarded menstruation," Mr. Cook explains, "one of the diseases recognized universally as insanity of women, and we will show you instances of it because they have occurred right here in our midst—in our own city—instances of ladies of the highest respectability, perfectly sound and sane, and who have completely stripped themselves, have become maniacs for two, three, four, or six hours, and after it was over they had no recollection of what had occurred."

We sit, heads high, unblushing, while the men stare at us, amazed that we can sit with straight spines as our bodies are exposed on the dock before so many male eyes. Mrs. Fair's madness is the consequence of a tipped womb and delayed menstruation: "Anteversion of the womb is where the upper part of the womb is thrown forwards towards the bladder, and in those cases lies nearly transverse," according to Dr. Trask.

Mr. Campbell: "Did not anteversion frequently result from excessive indulgence in sexual passion?"

Dr. Trask: "Yes, sir. You may find it as a frequent result of sexual indulgence when carried to excess, when carried to *an* excess. You find it in a great many prostitutes, but I do not know that it is found more there than among females who are not prostitutes."

Then, Dr. Tucker: "Her act was nonvolitional. It was not the act of volition. It was the act produced by the hysterical mania, which probably she had been laboring under for some time past, and which in that moment of frenzy, perhaps lighted up by other passions, mingled with it, caused her to commit the deed."

Was not eight years of deceit and callous treatment enough to cause such "hysterical mania"? We sit, we listen, while the doctors explain their use of the speculum and the graphic details of gynecological examination. The men in the courtroom stare at us, their eyes riveted to the backs of our necks, hoping to see our delicate natures recoil as we are stripped naked on the examination table. "Science knows no unclean thought," Mrs. Stevens says, "but I hardly believe what we witness here is the full expression of exalted science."

Sometimes I sit with my ears closed so as to avoid showing any signs of discomfit, to avoid displaying the slightest blush. It is as if our bodies contain the Via Dolorosa, and Mrs. Fair must walk the stations of the monthly cycle before she is allowed to have her menstrual blood drain from the cross.

Several times when I return to our rooming house in the evening, I vomit from the strain.

＊＋ ≡◆≡ ＋＊

Women and guns, guns and women—the talk in the court-room and the palaver in the press swirl around and around the two subjects as if a new discovery has been found: female vio-lence. The *Chronicle:* "The Fair-Crittenden tragedy threatens to call forth a battalion of female 'shootists' powerful enough and desperate enough to knock terror into the hearts of recre-ant husbands and gay deceivers generally." The *Chronicle* illus-trates the danger posed by such "amiable amazonians" with the example of Annie Meaghen, who this week leveled a six-shooter at her husband at the corner of Market and Dupont.

After one of her lectures Mrs. Stevens is accosted by former Assemblyman ——— who berates her threateningly. Someone slips Mrs. Stevens a derringer for her protection, which she ignores, immediately thrusting the revolver into her shawl, as she resumes the argument with the belligerent political bum-mer. However, word spreads that Mrs. Stevens had bran-dished the weapon at the weak and defenseless male, and the next day in court the spectators leave a wide path for the "female shootist," despite her public protestations that, rumors notwithstanding, the derringer, which was unsolicited, was

＊＋ ≡◆≡ ＋＊

never shown or employed and that she abhors the use of all violence.

It is as if the notion of "female shootist" knocks unimaginable terror into the hearts of the male populace, provoking the possibilities of even greater violence among them than they are typically accustomed to entertain. All of this is fanned even more by the sudden, extraordinary presence of Victoria Woodhull before the country. I set the type of her astonishing words demanding the vote in the *Pioneer:* "We mean treason; we mean secession—and on a thousand times grander scale than was that of the South. We are plotting revolution; we will overthrow this bogus Republic, and plant a government of righteousness in its stead!" I thrill at Mrs. Woodhull's words, her boldness, her fearlessness, but I quake at the results: The blood shed by the South's unholy secession is still not dry, and I wish for no more.

Mrs. Stevens notes how Judge Dwinelle allows Mr. Campbell "to indulge in the cruel sport of hurling against Mrs. Fair epithets, which a sensuous and vengeful crowd listens to with feelings of delight and joyful approbation. Where is the law that allows a counsel to vilify, abuse, and blackguard an unconvicted man or woman when on trial for crime?" But we continue to sit, along with Mrs. Fair, receiving outrageous insults, until, finally, there is a remarkable outburst.

As Mr. Cook questions Mrs. Fair concerning her intention in carrying a pistol on board the ferry, Mr. Campbell jumps to his feet to object, at which time Mrs. Fair tells the jury: "I am sure he was the only friend I had in the world. I would not have desired to have harmed him, and if he had been living now, gentlemen, when Mr. Campbell insulted me the other day, he would have made Mr. Campbell on his bended knees apologize for it."

We clap our hands and stamp our feet in approval, until Judge Dwinelle pounds his gavel, roaring, "Silence! The officers will bring the parties forward immediately that applauded. Bring them forward at once and have them sworn."

The bailiffs swim through the spectators like sharks, sniffing out who made the noise, while all sit in sudden silence.

Mrs. Fair: "Judge, it was my fault, probably."

Judge Dwinelle: "Just answer the questions, Madam. Of course you are not to blame for the disturbance."

Mrs. Fair: "Well, Judge, human nature could not stand it."

Finally, the bailiffs set upon Mr. Francis Hughes, who is brought to the bench, but he admits neither to applauding nor to having seen anyone else applaud. After he is released, one of the more dissolute "gentlemen" in the crowd points at Mrs. Stevens as the instigator, and she readily advances to the bench.

Mrs. Stevens: "Judge, I was not aware that I could not applaud in court."

Judge Dwinelle: "Did you applaud?"

Mrs. Stevens: "I said, 'Good.'"

"What is your name?"

"Mrs. Emily Pitts Stevens."

"You did applaud in court, did you?"

"I said, 'Good,' and I put my hand down on the desk like this."

"Did you make any noise?"

"I made no noise with my feet."

"Did you with your hand?"

"With my hand I did."

"You are fined twenty-five dollars."

Then Laura Fair interjects: "I will pay it."

Mrs. Stevens: "Thank you."

Forthwith the same dissolute peacock points out Mrs. Booth, sitting beside Mrs. Stevens. She too is called to the bench, admits stamping her foot, and Judge Dwinelle fines her twenty-five dollars as well. Once again, Laura Fair offers to pay the fine.

Judge Dwinelle: "You will have to draw heavily on your bank if you pay the fines of all of them."

Mrs. Fair: "I do not think, your Honor, these ladies understood the rules of the court."

Judge Dwinelle: "Well, they understand them now. I wish the officers now to keep a careful lookout, and arrest any person guilty of applauding on either side."

Judge Dwinelle finds the grace to void the fines at the end of the day, but he displays even more contempt when, a few days later, Mrs. Fair exclaims, "It's a lie!" This comes after Mrs. Crittenden testifies that Mrs. Fair came to her room at the Occidental Hotel to kneel at her knees and begged to be allowed to kiss her hand for forgiveness: "Madam," the adulterer's wife recreates her answer, "you may lead him to leave his family and live with you openly, though I do not think you can—I do not think he is yet so lost to honor and to the love of his children as to do that—but if you did, I assure you I will never apply for a divorce."

At the end of the day, Judge Dwinelle officiates that "a gross insult has been put upon a witness, which is a contempt of court," and he fines Mrs. Fair. The men in the audience murmur their approval, but we depart roiling in anger, and Mrs. Stevens writes:

> When Mrs. Fair, wearied and exhausted, nervous and irritable, not only from troubles of mind, but the trying labors of daily attendance upon court—enough to unnerve a person strong both in body and mind—became uncontrollably outraged at what appears to many an improbable statement by Mrs. Crittenden and burst out with, "It's a lie!" the Court seemed horribly shocked at her improper conduct—promptly

rebuked the prisoner, whom medical experts had pronounced at the trial as being subject to fits of hysterical mania, and fined her \$250.

Judge Dwinelle is so completely enveloped by his relations to the Bar, which from the first entertained towards Mrs. Fair feelings of the most bitter hatred, and by his association with the ruling classes, which have largely partaken of that spirit, and by the united flood of abuse poured out against her by the press generally . . ."

Enough. The scores of male violators remain in the courtroom unrebuked, while we return the next day to snickers of "It's a lie!" whispered again and again amid schoolboy giggles as we pass to our seats.

— ·— ≡◆≡ —· —

Each night of the trial I return to our lodging house at the corner of Greenwich and Stockton streets; a high, sunny locality, overlooking the bay on one side and the city on the other. It is a cozy habitation, nothing grand or pretentious about it, and it soothes me to sit by the window of my room to watch the sun go down beneath the Golden Gate. But when the darkness finally envelopes the bay a great wave of fear and trembling washes over me. I weep almost every night, and Sarah Wallis, my fellow typesetter with whom I share my little room, takes me in her arms to her bed and holds me, gently wiping the tears from my cheeks as I sob.

"There, there. No reason to weep," she says, holding me and rocking me and kissing the tears from my face until I fall asleep in her arms. The hard, confining city is to my back, while the soft, limitless expanse of sky and bay and ocean is to hers; and her sweet embraces revive me the way the airs of the Pacific refresh our troubled city with gentle tufts of fog . . .

— ·— ≡◆≡ —· —

Each morning we breakfast with Mrs. Stevens, who shares

— ·— ≡◆≡ —· —

rooms downstairs with her enlightened husband, whom we see only rarely as he usually leaves each morning before dawn to his business affairs. Our conversations are usually desultory, each of us brooding at the storm that awaits us that day in Judge Dwinelle's theater. This morning, however, Mrs. Stevens notes that my countenance remains sad, drawn.

"I must confess, Mrs. Stevens, that sometimes I lose heart, my spirits flag. Sometimes I feel that the world must be mad. We see the logic of equal rights as evident as the sun, just as we see the innocence of Mrs. Fair, and yet we are met with such contempt, such contumely, such bestial irrationality, that I feel we are walking through the darkest of nights."

"Do you wish to stay from the courtroom today, Hattie?"

"No, Mrs. Stevens, not in the least. Forgive me if what I said gave such an impression. I have become a warrior in a great battle just by sitting on a cold, hard bench, just by inserting my small form into forbidden realms; I would not miss the trial for the world. It is only that I grow weary at the benighted state of society."

Mrs. Stevens pauses to look at me over her cup of tea before she begins a softly spoken lecture: "Hattie, society rises from the zero of savageism up and upwards into warm and warmer regions of light, purity, and knowledge. That is the true order of human development. The nineteenth century is far from benighted, and yet it is just as far from being enlightened. 'We hold these truths to be self-evident . . .' That is what they said at the end of the last century; but what is self-evident, Hattie? Is anything, really, self-evident? Or is it made evident by Self? Only a short time ago did Jefferson and those other brilliant minds decide that equal rights were self-evident, whereas up to that time it was so very much self-evident that rights were only bestowed upon tyrants by their appropriation of the Deity. Woman's embrace of all of life is such a self-evident fact, so self-evident it does not need even to be argued. I suppose what Mrs. Woodhull says is true: that woman already has the right to vote, and that she has only been prevented from exercising such a right by a fraudulent government. What prevents us are the hard hearts and harder heads of a masculine Congress standing in our way. But I am sure that all that we hope and strive for will become self-evident someday, but for now, we must begin to light the lamps one at a time. Perhaps you shall live to see female suffrage, Hattie; I believe that I will not. But we all have to live in this marvelous nineteenth century with our feet planted firmly in the past, and our heads reaching far into the future."

Mrs. Stevens smiles at me with great tenderness as she nibbles her toast. "If you believe that what we seek is inevitable, my dear, then patient fortitude can only hasten its arrival," she concludes, then wipes her mouth with a napkin.

I nod and try to imagine my head high up above the clouds looking down upon the future, looking at a world without intoxicating liquors, without violence, wars, poverty, a world where women take up the reins of government on a higher and more scientific idea. But although I crave such a world, I fail to see it. I end up feeling only a certain vertigo, as if my head floats aimlessly like some wayward balloonist.

I begin to feel doubt—not in our cause, for I know it is just, and I require my rights just in order to survive—but I begin to doubt in the semblance of the world itself. What if society is not moving up and upwards towards fulfillment but remains flat, horizontal? What if the human spirit does not constantly ascend from savageism but rises and falls like the swells of the sea? What if humanity is like some kind of insect, a gnat, buzzing erratically, fitfully, with no apparent reason? Or what if society simply turns in a circle, like a snake swallowing its tail? How can we know that what we will achieve is not simply yet another form of evil, and not a greater good? What if we merely uncover new vileness as yet undisclosed within the folds of the future? What if all we do is a feeble slap at chaos and the inevitable is but . . . ?

It is at this point, I am told, that I faint and am carried to my room. I miss the trial that day, spending it instead in my bed gazing out my window at the bay, recovering my equilibrium. By the next morning I have no answers to the whirlwind of questions, no better grasp at reading the book of today by means of setting the type of the future. Still, I feel refreshed, rested, strong enough not to think of such conundrums at all, which is the way, I suppose, one must walk into the future. I do not speak these questions either, although the doubt remains, as Mrs. Stevens greets me kindly at the breakfast table.

"Are you feeling better today, my dear?"

"Yes, and I am ready to resume my bench."

— ·+· ≡◆≡ ·+· —

Indeed, Mrs. Fair once took the stage as an actress, although she was no Lola Montez; yes, Mrs. Fair, a Southerner, displayed sympathy for the secessionists, but she did not dance around the streets of Virginia City draped in the Confederate flag, as some may contend; yes, her husband shot his brains out, but Mr. Fair's suicide was accounted to his business affairs and not to any marital ones; yes, Mrs. Fair is the mother of a beautiful daughter, but Mr. Fair is the father of her child and not Mr. Crittenden; yes, Mrs. Fair impulsively wed Mr. Snyder, but it was only as a form of revenge upon A. P. Crittenden for dangling her life upon his promises, nor was the marriage ever consummated; yes, Mrs. Fair shot at Mr. Crittenden once before as she stood at the top of her stairs, but . . .

The atmosphere around the trial is an interminable swirl of rumors, scandals, conjectures, and lies spewing from the mouths of weak-minded gentlemen. From the glistening beaver stovepipe to the meek moustache, from the immaculate

— ·+· ≡◆≡ ·+· —

necktie to the lavender kids, from the lavender kids to the excruciating patent leather boots, there are thousands of such creatures in the city; and these battalions of be-whiskered and be-kidded effetes, many of them by this time more famous than Emperor Norton, and more wealthy than Friedlander, join the cruder vulgarians of their sex in endless conversation over the imagined affairs of Mrs. Fair. These weak-minded gentlemen open the newspapers and ignore the reports on the Ku-Kluxer outrages in Mississippi; they close their ears to the arguments over annexing Santo Domingo; they sniff at the titanic battles between the Communards and the Versaillists; instead, they turn to each day's transcript of lurid testimony; they linger over headlines that announce "Spicy & Interesting Letters from Mrs. Fair to Crittenden," tittering like Peeping Toms at the passions of others.

"Oh! I will try not to grieve you," writes Mrs. Fair in a letter to her lover, as read to the Court by the prosecutor, Mr. Campbell. "And when you tell me she is gone, and I may come back—Oh! then how I will try to make my poor darling happy again. How I *will* make the dear old rooms ring with music, happy music, heart music. Let her take it all—the dear old bed, the chairs in which you have held me in your arms. Yes, let her take *them*. She *can't* take your heart, and she *shan't* take your happiness. We will consecrate the new furniture.

"Now answer me candidly, darling—do you think your dear body will or can ever seem so purely and entirely mine as before it rested upon the same bed with another?"

Mr. Campbell looks at the jury to remark archly that "her idea of consecration is a little different from that which is generally received in Christian communities." Then the prosecutor continues: "You shall kiss me in every corner of each room, hold me in your arms in each chair, lie by me on the sofa, hang over me at the piano, and sleep with me in the bed. There, I defy her to prevent it, you darling!"

Again the masculine throng ogles us expectantly as we listen to Mr. Campbell's recitation. How can "respectable" ladies listen to such explicit words of sexual passion, of "consecrating beds," of "You shall kiss me in every corner of each room . . . and sleep with me in the bed"? If anything, I find the letters somewhat sad, somewhat silly at times, but not at all repulsive. What is repulsive is Crittenden's constant toying with Mrs. Fair's evident gullibility, although Mr. Campbell, of course, opines that "had not he been blinded by the most extraordinary infatuation, Crittenden would have read her true character in every line of that letter, and he would have fled from her as from a pestilence."

Yes, such a "pestilence," to have been gulled into believing, as Mrs. Fair testifies, that "I was his wife, and his only wife."

Mr. Campbell: "I beg your pardon—what did you say?"

Mrs. Fair: "I was Mr. Crittenden's wife."

"You were?"

"Yes, sir."

"When were you married to him?"

"Well, God married me to him when we were both born. God made me for him, and he for me. My standing up before Dr. Scott did not make me Mr. Snyder's wife . . . That was adultery, when I married Mr. Snyder."

The male assemblage begins to murmur, as Judge Dwinelle admonishes the witness: "Stop! Mrs. Fair! Just answer the question."

Campbell presses on: "Well, standing up before Dr. Scott did not make you Mr. Snyder's wife?"

"Not in the sight of God, sir, because I did not love him nor he me."

With a low smile, the prosecutor inquires further: "When

did you first get this impression about being married when you were born?"

"I mean by that that I believe there is but one person born for another in this world, because I felt so differently towards Mr. Crittenden than I did towards any other human being on earth. I do not believe God put such feelings for a man in a woman's heart, if that man is not intended for her husband. I would have been willing to have died for him anytime."

Mr. Campbell: "In other words, you repudiate the ordinary institution of marriage?"

"No, sir, I do not at all."

"You do not at all?"

Mrs. Fair: "I do not repudiate it, but I simply say, in the sight of God, standing up before a minister does not always make us married. If we go there with no love, it is not a marriage—in the sight of God, it cannot be."

Mr. Campbell: "At the time you were living with him and considered yourself his wife, do you mean that expression in the fullest and broadest sense of the term *wife?*"

"I mean that I was in the purest and most holy and fullest sense of the word his wife."

"The fullest sense of the word?"

"The purest and most holy sense of that word *wife.*"

"I understand that—I ask this question merely in order to be fully understood—I understand that as embracing all the relations existing between husband and wife?"

"How is that?"

"*All* the relations of husband and wife?"

"I said, in the fullest and purest and most holy name of wife and husband in the fullest extent."

"In the fullest extent?"

"Wife—yes, sir."

The male throng is driven to a virtual frenzy with excitement at her words; the journalists are almost unable to contain their glee; the pulpits can barely sputter their denunciations. Why, the South can rise again; shouts of "Gold discovered in Oakland!" can be crowed from every rooftop; endless boat-loads of Chinamen can stream down the docks—still, such astonishing news would not be heard or perceived above the clanging bells of public opinion; for Mrs. Fair has filled San Francisco with the reverberations of a delicious, fascinating, overwhelming horror; no matter what "holy name" of marriage she pronounces, no matter what Mrs. Fair signifies by her curious ideas, in the eyes of the city she proclaims only one thing: FREE LOVE!

May God save San Francisco!

In his final arguments Mr. Campbell pronounces the accusation fully: Mrs. Fair is guilty of nothing but "free love":

"I like the true strong-minded woman," the prosecutor intones, by way of comparison. "I love and reverence her—the woman of cultivated intellect, of a pure heart, of honest impulses; sensible to her duty to her husband, to her children, to all her relatives, and to mankind in general; the woman who walks in the paths of charity and kindness, who seeks to reclaim the fallen," on and on and so forth.

But then the lawyer advances to "another class of so-called strong-minded women," whom he excoriates as women "who have a mission to tame and subdue the brute man, to reduce him to absolute obedience and subjection." As he speaks, he regularly glances between the jury, the accused, and the women of the *Pioneer*, so as to make clear the full extent of the conspiracy these gentlemen are called upon to judge. He lashes this "class of women who think the ordinary humdrum relations of society are not adapted to their superior intellectuality; that these common rules that would attach the husband to the wife, and which would impose upon earthly marriages certain obligations and certain duties—that these human laws are oppressive upon the other sex; that man is a kind of creature whose mission it is to trample upon woman; who never attend to their own business, but are always anxious to interfere in the business of others; who are not satisfied with any existing social relations, or any ordinarily accepted view of social rights and social duties; who have a 'mission' upon earth to make themselves and everybody else miserable—a class of women who are always prating about domestic duties, but yet go about the streets with unclean petticoats and dirty stockings; a class of women who think it all right that every woman should seek her 'affinity'—that she may marry whom she pleases in the meantime—that that is a mere earthly arrangement; that she may have children by the half a dozen, and then she discovers that though she has already been married six times or four times, she has a mission from heaven compelling her to marry some other woman's husband, and that God Almighty (as has been developed by *this* woman in her correspondence) has decreed that that man, though he has been married for twenty-five years . . . that she has a right to take that man from his wife and his children, and appropriate him to her own use, and live with him just so long as she thinks that marriage made in heaven lasts. She may change her mind; she may discover her mistake; the singular notion which led her to unite with this affinity may have passed away, and she may meet another man whom she discovers to be her affinity also, and *he* may have a wife and children. And so we may go on with this progressive doctrine of affinities, until we destroy all at once all the sanctity of the family relations, or peace, or comfort, or security of the husband and the wife, and the parent and child, until we uproot the foundations of society, until we produce a perfect Pandemonium upon earth. And that is progress.'"

We sit, our eyes turned steely, as this torrent of abuse, this flood of invective, distortion, and deception rushes about our ears. The entire courtroom is waiting for us to raise shrill voices, to shout our objections, but we keep silent, impassive, stolid, intently eyeing the bilious prosecutor as he panders to the weak-minded men.

Later, back at our offices, Mrs. Stevens fumes as I have never seen her before. "My God, this woman sought nothing but to be married to that duplicitous donkey, and Mr. Campbell prates on about how she threatens the sanctity of marriage—of all civilization! Such an outrage! And we, without being called to the witness chair, are submitted as unspoken evidence of such a dire threat, we who have an 'affinity' for dirty stockings and unclean petticoats! I pray to God that we make Mr. Campbell choke on his own words!"

Mrs. Stevens storms out to her quarters to write her counterattack, words that later I fling off my fingers like meteors:

> To us it is a matter of astonishment that the press and public in sympathy with the Crittendens have the boldness and effrontery to charge upon us and our associates an encouragement of the system of "free-loveism," of which they assert that Mrs. Fair is the embodiment and representative. We hurl this charge, with indignant scorn, back in the teeth of those foul-mouthed defamers. They are the encouragers of his lust and the virtual advocates of and apologists for a disgustingly rotten system of masculine free-love practice.
>
> It was A. P. Crittenden, that notorious roue and adulterer, who advanced the unholy doctrine of free love as a married man living in open adultery with Mrs. Fair in the principal towns of two states. Still, the best San Francisco society had its arms open for the warm reception of this free-lover and his wife and family, who were cognizant of his guilty course and who appeared to be in intimate terms with his paramour from motives of policy, craving his supporting money and his high social standing . . .
>
> If this jury is composed of real men, if this jury can distinguish itself from the weak-minded effetes and ninnies who thirst for Mrs. Fair's blood, it will have the courage to do its

duty regardless of the madness of mobs and ravings of the public press. These twelve honorable men can determine that no man, however wealthy, powerful, and intellectual, can trample on the sacred rights of his family and hope to receive the sympathy of American freemen; that any man of that character who enters into the household of another family, and by his powerful arts betrays and seduces a member of that family, does so at the peril of his life, as Mrs. Fair so readily demonstrated. And they will say that those associations of men which are bound together by sacred and revolting oaths to defend and protect one another, right or wrong, no matter what their debaucheries and crimes may be, are marked in this community with the brand of Cain; that those fashionable and wealthy clubs from which human hyenas sally forth in search of victims upon whom to gratify their unholy and accursed lusts, that these wealthy and lecherous dogs must beware and tremble! This jury will say to the poor men, that their wives, daughters, and sisters are not to be the victims of the lust of the wealthy and powerful, and if they are such victims, the seducers must forfeit their lives, must fall like wild beasts caught in the fold. Through a verdict of innocence by reason of emotional insanity, this jury will throw around Home and its sacred influences a barrier that will deter moneyed villains from carrying out their base and damnable designs.

Here is a poor, wretched, friendless woman—a woman whom none of her sex had treated kindly in many years—a woman with health ruined by dissipation, who, in a fit of ungovernable anger, inspired by jealousy, kills the learned "universally respected man" whose acts were identical with hers, whose excuse for these acts was, to hers, as a grain of sand to a mountain of granite. Hang this woman, and the very name of San Francisco will be odious for ages to come!

＊＋ ☰◆☰ ＋＊

The verdict: Guilty.

Such a verdict is not entirely unanticipated, given the ugly, vindictive character of the trial; but what is so unexpected, so grievous, so hideous, is the fact that the jury took barely more

＊＋ ☰◆☰ ＋＊

than half an hour to reach their blood-curdling verdict. As they explain, the foreman took a straw vote at the start of deliberations and found to the surprise of all a unanimity of opinion. Days of testimony, of raucous, vicious public debate—all of this accounts for nothing, not even for a pause for reconsideration, not even for a moment of hesitation, of doubt, amongst these twelve men. Mrs. Fair's mother turns to the reporters and cries, "You've got what you want now, haven't you? You've got her hung. It gives you great joy, I hope." Now the "wealthy and lecherous dogs" can remain free to roam without fear—"The majesty of the law is vindicated," intones the *Chronicle*—for Mrs. Fair will be the first woman in California to hang in defense of a man's right to seduce a woman and drive her mad.

Exhausted, I am again filled with that strange doubt of the world, and I take to my bed once more. There I watch the fog sweep over North Beach like giant blank white glaciers. I wish nothing more than to return to my typesetting bench and to absent myself from the presence of Judge Dwinelle, of the weak-minded fools, of the press, of all the savage beasts of decorum, once and for all.

It is just at this moment that Emily Pitts Stevens asks me to write several contributions to the newspaper. I have never written before, except for letters and in my journal. The thought of holding up articles and other literary creations to public scrutiny is more than a little frightening. But then I think that writing may be like typesetting, like pulling letters from different parts of the job case, and that perhaps I can feel words first in my hands before I need to have them in my brains. The thought of it raises me up from dejection. I decide to try.

Laura Fair's Orphan Child

They've placed her in the felon's cell,
And closely watch'd she'll be,

For a lurking doubt does still exist
   As to her sanity.

Her wasted form will there remain
   With dangling chains around;
But, 'reft of reason, she'll know no pain,
   Nor hear their clanging sound.

The gallows will take her life away,
   She with a thud will fall;
But not alone she hangs that day:
   With her dies Woman all.

The Law may shout a victory,
   And from her blood exact,
But all who watch her agony
   See murder in Law's fact.

Her orphan child will wander 'round
   Without caress or care,
With stigma branded on her brow,
   Which heretofore was Fair.

All those who know when madness claims
   To right the world by pain
Become Fair's Orphan Child, sans blame:
   Our destiny proclaim!

God help the little Orphan Child,
   Struck by an insane blow,
That She may safely through the Wild
   Unto Her Canaan go.

Mrs. Fair's Picture

The picture palace of William Show displays a correct picture
of Mrs. Fair, and hundreds of people have visited the gallery,
all eager to gaze upon a good likeness of the convicted woman.

For three days the crowd poured in, and on the fourth day the picture was placed in the show window at the foot of the stairs. All week at any hour a crowd is pressed against the glass to gaze upon the sweet face that looks from the canvas.

It seems that everyone in San Francisco passes the picture, drawn as to a magnet. And even those who unjustly and vindictively condemned her in their hearts look with surprise upon the womanly face. There is a shock of recognition, of feeling, of inexpressible sentiment. Few men or women, possessed of heart and feeling, can look into the clear eyes of the picture, which reveal a sensitive nature and a woman's soul, without being both merciful and charitable.

The painting is a perfect likeness—except that it does not show how her face is lined with care and suffering, how it grows whiter and whiter in the damp cell at County Jail as she awaits her appeal. The impress of an agony few can realize rests upon her features. Her hands, emaciated and bloodless, when pressed in welcoming the visitors who call, feel akin to death in their coldness. Reader! when you gaze through the glass upon the picture, think of Mrs. Fair as she is now, shivering day after day with cold, bowed to the very dust with grief. She is ruined at the summer age of thirty-three, and if she dies she will achieve that sorrow and suffering known only to such who have "suffered likewise."

—■◆■—

On the eve of execution, Mrs. Elizabeth Cady Stanton and Miss Susan B. Anthony arrive in San Francisco to lecture on the Power of the Ballot. Mrs. Stevens takes them to visit Mrs. Fair in the County Jail. Their lecture is anticipated with excitement, the local newspapers taking up their visit with considerably more respect than they regard the activities of local suffragists. After all, they are individuals of great national prominence, and that alone piques their curiosity.

—■◆■—

Miss Anthony speaks on the ballot, on the need for woman's suffrage as the means for general social reform. As she appeals to men to rise above bigotry and ignorance to protect the rights of all women as if each were of their own blood, she pauses. She peers out at the audience, then adds, "If all men had protected all women as they would have their own wives and daughters protected, you would have no Laura Fair in your jail tonight."

Dashaway Hall explodes with hisses, seemingly from every corner of the house. Afterwards, Miss Anthony tells us that it was the same sound she heard in the antislavery days before the war. She responds in the same way, by standing still, until there comes a lull. Again she says, "If all men had protected all women as they would have their own wives and daughters protected, you would have no Laura Fair in your jail tonight."

Once more a storm of hisses rages through the house, although this time cheers could also be discerned above the din. She waits for silence again, then says it yet a third time. Her courage impresses the audience, wins over their admiration so that it breaks out into a roar of applause at her words, all hisses overcome.

Still, she waits for silence once more, then says, "I declare to you that woman must not depend upon the protection of man, but must be taught to protect herself, and there I take my stand."

The applause and cheers are thunderous.

Perhaps it is due to this visit that opinions begin to change slightly, I do not know. Soon after, there is a stay of execution and the possibility of a new trial. But whatever does change, it is at first imperceptible, for Miss Anthony and Mrs. Stanton must cut short their speaking tour because of the outrage, setting out on a sudden trip to Yosemite. "Never in all my hard experiences have I been under such fire," Miss Anthony remarks.

The California Supreme Court orders a new trial—for "frivolous" reasons, the *Chronicle* fumes. Once again, the witnesses are paraded through the court; once again, the women of the *Pioneer* observe. Mr. Campbell is back, but Mr. Cook is dead, and of Mrs. Fair's former defense counsel only Leander Quint returns. Judge T. B. Reardon mercifully takes Judge Dwinelle's place. Again there are the crowds, the prosecutor's slanders, the defense's argument of emotional insanity. Everything seems as charged as before, but perhaps only because the spectacle is repeated, is old news—and those who thirst for scandal can drink more deeply at Victoria Woodhull's well— the reaction is slightly milder, the blood frenzy is a little less unrestrained. Certainly, Judge Reardon allows for more decency and respect of a woman's feelings than Judge Dwinelle could even comprehend.

Again, the jury goes out to its deliberations. But this time they do not return after forty minutes; they remain sequestered, evidently torn. We are praying for a hung jury, and we know that even many of those who call for her blood privately desire it, for then they feel the tormented woman can be freed, but without having to be exonerated. The jury deliberates past midnight and into the next morning; throughout the next day their only word is that of the foreman sending out for a gallon of whisky. Then on Monday morning, September 30, 1872, after sixty-five hours, the jury finally returns with its verdict: *Not Guilty!*

At the foreman's announcement a low, thrilling moan can be heard in the courtroom, and in an instant two thin, white, chalklike wrists are clasped around her lawyer Judge Curtis' neck, Mrs. Fair's golden hair streaming on his breast. She was as senseless as a corpse, clutching her lawyer. Judge Curtis lifts his lifeless burden to a settee and gently lays her down. We rush over with water to revive her, which she soon does, although she is as yet insensible, unable to comprehend the turn affairs have taken.

———— ❈✦❈ ————

Mrs. Emily Pitts Stevens writes:

This is a triumph of Justice and Mercy paralleled by the triumph of Christ over the howling hypocrites and lecherous liars who thirsted for the blood of the woman charged with adultery. What is this later triumph? A jury of twelve honest, fearless, heroic men, after due and solemn contemplation lasting sixty-five hours, did their duty. In their own hearts, before their fellow creatures and in the sight of God, they can walk the streets of San Francisco feeling that their verdict was just, and knowing that they are respected, loved, and reverenced by every man and woman to whom Justice and Mercy are the sweetest, noblest, and holiest attributes of our common natures.

The press has howled against the verdict. The *Bulletin*, nurtured in blood and never happy except when its accursed fangs are tearing out human hearts, thirsted for the blood of Mrs. Fair. It howls like a madman, raves like a lunatic, and throws itself into an insane frenzy because the poor woman was not tortured to death. The *Alta*, no less atrocious in its thirst for blood, has displayed its tigerlike instincts. The little Catholic organ, price two cents, has shown its currish teeth and snarled with characteristic infirmity. This receptacle of bigotry, intolerance, and malice represents the Inquisitorial jackals. We need not mention other journals whose course has been no less vindictive and cruel. Their editors in every case have denounced the jury as being composed of idiots, fools, and worse.

The former jury tried her under the shadow of an infuriated mob and, without reason or deliberation, condemned her to death. The present jury tried her under the very shadow of God, and reasoned and deliberated like men upon her life or death. Those composing this jury were resolute, heroic souls. Their noble Verdict of *Not Guilty* will consecrate their names

———— ❈✦❈ ————

and memories in the heart of every American woman who has been wronged, violated, and outraged by the perfidy of her betrayers and seducers. Is not the verdict of the press the result of malice, hate, envy, and all the characteristics which govern unreasoning and brutal natures? And in the name of God, if San Francisco is to be governed by "idiots," who have yet the consciousness that such a thing as mercy exists, or by human brutal natures, who thirst for human blood, let us be governed by "idiots." Yes, let merciful idiots rule! Let human hyenas be accursed in the sight of man and the sight of God!

San Francisco is by no means ruled by merciful idiots. But with the acquittal, at least the celebrated murder case is no longer the overriding focus of our activities. The presidential elections dominate us now, with Mrs. Stevens proclaiming George Francis Train as "The New Comet in the Sky," along with all the talk about Grant, Greeley, and that quixotic madness of Victoria Woodhull running for president with Frederick Douglass. Still, Mrs. Fair is not entirely forced out of our minds.

It seems that a demon of ill fortune still pursues her, or, at least, Jimmy Crittenden does. The dead man's son followed Mrs. Fair until her escort, Judge Tyler, cocked his pistol and snarled that if he made the least motion to injure Mrs. Fair he would "blow a hole through you big enough to pass a rail stake through."

She is pursued by more than the dead man's son, however. She is publicly reviled; men smirk at her and treat her discourteously on streetcars, while even the majority of those women who wished her freed prefer that she absent herself from their sight. No longer a martyr, the contradictory, conflicted, tawdry woman with curious ideas is suddenly less magnetic. She is recognized for what she seems to have been all along—a sexual monstrosity—and cast off. Nor does Mrs.

Fair show any interest in joining or working with the *Pioneer*, preferring instead to war against the world alone. In this spirit, Mrs. Fair enters into numerous disputes and endless litigation with her lawyers, even a lawsuit with her own mother, which dispute is settled only when the daughter rushes to the mother's bedside after she swallows half an ounce of laudanum.

Worst of all, when Mrs. Fair attempts to give a lecture to explain her case at Platt's Music Hall, the owners shut it down out of fear of violent mobs. We launch a protest to protect her freedom of speech, but she chooses to flee to Sacramento to give "Wolves in the Fold." Her lecture sets out to prove that "the base slanders heaped upon me by my revilers and enemies are deliberate, premeditated, and false, from alpha to omega." When the crowd in Sacramento refuses to pay one dollar each to hear her in the vacant saloon she has hired, she flings open the doors free of charge to all, her audience comprising mainly the usual loungers, drunks, and derelicts in the vicinity, as she resolutely delivers her lecture.

When "Wolves in the Fold" is published, I will read it with great relish, as I imagine she will unburden much of what oppressed her during the trial. I do know, from the Sacramento newspapers, that she has at least called Judge Dwinelle "a judicial pettifogger," and Mr. Campbell she insists is "a rake with a record of forty years of licentious debauchery." What next for Mrs. Fair I can only guess—except that I imagine she will wisely establish a new home far from San Francisco where she will find comfort in anonymity and joy in being the mother to her beautiful daughter.

For myself, I try to think back over my own experience of this ordeal. How difficult it is sometimes just to sit in a room, even to enter it. All the same, it seems comical, really. The esteemed Court is but a zone for controlled warfare at the same time that it is just another form of theater, a preposterous acting out of ideas and a talking out of flesh. Perhaps up to now all the roles have been played by men, but Mrs. Fair and the women of the *Pioneer* have shown it will henceforth be otherwise.

All this is an accomplishment, I suppose, which, along with the triumph of Mrs. Fair's acquittal, will always be remembered by San Francisco. I have changed so immeasurably, discovering courage I never thought was buried within me, as we braved the smirks of peacocks and the howls of hyenas. I think of all these notes, these fragments of experience I have been writing, these thoughts of someone who feels words first in her hands before her brains, and I marvel at how I have begun to invent words. I remember, too, the doubts I have held, still hold. For I am not now any more certain of the inevitable trend of history; I am certain only that, for a brief instant, I and all the women of the *Pioneer* forced ourselves within that current by merely sitting on a bench . . .

Last night I lay in bed while Sarah Wallis comforted me as in the days of the trial. In the morning I wake early to sit alone, and I gaze out my window while poor exhausted Sarah sleeps. I can see the hills, the clear, fogless morning light brightening the North Beach hills, and I watch the street stir beneath. I put my hand on the glass and feel the shock of its morning coldness. I can sense the window pressing against my palm, and I push harder and harder against its transparent surface, until the glass, able to take no more, shatters as I reach through to the other side. Sarah wakes with a start at the sound and screams at the sight of blood streaming from my hand, but I can only laugh at her frightened expression. "Don't worry," I tell her, "the window is not yet broken."

Spite Fence

Concerning Charles Crocker, His Fence,
and the Troubles of 1877

Charles Crocker

I was never one to be outdone. When Stanford and Hopkins
began building their big mansions on the California Street
Hill, I came up with my own plan of action. I bought the site
of my house on ground a shade higher than my partners and
a block west of them on the hill. Stanford built his place out
of redwood, with marble steps that lead into a grand circular
entrance hall, and he even has that stone floor in the hall that's
got the signs of the zodiac inlaid in black marble, and over-
head he has that wonderful glass dome that gives off an amber
glow. Stanford's sitting room is truly magnificent, filled up
with all that East Indian furniture, and its windows on the
Powell and Pine corner overlook the entire business section of
the city. Meanwhile, Mark Hopkins throws up the brainchild
his wife concocts from all the books she's read. Well, I was
amazed. It turns out to be a spectacular collection of towers
and gables and steeples, and with a drawing room as big as the
Chambers in the Palace of the Doges. I have never seen the
Palace of the Doges, but I figure those Chambers must be very
big indeed if they measure close to Hopkins' drawing room.

How was I to compete? Well, I got the architect Arthur
Brown to draw up a splendid mansion for me. What he did
was all in wood, and he called it "early Renaissance." Brown
put in the little theater, the library, the billiard room, and a

huge 12,500 square feet of floor space. But I asked him particularly to add something special, something that would blow
up the competition, so he put in that seventy-five-foot tower.
My own tower! You must climb to the top of the tower with
me and take a look at the view when we are done with this
interview. You can see clear to Mount Diablo, Tamalpais, the
Mission Hills, just like you're standing on the top of a mast on
the rolls of the sea looking out at the other waves, except our
frigate is forever at the crest of a frozen wave in a frozen sea.
From my tower you can survey the City and the Bay as if you
were taking in the entire monumental job it's supposed to be.
Perhaps it befits Stanford to keep his perch over Montgomery
Street, just as it may befit old Hopkins to play the Venetian.
They may be supreme in their pursuits, financial or political,
but I am supreme on the road. I build the railroads. From my
tower you can survey the entire City as it washes up and down
the hills just like it's one big job, and you can supervise the
construction of all of it, and all while standing *over* the shoulders of Stanford, Hopkins, and everyone else!

I would have been happier than a condor in the sky—
except for that crazy undertaker Nicholas Yung. When my
people approached him to buy his property on the block, he
said he was not anxious to leave, and he declined the offer. He
says his daughters were all born in their house, they like the
view of the Bay, they don't want to move. Mind you, I had
known Mr. Yung previously, was welcomed in his house
often, admired his family. I believed he was an honorable
man, so I certainly did not anticipate him starting a dispute.
When I heard he turned down the offer, I judged him to be
no more than a keen businessman, and, even though I offered
him a fair price for the property, I could come up with a little
extra just to be neighborly. Well, he still says no, and he
moans and groans about how his daughters so love the place
and the beautiful environs, so I offer to trade off some fine

property in the Mission District, but that was not enough. Now, I figured I had a tough bargainer on my hands, so I personally visit Yung and explain to him that I must have the property in order to build on the entire block. I explain that his small parcel is all that stands in the way of a successful project, and that I'm ready to pay him way over the appraised value, offering him $6,000—a too generous amount, if you ask me. Not only does he reject my offer, but he insults me! I know full well when my cheeks have been slapped, and I could tell that the little Prussian undertaker was only interested in digging his own grave. I had met bigger enemies than Nicholas Yung. I just went ahead on the work on the house, leaving the space of his property on the Sacramento Street side to be built up later. I ordered the men to blast away the rock for the foundation. I said they could be as "relaxed" as they wanted with the charges so as to let the rocks fly freely towards Yung's house. He still would not budge. But I figured Yung would give in after I put up my house, so I just went about my business building my mansion, all the while ignoring the little weasel.

I have often said that in no enterprise that I have taken up, where I superintended it myself, was I ever unsuccessful. I occupied myself on supervising the construction of that mansion, and it turned out as successful as all my other enterprises. I don't know anything much about mansion building, but I knew I could do it. When I started work on the railroad, I could not have measured a cut any more than I could have flown, but I built the railroad. When I started, they ridiculed me: "Why, Crocker, are you crazy? You think of building a railroad across these mountains? Why, you have got a good business, why do you want more?" "Well," said I, "I am going to build this railroad." So this time I just said, "I am going to build my mansion, supervise it myself. I am going to climb the tower that I build myself."

I enjoyed myself mightily putting up that house. When I was building the railroad I used to go up and down the road in my car like a mad bull, stepping along wherever there was anything going amiss and raising old nick with the boys that were not up to time. I went charging up and down that house in the same manner, watching, working, climbing over the lumber, managing the men. When I took the first contract to build on that railroad, they wanted to know what experience I had. I told them I had all the experience necessary. I knew how to manage men. I had worked them in the ore beds, in the coal pits, and worked them all sorts of ways, and had worked myself right along with them. And where did I learn those valuable lessons? Why, in Marshall County, Indiana, when I was a young man, first doing forge work, digging ore, burning coal, sixteen hours a day for $11 per month. Working the men to put up that mansion was as familiar to me as the back of my own hand. I had a grand time.

In any case, when I was nearly done I went back to Mr. Yung in person to make my offer again. The undertaker finally says he's willing to sell—but then he concedes the property for $12,000, saying that no amount of money could compensate for what it means for him and his family to lose such a beloved home. Balderdash! I called the man an extortionist to his face. Then he was brazen enough to tell me that he did not consider such a price exorbitant, "considering James Flood paid $25,000 for a similar lot on California Street." The man was absolutely preposterous! I will not have a knife held to my throat by some highway bandit! Nicholas Yung was scraping for a fight, but he was fooling with the wrong man. I've wrestled with far tougher brutes than this undertaker can ever imagine.

That's when I built the fence. All I aimed to do was to show him a little muscle until he comes to his senses. I had the men build it around all the three sides of Yung's house that face my property. Admittedly, there are other fences on the hill. There's the granite one surrounding Stanford and Hopkins, built by the railroad's stone masons, that looks like a medieval castle with battlements and towers. James Flood got his brownstone place surrounded with a gigantic bronze fence that cost him $50,000. No, Nicholas Yung did not get such a mighty fine fence. I had the boys put up a plain, unpainted plank fence with no spaces between the planks and no fancy woodwork. And I wanted that fence to shoot up high above his house—forty feet high! I wanted it that high so it would tower over Yung's place and make his house look like a little shack in a gulch. I wanted him to sit in total darkness even in the bright blaze of day. He would be living at the bottom of a dark, dank well at the same time that I would be able to climb my tower to oversee the City. How's that for a rub? If that's where the stubborn fool wants to live, so be it. He would not be reasonable, so the undertaker had to dig his own grave. Of course, as you know, he can relent at any time and get paid handsomely—and fairly—for his property. Then he could stop mistreating his family and move to a more fitting location to raise his girls. But the man is crazy.

After I finished the house I took off for Europe on a furniture-buying expedition—just about emptied out the Medicis of all their chairs and armoires and whatnot. I don't know much about art, but I picked up some fine pictures—a Meissonier, "The Smoker," cost me $12,000. But when I came back, Yung was still there at the bottom of his well, just as obstinate as ever. Then comes all that trouble, with crowds of people climbing the hill in order to see Crocker's spite fence, but I just go ahead with life just as I intend to live it, like throwing that big party for our Silver Wedding Anniversary. I don't mind having people gawk at Yung's house—it'll make him give in quicker. Even all that excitement with Dennis Kearney and his hoodlums don't bother me much. I have all the protection I need, and those loudmouth agitator types will be stirring up trouble for a successful man no matter what he does. But I imagine old Nicholas Yung must be thinking pretty hard right now about his tender daughters, about them having to see those drunken communistic scum trooping up the hill to take their papa's side. Mark my words, he'll be giving in soon enough. And if he doesn't—well, that's his tough luck.

I want you to climb up the tower with me now. I think I've said all I can. You will marvel at the view from up there, I guarantee it. You probably won't believe a man as big as I am can even climb up these stairs. Chinaman weighed me in China, called me a "four-picul man." That's 274 pounds. But I'm up there in my tower with my spyglass looking out over the city two, three, four times a day every day when I'm at home. I especially fancy climbing up at dawn. Can you imagine that? I'm a big man, but it's a big world.

Gertrude Yung Miller

My father bought the lot on Sacramento Street from a banker, Jesse Seligman, sometime in the fifties. When my sisters and I were growing up, we were not very wealthy, but we lived comfortably. Papa earned his income from the Railroad Iron Works, which did very well supplying the Nevada silver mines with equipment, and then he bought a partnership in a funeral home, Craig, Golden, and Yung on Sacramento Street. When we first moved into our house, a carriage could barely get up the hill. It was like living in an isolated castle on a craggy mountaintop. The view was stunning, and we were almost entirely by ourselves, as if we were living in the country, except that we were high above the city while not far from it. But by the early seventies they began operating the cable car, and the city began to catch up to our hill. Suddenly, the California

Street Hill became very fashionable, and all the millionaires wanted to build their mansions on it. It became "Nob" Hill overnight.

Papa left Germany after the troubles in 1848. He came to America to get away from tyrants and to have his family live proper, cultured lives. He wanted peace and freedom. For him, America was everything. It was only here that he could live on top of his hill, a free man. We were quiet, unostentatious people, very happy, and we left everyone else alone. When he came to San Francisco, he changed his name from Jung to make it easier for Americans.

The sunlight on the top of that hill filled everything. Every room of that house was sunny, bright, airy. It was a wonderful childhood we had because of that house, the sun always filling our hearts. So many times we would look down upon the fog clinging to the valleys below. Every day Mama would close the drapes to protect the velvet-covered chairs from the afternoon sun, and we would sip our tea. We attended concerts and enjoyed plays, riding down from our hill. We lived as sedately as respectable people did in those days, especially ones with four daughters who were of marriageable age.

We met Mr. Crocker several times even before all the trouble began. He visited Mama and Papa when he first was looking for property on the hill. By then Papa had come to accept the inevitable intrusion of the city, so he harbored no ill feelings to the magnate when he would visit. Actually, Papa liked Mr. Crocker at first. He said the man was crude but filled with sheer daring, gusto. Papa also said that Crocker thought very much of himself. All I remember today of Mr. Crocker is a huge mountain of flesh moving to greet me and my sisters. I had never seen such a big man. In fact, I felt I could barely see him when I met him, he so filled the space before me and above me. After the trouble began, I never saw Mr. Crocker again, although I do remember hearing his booming voice as he and my father argued by the front door while we hid in the kitchen.

I've read that one of his railroad men said that Crocker was used to getting his way. Crocker would obtain the right-of-way when he built his railroads because he was given the right to take private property without the consent of the owner just by paying the appraised value. I suppose that Mr. Crocker did get used to such a thing, and I imagine he thought he could do the same with Papa. But Papa did not want to move. We had such a wonderful life in our house, my Papa did not see any reason we should leave. And if he were to sell his property, he would be the one to fix the price. All of us were mournful about the prospect of leaving. We were resigned to having neighbors, but we didn't think that meant we had to move. But Mr. Crocker kept insisting, coming back again and again with more offers. But the more insistent Mr. Crocker became, the more calm and tranquil Papa would become. From behind the kitchen door we would hear Crocker roar, and then we would hear Papa's calm, even voice responding. His quiet stubbornness must have been terribly infuriating to Mr. Crocker, like banging his head against a wall. One time when he came with yet another offer, my father greeted him in German, "*Es ist gar hübsch von einem grossen Herrn so menschlich mit dem Teufel selbst zu sprechen.*" That means, "It's very handsome of so great a lord to talk with the devil as man to man," and when Crocker finally got Papa to tell him in English what he had said he was furious.

Meanwhile, Crocker just went ahead building his house. You couldn't imagine how noisy it was. There's plenty of rock on the California Street Hill, so they had to dynamite for a foundation. For a while it felt as if cannons were being aimed at our castle and we were under siege. Then we saw the building go up. We were horrified to learn that he designed his mansion so that we would be tucked into our lot as if we were pushed into a miner's pocket. We were going to be cut off from our beloved view, from the sunlight of our childhood. I remember sitting with my sisters as my mother told my father that perhaps he should settle with Mr. Crocker because we certainly would not be able to live like this. That's the time when Crocker came with one price and Papa offered to sell the property for twice the amount. It was a lot of money, $12,000, but Papa knew of people getting even higher amounts for their lots. He still insisted that he would not be bullied by the millionaire, that this was America, that Crocker was no baron.

That's when the fence went up. One day wagons and carpenters and other workingmen showed up, and they began hammering away until an immense plain wooden fence towered over us from all three sides of Crocker's property. To tell you we were astonished would not be adequate. We were stunned; I should say we were even awed by the sight. We could only see the sky when we craned our necks out the window and twisted our faces up. We could not believe it, nor could we believe the audacity of the man, the arrogance and lack of sentiment. A man so fabulously rich could not strike a fair bargain, so he resorted to such an incredible, unthinkable act against an entire family, although I suppose he probably thought it was merely punishment that fit Papa's own crime of holding out. Maybe he thought Papa would be dashing over right away, overjoyed to take his $6,000. Of course, this fence just had the opposite effect on my father. He vowed that he would never sell his property to that Croesus for anything less than his price. In his typically understated fashion, Papa's only response was to send a note to Mr. Crocker. I believe all it said was, "$12,000."

The fence soon became a sight to behold by the whole city. People came climbing up Nob Hill or hanging off the cable car to stand before our house and gaze in awe at the monstrous fence towering over our little home. We felt we were living in a fish bowl, a very dark one, for every time we left the house the crowd would murmur that there went the poor man's daughters. They called it Crocker's "spite fence" or "Crocker's crime," and my father was painted in the press as the common man violated by a bloated bear. The fence became notorious, a Barnum attraction, and people came because they loved to be shocked into loathing the railroad magnate. One of his lawyers, a Mr. Cohen, was on trial for stealing railroad money, and he would lacerate his old boss with sarcasm. He was the one who said, "If Charlie had the brains we all believed he had, he could have charged the spectators two bits apiece and bought the lot a dozen times over with the profits."

How gloomy our house became, how sad. All we could see out our windows was the blank wood of the rich man's fury. The darkness made us so very melancholy, and the constant public surveillance made it very difficult indeed for any available gentleman to join the Yung girls at tea. However, we never complained to Papa. When the fence went up, we realized that this fight was more than a little business squabble, and that family honor required that we stick together. Mr. Crocker really thought he could bully the entire world into doing his own bidding. My Papa, small and quiet and unostentatious as he was, was called upon to battle a Titan who had been driven mad by a little man's willpower. We were going to stick by Papa's side even if it meant we had to live at the bottom of a pit. As I said, never once did we complain to Papa, although I confess we would privately weep to each other that we would end up as spinsters honored for our devotion to our Papa but lonely and barren nonetheless.

Then came all the troubles in 1877. There was a depression then, probably even worse than the one now. Workingmen all over the country were hungry, unemployed, living in the streets. Then came what they called the July days. The Molly Maguires or other communistic types stirred up a railroad strike back East—Baltimore and such places. Soon mobs were burning down every single city in the country. San Francisco didn't escape the turmoil. There were about four days and nights of riots and fires here. Some Chinamen were killed, and several Chinese laundries were burned down. They called up William T. Coleman from the old Committee of Vigilance days to protect the city. They named the new vigilantes the "Committee of Safety," but everyone called them the "Pick-Handle Brigade" because they were all armed with hickory ax handles. The workingmen hated the Chinese because they were coolies, they worked for much less than white men, and they didn't like Mr. Crocker because he was the capitalist who brought the Chinese to work on the railroad in the first place. "Crocker's pets," they called them. Dennis Kearney started making his fiery speeches in the sandlots at that time. "The Chinese must go," that's what he was saying back then, and Kearney became a very powerful man for a few years. His party even elected the mayor.

In any case, Kearney and his Workingman's Party actually held a mass meeting on the top of Nob Hill. It was October 29th that they held it, at night. Thousands and thousands of this rabble of disgruntled, angry workingmen congregated on the hill, marching past our house. It's a steep hill, so the fact that they had the grit to climb up at eight in the evening to listen to speakers in a cutting night wind was some accomplishment. Of course, we were not the targets of their wrath; we were just victims of Crocker's megalomania. But the blood and flames from the July days were fresh in everyone's memory. Afterwards, we learned that Stanford had employed a hundred men with batons under their coats to mingle with the crowds. Crocker's house had five hundred rifles stacked and soldiers hidden in his hallways, just in case. The workingmen set fires in the lime barrels that were still around Mr. Crocker's house from the construction, and in that diabolical light they yelled and shook their fists at the fence. Papa stood in our door, shouting, "Go home! This fence has nothing to do with you! It's not your fight!" and things like that, until he was hoarse. We had never heard him shout like that, but it was no use. Kearney and his agitators were determined for their own reasons to hate that spite fence no matter what Papa said. I did not hear any of the speeches that night, naturally, although we read about them in the next day's newspapers. Kearney launched into what was by then his usual rant against the capitalists and the Chinese, although he made one particular remark that drew our especial attention. Kearney demanded that Crocker tear down the fence by Thanksgiving Day or he and the workingmen would tear it down for him. After a while, the demonstration broke up. We were terribly frightened, and I cannot tell you how greatly relieved we were when our "friends" decided to end their visit. At the end of the rally, the thousands of men began stampeding down California Street, heading towards Chinatown. But nothing happened. There was no violence, and at the bottom of the hill the agitators dissolved into the night.

When next morning came, everything was normal, and the small crowd gathered as usual in front of our house to view the notorious fence. Now our house had become even more of an attraction, for not only was the fence a monument to Crocker's spite but Kearney's threat to tear it down made it a symbol of the workingmen's anger and their defiance of the rich. We had to live for nearly a month waiting for Kearney to make his threat good, while the tourists came to watch where the fence "used to be" even before it "was."

Dennis Kearney

The monopolists who make their money by employing cheap labor had better watch out. They have built themselves fine residences on Nob Hill and erected flagstaffs on their roofs—let them take care that they have not erected their own gallows. I want Stanford and the press to understand that if I give an order to hang Crocker, it will be done. When the Chinese question is settled, we can discuss whether it would be better to hang, shoot, or cut the capitalists to pieces. The City will be leveled to ashes and the ruins filled in with the roasted bodies. Bullets will replace ballots. San Francisco will meet the fate of burning Moscow. Bring guns to the sandlots and form military companies—blow up the Pacific Mail docks. The Central Pacific men are thieves, and will soon feel the power of the workingmen. When I have thoroughly organized the party, we will march through the city and compel the thieves to give up their plunder. I will lead you to the City Hall, clean out the police force, hang the prosecuting attorney, burn every book that has a particle of law in it, and then enact new laws for the workingmen. Judge Lynch is the only judge we want. Don't these capitalists know that the Anglo-Saxon spirit is not dead, that the doctrine of the survival of the fittest is hourly growing more salient, and that we are superior to these moon-eyed Mongolians and will survive them? We don't want to send little boys to burn washhouses. We want organization to drive out these Chinese lepers, and we will drive them out, despite the police, the military, and the hoodlum Committee of Safety. I will give the Central Pacific just three months to discharge their Chinamen, and if that is not done, Stanford and his crowd will have to take the consequences. I will give Crocker until November 29th to take down the fence around Yung's house, and if he does not do it, I will lead the workingmen up there and tear it down. Take down that fence, Crocker, or I'll beat you over the head with the boards—I'll give you the worst beating with sticks that a man ever got!

Letter from Chinese Six Companies
to Mayor Andrew Jackson Bryant

November 3, 1877

To Andrew Jackson Bryant, Mayor of the City and County of San Francisco

Sir:

We, the undersigned Presidents of the Chinese Six Companies of this city and state, desire to call your immediate attention to a state of things which seems to us to threaten the lives and property of the Chinese residents, as well as the peace and good name of this municipality.

In the multitude of responsibilities which tax your time and strength, it may possibly have escaped your notice that large gatherings of the idle and irresponsible elements of the population of this city are nightly addressed in the open streets by speakers who use the most violent, inflammatory, and incendiary language, threatening in plainest terms to burn and pillage the Chinese quarter and kill our people, unless, at their bidding, we leave this "free Republic." The continuance of these things for many days, with increasing fury, without any check or hindrance by the authorities, is causing the Chinese people great anxiety, and in the immediate danger which seems again to threaten us as well as to threaten the peace and good name of the city, we (as on former occasions) appeal to you, the Mayor and chief magistrate of this municipality, to protect us, to the full extent of your power, in all our peaceful, constitutional, and treaty rights against all unlawful violence and all riotous proceedings now threatening us. We would deprecate the results of mob violence, for we not only value our property and cherish our lives, which now seem in jeopardy, but we should also regret to have the good name of this Christian civilization tarnished by the riotous proceedings of its own citizens against the "Chinese heathen." As a rule, our countrymen are better acquainted with peaceful vocations than with scenes of strife, yet we are not ignorant that self-defense is the common right of all men, and should a riotous attack be made upon the Chinese quarter, we should have neither the power nor the disposition to restrain our countrymen from defending themselves to the last extremity and selling their lives as dearly as possible.

But we trust and believe that it is entirely within the scope of your Honor's power and in accordance with your high sense of justice to prevent these threatened evils. That we may do all in our power, as good citizens, to preserve the peace and avert a riot, we most respectfully submit these statements and make this earnest appeal to your Honor.

Respectfully submitted,

> Lin Cheok Fung, Pres. Sam Yup Co.
> Lo Sing Ho, Pres. Kong Chow Co.
> Lan Kong Cha, Pres. Ning Ying Co.
> Chan Fung Chin, Pres. Yen Wo Co.
> Lee Cheong Tip, Pres. Mop Wo Co.
> Lee Jen Yeun, Pres. Yeeng Wo Co.

John McCabe

Oh yes, I remember the demonstration on Nob Hill. It was something else, it was. Things was mighty exciting in those days, and that meeting in front of Crocker's fence and Stanford's palace—you can still see how splendid and Godawful ugly those mansions are, like taking a regular house and throwing in eight times the amount of windows and carvings and towers and whatnot and blowing it up like a balloon, that's how gargantuan they are, big and bloated like Crocker himself. Looking at those monstrosities is enough to make you madder than a bull and having a meeting there with thousands of hungry workingmen—well, that was like throwing a match in a bucket of gasoline.

But things was burning pretty much already, and I figure you need to go back at least to the July days to get a sense of things. That depression was something terrible, and it was only made worse by the drought. Thousands and thousands of men were out of work, they were literally starving, even the Comstock mines was shutting down and the rich was getting ruined. Before the depression they said there was a hundred millionaires in California, but in no time they was reduced to less than fifty, not that I felt too sorry for 'em. Anyway, all of these poor souls from the mines and the farms and the small towns kept pouring into San Francisco hoping for some kind of job or at least a handout. They wanted a job or bread or at least a night in jail. I'll tell you, the revolution was just waiting to explode.

That's when the railroads cut their wages by ten percent—cut 'em, mind you! Well, the fighting in Pittsburgh and Baltimore and the other Eastern cities was something unheard of. It looked like it was going to be the Civil War all over again, except this time it was going to be free white labor fighting to cut loose from its chains. The Central Pacific had the good sense to rescind their pay cut right after they got the news of the riots back East, so it took a week or so before the rebellion broke out here.

At that time I was talking with the boys in the Workingman's Party—that's the Workingman's Party of the United States, not Kearney's outfit that came later. They were the socialistic types—some Germans, although mostly Irishmen,

Americans, and others. These fellows were more Marxian than those who followed Lassalle's thinking. I was interested in organizing the trade unions, which the Marxians thought was just the right thing for getting the workingmen educated in the class fight. The Lassalleans didn't care for unions since they thought they was just doing the bidding of the capitalists. In any case, I was seriously considering the advisability of applying for membership to that organization, and I considered P. J. Healy, the local organizer, to be the right man in the right place. Several of us were gravitating to the party, notably Frank Roney, Sigmund Danielewicz, Jim Flaherty, a bunch of us, although none of us had joined up yet.

Well, when the July days was happening, labor in San Francisco was pretty much without any leadership. There was General Winn and his Mechanics Council, but they were pretty much washed up. There was some unions and anti-coolie clubs and other ward clubs, but they had no focus, and many of them had hardly seen any socialistic propaganda, didn't know a damn thing except they hated the capitalists and the Mongolians, so you couldn't expect much from them. So the Workingman's Party decided to step in and give a voice to the class. Mind you, the party had been organizing meetings all over the country, trying to lead the riots into a real confrontation with the capitalists for real demands—and they did mighty well in St. Louis, for example, just about taking over the city—so it was just natural they would try the same in San Francisco.

So on July 23rd they called for a rally in the sandlot next to the City Hall. Thousands showed up, and Healy and the others started making speeches about the eight-hour day and nationalizing the railroads. But pretty soon a brass band from one of the anti-coolie clubs marched by, then some boys started hollering about cheap Chinese labor, and pretty soon some of the hoodlum types started to break off to hunt for

Chinamen. In no time the rally was gone. It had turned into an insane mob smashing Chinese washhouses, beating up Chinamen, and aiming to burn down Chinatown. I think they must have smashed up twenty or thirty washhouses, just delighting to maul any Chinese that got in their way.

We simply stood there in the sandlot with the boys from the Workingman's Party, just staring at each other and scratching our heads wondering what in hell's bells had happened. It was as if somebody had taken over the crowd, but we didn't see who it was, except that maybe it was that crazy mind a mob can get all of its own. And there we stood in the empty sandlot with the leaders of the revolution, trying to figure out who the hell had stolen the goddamn revolution. After a while, me and Danielewicz, we followed after the mob, trying at least to talk the boys out of getting themselves killed over a Chinaman's dirty laundry.

Well, it was amazing how the authorities came together out of fear of the rioters. The mayor, Andrew Jackson Bryant, was from the Democracy, but he just forgot his election blather and teamed up with the Republicans to put down the workingmen. Bryant simply handed over his power to William T. Coleman, the capitalist who had organized the vigilantes back in '56. Coleman passed out six thousand pickax handles to his volunteers and had the Navy move in with gunboats and Gatling guns—he just mobilized an entire army overnight, his Pick-Handle Brigade, to protect both the Republican and Democratic moneybags. Coleman blamed the riot on hoodlums, thieves, and what he called "a small sprinkling of Communists or Internationalists who hope to usher in the millennium by a judicious use of the torch." Even back in those days the true labor fighters was always a "small sprinkling," like he said, even though that "small sprinkling" didn't do a damn thing to start the riot and even tried to stop the men from running off like wild animals.

Well, the battles went on for nights, with fires getting set and Chinamen getting killed and the boys fighting the police and the Pick-Handle Brigade. The big battle was at the lumberyard by the docks of the Pacific Mail Steamship Company. They was the ones bringing in the coolies to work for the Crockers and the Stanfords. Every day you could watch the Chinamen trooping off the steamships coming to take jobs from the white workingmen because John Chinaman was willing to work so cheap, so the Pacific Mail was a big target of the mob's hate. They set the lumberyard on fire, and when the firemen came to put out the fire there was a pitched battle on Rincon Hill. Several workingmen ended up getting killed that night. I was there, even though I thought they was crazy, because that was where the workingmen were. My philosophy is to be where the fight is. But that was about it, the end of the July days. After that big battle, things calmed down for a time: the mob went to sleep, the men all disappeared, the Navy sailed back to Mare Island, and Coleman collected his ax handles.

Of course, all this only meant that the pot was getting ready to boil again. Soon there was meetings in the sandlots again. Nothing practical got accomplished, nothing but denunciations and fostering hatred for the Chinese. It was a customary thing, these sandlot meetings, and all manner of questions would be debated, and anyone who chose could take part in the discussion. Then one day Dennis Kearney gets up and starts to speak at these meetings. You would not believe what kind of frenzy he worked himself into, but he starts telling the boys that what they need is twenty thousand well-armed and well-organized workingmen to demand and take what they wished no matter what the Pick-Handle Brigade or the Navy would do. He told the boys what they needed was a few fires to clear the atmosphere, that they needed to hang the capitalists and drive out the Chinese on their own. When some of the leaders complained that his dangerous talk could end up getting decent workingmen jailed or killed, Kearney just turned on them, shouting to the crowd that "you will have to mob those white Sioux and white pigtail-men first. You will have to shoot them down on the streets before you begin on the Chinese." The crowd roared with him, took over the platform, and Kearney just bulldozed himself into becoming the king of labor, whereupon he announced that he was the head of the Workingman's Party of California and asked everyone to join. You should have seen the faces of those Marxians—they were amazed how this demagogue stole even the name of their party—but there was nothing they could do about it. Kearney was the man of the hour, and "the Chinese must go" was the slogan.

Right from the start I never trusted Kearney too much. He came to San Francisco in '68, but the fact that he was from the old country did not automatically make me like him. For one, although he had been a sailor, he wasn't even a real workingman. He was a drayman, owned his own teams, and he had even joined up with Coleman's Pick-Handle Brigade. I don't know what made him a convert on the road to Damascus, except maybe he saw which way the winds were blowing. He wasn't even much of a speaker before. He'd give speeches at the Lyceum for Self-Education before all the troubles, soporific speeches mainly about how his own guts and gumption made him successful and how the workingmen had to follow his own example. No one paid him any mind; he couldn't have even commanded a flea's attention, much less a mob's. But all of a sudden there he was booming and bellowing, venting the pent-up anger of the hungry, saying just what everyone wanted to hear with no pussyfooting—the most daringest, the most craziest man in San Francisco.

Now I know for a fact that when Kearney appointed himself head of the Workingman's Party, he took the precaution of having his speeches prepared for him by a reporter for the *Chronicle*. That's right. Chester Hull was his name, a newspaperman well known in Nevada. "Monumental Liar" was the way he used to sign his articles in Virginia City. Hull kept on dashing off those speeches, making each one more incendiary than the last. Hull told me personally that he never dreamed that Kearney would deliver them just as he had written them, but that's just what Kearney did, although from time to time Kearney dovetailed a trifle of his own words into them. So there was this "Monumental Liar" putting fiery words into the mouth of a monumental liar—but I suppose the workers are always ready to be fooled when they're desperate from hunger. Why, Kearney for a time even got a campaign going to get people to cancel their subscriptions to the *Call* in favor of the *Chronicle*. Naturally, the *Chronicle* ran all his speeches, giving him plenty of advertising. That was before Charles DeYoung, the publisher of the *Chronicle*, turned on the Workingman's Party for running Reverend Kalloch for mayor instead of allowing DeYoung to pick his own man. DeYoung shot Kalloch down, only to end up getting killed by Kalloch's son—but I'm getting ahead of myself. I believe Hull wrote Kearney's speeches for a lark, although I wager DeYoung must have given him the nod to do it, and some money too. You might say DeYoung ended up getting killed by his own words, since he betrayed his own creation.

Then came the mass meeting on the top of Nob Hill. It was like some kind of theater show, with Crocker's fence and all the big mansions a perfect stage set. It was brilliant as far as political tactics went, with thousands standing around barrels that had been set afire on top of that hill, the huge, wild animal of the masses growling in the flickering light. There we were, all the laboring classes, those who were starving in the midst of California's plenty, stuffing our impudent words down the throats of the bloated bastards themselves. Kearney made one of his fiery speeches, peppering it with a rollicking nomination for the leaders of the Fourth Ward of the Workingman's Party: He appointed Leland Stanford to be president, Charles Crocker to be secretary, Mark Hopkins to be sergeant at arms, and he declared that the meeting had been called in front of their homes just for their convenience. He invited them to come out to accept their new positions. All of this caused gales of laughter. And then he said, "However, for the position of treasurer of the Fourth Ward, I will appoint some laboring man, since I wouldn't trust you thieves with a penny of the party's money!" How the crowd roared at the whole joke! It was marvelous fun, and it must have put some real fright into those capitalists. Then Kearney launched into another one of his tirades against the rich and the Chinese, finally demanding that Crocker tear down the fence he had put up around Yung's house in thirty days or else the workingmen would come back and tear it down themselves. All the mansions were darkened. Only Nicholas Yung seemed to be at home, and he stood in his doorway shouting. I couldn't hear what he said, but I could tell that he was none too happy to have so many people by his front door. When the rally came to an end, the crowd went running down California Street, went rolling down the street in one mass. Of course, how else could you get down such a steep hill except by picking up some momentum? Yet, despite the hot words, no one made an attempt on Chinatown that night.

A few days later Kearney was addressing another sandlot meeting, when the police suddenly appeared and arrested him. I figure the meeting on top of Nob Hill must have been the last straw. Mayor Bryant, District Attorney Daniel Murphy, and Chief of Police Kirkpatrick became alarmed at Kearney's apparent progress and resolved to nip it in the bud. I believe the capitalists wanted Kearney's arrest to turn into a riot so they could suppress the movement with no restraints, but

Kearney had the presence of mind to cool the passions of his followers and to walk calmly to jail. Instead of stopping the meetings, Kearney's arrest only increased the interest in them, particularly when his arrest was followed by the arrests of the other leaders of the Workingman's Party and by a gag law making just about any speech a felony to incite a riot.

The actions of the city authorities in attempting to suppress free speech so angered me that I gave up on the Workingman's Party of the United States and instead joined the Eighth Ward Club of the Workingman's Party of California. The night I joined, a large number of others also joined, principally as a protest at the high-handed arrests. Naturally, I did not agree with Kearney's violent speeches, particularly what he said about the Chinese, but I joined anyway, as did Frank Roney and many other solid trade union organizers. Sigmund Danielewicz refused to join, though. He said he was a Jew, a race that had been persecuted for hundreds of years and was still persecuted, so he wouldn't join in bothering any-one else. Besides, he said, no socialist would ever betray the brotherhood of man. He was right, of course, but he was not very practical. Danielewicz ended up being one of the main-stays of the sailors' union, but he'd often get plenty close to get-ting himself lynched for sounding like one of those "white pigtail-men."

All of the talk against the Chinese was nonsense, and the restrictions and harsh treatment advocated against them was brutal. No self-respecting civilized people would dream of imposing such outrages upon the members of any race within their midst. The main objection to them that held any water was that they were cheap workers. In this respect they were much like the immigrants arriving on the Atlantic side of the continent. When the Irishman was driven to America by famine and landlord oppression, he first worked as a cheap laborer and became the target of rocks and brickbats by the native Americans. But after a while he was no longer a cheap laborer; he held office, conducted business, entered the professions, and he became a good American with the vested right to jeer at the cheap laboring German who succeeded him. Then, after the German asserted himself, both pitched into the Italian. It seems that to assail and assault and oppress one part of humanity is the delight, inherent right, and practice of another part. But as a cheaper laborer than the others—who had an impossible time learning the language and ways of his new home—the Chinaman was hailed as a veritable godsend by the exploiting employers. The fact is that John Chinaman will never fit in; there is an impenetrable barrier between him and his new land. As a result, he will always be manipulated by the capitalists to break strikes and lower the wages of the white workers. While I was not interested in Kearney's harangue about the Chinese, he did voice a lot of things on the minds of workingmen, such as the eight-hour day, and it was true that the importation of coolie labor, in which the American capitalists handsomely paid the wealthy classes of the Chinese to enslave their fellow countrymen, was vile. There was—and is—a problem of Asiatic labor, but I was always in favor of sensible policies of exclusion and deportation, not violence.

Both Roney and I figured that we would try to make the party as robust and as progressive as the times and circumstances would allow. It was an essentially anti-Chinese party, and, as I said, we never warmed to that feature of the agitation. We realized the cry was superficial, but we agreed to sail under such a flag in order that we might in time have other, more important issues considered by the people. One day perhaps the workingmen will all think like Danielewicz. But, like I said, I always went where the fight was, and the Workingman's Party was it, at least until it disappeared a few years later. Why, the Republicans were shivering in their boots, and all that was left of the Democrats for a time was nothing but a smudge of grease.

The spite fence? Well, Kearney was released from jail in time for the massive Thanksgiving Day parade of the Workingman's Party. He rode one of his dray horses like Napoleon, although he wore a plain suit without decking himself out with ribbons and medals. I estimate there was ten thousand at the parade, a mighty assemblage, and not just rabble and the anti-coolie clubs but stable, skilled workers too. Still, no one made a move to climb Nob Hill. No, Kearney let his threat stand, since the authorities was just waiting to round him up along with everybody else the minute anyone got close to Crocker's fence. After that, the fence was pretty much forgotten, what with elections and the state constitutional convention right at hand. You can still see the fence today. And now with Kearney gone and things calmed down—I hear he's a grain merchant in the Valley working with the railroad, a class traitor as I always suspected he would turn out—the fence is just one more strange sight in a strange city. For a moment it served as a stage set for a grand, dramatic gesture. Well, gestures never fed a belly yet, and it didn't feed anyone in '77 either. Labor's come a long way since then, but we still ain't torn down capital's spite fence.

Jackson Lin

November 3, 1877

To: Andrew Jackson Bryant, Mayor of the City and County of San Francisco

Sir:

I am writing to you as a Chinese resident of San Francisco concerning the recent violent threats against our people from the riotous, unstable elements of the population of the city. I am only representing myself, humbly aware that both of us share the same illustrious namesake. As a native-born American (my father was one of the first "China Boys" welcomed to San Francisco), I was named after the street of my birth in the Chinese quarter and not after the honorable president. But I too am cognizant of the great words and deeds of "Old Hickory" in achieving the full expanse of democracy in this great Flowery Flag nation, and it is therefore in the spirit of our namesake that I address you.

I shall not present elaborate arguments pertaining to the present crisis; I shall not enumerate the value of the Chinese in building railroads, reclaiming swamp lands, opening new agricultural districts, and accomplishing other achievements that have inestimably contributed to California's prosperity. I too sympathize with the white workingman who suffers poverty from crushing opposition or even competition. If, therefore, it were true that the presence of the Chinese in California were a block to the prosperous advancement of our working class, I would not raise my voice against the unchristian and inhumane crusade now launched against us. But who are they who make the infamous demand that we must go? For the greater part they are themselves foreigners who came but yesterday from lands of oppression in abject poverty; they are ignorant agrarians who today are so ungrateful and insolent as to demand from the same beneficent American government, which, in its excessive magnanimity, endowed them with political rights and privileges, that it refuse to the Chinese even a small share of that hospitality which was so liberally accorded them . . .

I never finished my letter, since I could not maintain the firm yet dignified tone I was able to exhibit when I wrote the appeal to Mayor Bryant on behalf of the Chinese Six Companies. I put it down and went to join Old Lee for tea in the back of his boarded-up apothecary. There, sipping tea, Old Lee entertained me with stories from his village. I found one of the tales particularly appealing and, in a certain fashion, pertinent. Afterwards, when I returned to my room, I wrote it out as best I could in English. Here, then, is:

The Cannibal Demon

Once, in days long gone, in a lonely, isolated region, three sons brought the dead body of their father to be buried. In accordance with the ancient customs of the region, the sons built a house in the wilderness so that they might keep company with their father's spirit.

On the first night, when the eldest son sat alone as both companion and guard of their father's body, a demon came to him from out of the darkness and silence. The demon came before him and said, "I have come to eat you."

The eldest son was terrified and did not know what to do to save himself. At last he said, "If you must eat me, why not wait until tomorrow night?" To this the demon agreed and vanished in a cloud of smoke.

The second son took his turn at watch on the next night. He too was startled to see the fierce and horrible demon when he made his return visit. To the second son the demon said, "I shall eat you tonight." The second son was speechless, but he finally managed to think of the same answer that his brother had made. "Demon, why not wait? Tomorrow I shall really let you eat me." Again the demon agreed and disappeared.

On the third night came the turn of the youngest son to watch their father's body. He had heard what had happened on the previous two nights from his brothers, and he was determined to protect himself against the demon. So, taking with him a long whip and a sharp knife, he hid behind the door of the house in the wilderness to await the demon's return. When the demon finally arrived for the promised feast, the youngest son quickly lunged at him with the long whip and wrapped it tightly about his neck. The boy then took out his knife, ready to kill the demon, but the demon knelt before him in tears, pleading, "Free me! Let me go! Don't kill me! I will give you my precious drum if you let me go!"

"What good can that little drum do for me?" demanded the boy.

"Make any wish you want, then tap the drum a few times and your wish will be granted," replied the demon.

The third son agreed to take the drum, and he released the demon. He went home to his brothers, who were amazed to see him still alive, and he told them the story of how he acquired the magic drum. His brothers were jealous and envious, and they immediately provided themselves with whips and knives and went out to the little house to wait for the demon, planning to acquire some valuables for themselves.

But the demon, infuriated at the loss of his drum, was also prepared. He armed himself with a knife and returned to the house in the wilderness to recapture the drum he had lost. So when, in the darkness, the first and second sons attacked him and curled their whiplashes around his neck, the demon turned and slashed them to pieces. The frightened men began to flee, but the demon easily overcame them, laughing at their terror. The long delay, as well as his anger, only served to increase the pleasure of the demon's meal.

⊷ ▰◆▰ ⊶

All of Chinatown lived in terror. All the stores were barricaded, no one dared step outside Chinatown's boundaries, while the hired "specials" joined unemployed laborers in keeping watch from the rooftops for signs of attack. All of us ate the same bitterness—rich and poor, merchant and highbinder, laundryman and prostitute—for we were all "heathen Chinee" in the eyes of the ignorant foreign devils. We had already seen much violence during the July days—we saw washhouses set on fire and Chinese laundrymen thrown into the flames; we saw Chinese who set foot outside our quarters pounced upon by thugs and beaten unmercifully—and we expected worse to come. All of Chinatown was an armed camp. No one can say how many guns were cleaned and loaded—I even believe one of the *tongs* secretly readied a Gatling gun. As I wrote in the Six Companies' appeal to Mayor Bryant, we were prepared to defend ourselves "to the last extremity." Dennis Kearney and his hoodlums had no idea how dearly we would sell our lives, for if the Chinese "must go," then he and his minions would have to go with us.

That was when I got the crazy idea to climb Nob Hill in order to see Crocker's spite fence. I had met Charles Crocker before, when I worked as a translator for the Bank of California. I was hired because he was interested in the China trade. A huge man, he displayed no airs and did not seem any more brusque with me than he was with any of his other employees—which meant that he was thoroughly and crudely domineering, although ingenuously so. "They don't understand," he said, concerning the white laborers' objections to hiring Chinese. "Chinese labor elevates the white worker, gives him a better and higher level of status and pay. If it weren't for the Chinese being so willing to take on the meanest jobs, the white man would have to fill those positions. Chinese labor is a blessing to the white workingman, if the damn fool would only realize it." At that time I said nothing and went on with translating his negotiations with the Sam Yup Company. Now the men he sought to "elevate" wanted to spit at his benevolence.

I had heard of the spite fence that Crocker had built around undertaker Yung's house because of his refusal to sell his land. Everyone in San Francisco had heard of it. I knew it was on top of that great hill that overshadowed Chinatown, only a short climb from Dupont Street, but hardly any Chinese dared to see that fence, except perhaps Crocker's houseboy, especially after Dennis Kearney convened that huge rally at the top of the hill a few days before. With the loud, murderous threats made against us every day, the thought of leaving Chinatown at all seemed to be a virtual act of suicide.

I cannot explain why I decided to see the fence, particularly in that dangerous atmosphere. Perhaps one of Old Lee's demons possessed my spirit. Nevertheless, I felt an overpowering compulsion to do it. That night I put on the Western suit I would wear sometimes for work, coiled my queue underneath my hat, and in the dark before dawn I made my way up California Street. In the safety of darkness I would be taken for a white man, perhaps a capitalist rising before dawn to oversee his great enterprise. Hardly anyone stirred at that hour, and I reached the top of the hill shortly.

I paused before the great fence. It must have been the tallest plank fence on the Pacific Coast, if not in the entire country. The first glimmers of dawn turned everything gray, except for the fence and the small house beneath it, both of which remained in the deepest of black. Yung's house seemed entirely entombed, buried at the very bottom of a mine shaft. There it was, a monument to—to what? To spite? Yes, but also to folly, to division, to perversity, a monument to all the strangeness of the foreign devils. I found myself almost becoming giddy, and I was afraid I would start laughing out loud at the sight of such a stupendous, crazy thing.

I glanced towards Crocker's mansion. Against the sky I could just make out the millionaire's square tower with its mansard roof high above the fence. Suddenly I thought I could discern in the dim light the outline of Crocker's large shape in the tower's dormer window. There, in the dawn light, he had climbed to view his great works at the break of day. I felt I had to flee right away. The sight of that huge man in his toy tower almost caused me again to burst out in laughter. Besides, the sun was becoming brighter, and soon I would no longer be a white man in my suit.

As I started to make my way down the hill, my eye suddenly caught the dull glint of something white in the gutter, what appeared to be a small handbill. I don't know why I felt compelled to take such a memento of my excursion, but I bent over and stuffed the paper into my pocket. By the time I reached Dupont Street, the usual early morning bustle of produce merchants, farmers, fishermen, and butchers had begun. Old Lee was up as well, and he welcomed me as he always did to the back of his store. He had seen me many times in Western clothes—he knew that I sometimes had to make myself so uncomfortable as part of my employment as a translator—so he was not surprised to see me in my costume. I thanked him for his hospitality and for his tea. I told him the story of my adventure, drawing forth the crumpled handbill to read my souvenir from my visit to the fence.

THE TENTH WARD CIGAR DEPOT
—236 Sixth Street

Cigars by all White Labor made.
Workingmen, the place to trade
Is at Miller's. Yes, indeed!
Use no nasty Chinese weed,

But smoke a real White Man's cigar.
Miller sells them near and far,
He'll to all your wants attend,
Miller's is the workingman's friend.
Cigars—the BEST—at prices low.
Miller swears, "Chinese Must Go!"

I could no longer resist. I expelled the laughter I had so bottled up before Crocker's fence. Old Lee was perplexed and asked me what was so humorous about the piece of paper. I translated the handbill for him.

"Why are you laughing at such a hateful piece of dung?" he asked when I was done.

"I know this Mr. Miller, for I have translated for some of our cigar manufacturers who have done business with him. He is so successful that he cannot produce enough cigars, so he is forced to buy 'nasty Chinese weed' in order to meet his demand. Not only is his verse bad, but the man is a fraud."

Old Lee gave me a perplexed look for a moment, then he too broke out into broad laughter.

"Old Lee," I said, "the foreign devils need us too badly— Kearney needs us, Miller needs us, Crocker needs us, everyone needs the Chinese, each for their own reasons. The cowardly mob will never attack Chinatown. Without the Chinese, how will they arouse their hatred, or elect their mayors, or make their cigars, or build their railroads? *How can the Chinese go?*"

Old Lee just stared at me. "What nonsense are you saying?"

I just began to laugh again, and as I laughed I felt the demon that had possessed me go flying from out my mouth.

Gertrude Yung Miller

Dennis Kearney never did follow through with his threat to tear down the fence. The Kearney excitement passed, and he and his hoodlums went on to bigger and better things, until he disappeared. But life for us was miserable. The flowers in our garden all died, and our lawn turned brown, while inside the house everything felt perpetually damp. Our lives seemed to turn to gloom in our house, as if we were living in Papa's funeral home. We were so unhappy living in such utter darkness, we could not hide it, no matter how we tried, and I knew Papa was trying to think of a way out. I believe my father finally got his idea on how to deal with the situation when he saw a color cartoon printed in the *Wasp* making fun of the fence. It was called "Revenge of Mr. Yung" and showed Papa cranking our house up on jacks while Crocker watched from the window of his mansion. The joke was that Papa would crank himself up above the fence and then look down on his tormentor, which would be his revenge. Well, Papa did just that, in a manner of speaking. He cranked up the house on jacks, then he moved it to a new plot in the Mission District. Mr. Crocker's fence now surrounded only an empty lot that Papa had graded over. You would think that since we were gone, Crocker would tear it down. But he didn't. He just lowered the fence some, keeping our little rectangle of gravel surrounded by plain plank boards.

Nothing could ever replace our house on the hilltop, but our lives were much better in the Mission District. At least we still had our old home, and everything came back to life again. The Mission District is free of fog most of the time, so the bright sunlight was back. The young gentlemen came calling again, and we went on with our lives as before all the trouble. But even with our house gone, people still went up the California Street Hill in order to look at the spite fence. We went back a few times ourselves, just to see our old hill, and it amazed me to watch all the people contemplate three blank walls around an empty patch. A hole can mean a lot if people want it to.

My father died a short time later, in 1880, and even then Crocker would not tear down the fence. My mother inherited a considerable estate from Papa, and we were comfortable enough, so Mama preferred to keep the walled-up lot rather than sell it. Other people came to her about the property. Several times advertising firms wanted to use the lot for big signs selling coffee and other things. Once Mama received an offer to lease the lot for a Chinese laundry. Yes, a Chinese laundry! That would have been some revenge, indeed. Mama turned down all these offers, however, and with wonderful dignity she told a newspaperman: "Carrying out the policy of my husband, I do not care to retaliate for the meanness shown by Mr. Crocker. There are some things to which people like ourselves do not care to stoop. I would have had revenge, but I declined these offers."

When Mr. Crocker died in 1888, we thought that the feud would come to an end. But Crocker's heirs refused to tear down the fence; they just kept up the same vengeful attitude as before, so Mama simply held onto the property. In 1895 she went to the authorities with a request to have the fence removed. The Board of Supervisors voted to support her, saying that the fence had made the house uninhabitable and the land valueless, which "worked a great injury to Mrs. Yung and deprived her of constitutional rights." Well, the City Attorney ruled that the Supervisors had no power to interfere with private property, despite their vote. And so the property and the fence remained as they were right up until Mama passed away in 1901.

After her death the property came into the hands of the four of us. By then I was married to Dr. Miller. He was the son of a successful cigar manufacturer, the proprietor of the Tenth Ward Cigar Depot, as well as other businesses. I made sure that my husband, his family, and our children had nothing to do with all this vindictiveness. With the death of my mother, my sisters and I decided that enough was enough. We did not want this silly curse to go on down through the generations, and we hoped that by selling the lot to a third party we could end the feud. When the FOR SALE sign went up, the newspapers did not fail to note it: "When the lot has been sold to someone not of the Yung blood, it may be that the Crockers will drop their legacy of hatred and let the spite fence, inartistic monument of resentment, be torn down." Yes, I remember that apt description, "inartistic monument of resentment."

In 1904 Thomas Balfour bought the property. He was a retiring, modest bachelor who said he wanted it for investment purposes. Well, we thought it would eventually end up in the hands of the Crockers, but we didn't mind. We were not interested in prolonging the agony, but at least we would honor our parents by not being the ones to make the transaction. As the newspaper said, "Now the great, unsightly fence, wearied with its years of wickedness is to go to the ground." We avoided dealing with the Crockers all the way to the end, although twenty-five or so years after his mean, despicable fence went up, Mr. Crocker would have his victory.

But fate has a way of turning everything upside down. When the 1906 earthquake destroyed the city, Crocker's mansion went up in flames. His entire wooden monstrosity—one architect had even called it a "delirium of a woodcarver"—was gone. Even his great high tower was nothing but a heap of ashes. For years their entire property was just as leveled as our little lot had been.

Now I understand that the Crocker family has donated all their property to the Episcopal Church in order for them to build their cathedral. The Crockers say they're glad "to dedicate the land to hallowed use." I hope they're trying to expiate their guilt. After all the meanness, after all that coveting worse than Ahab's lust for Naboth's vineyard, after decades of that insane spite fence, the walls of God's house will now enclose the entire block. The Episcopalians intend to call it Grace Cathedral.

Calamity and Crime

The Great Earthquake and Fire

◆◆◆◆

From *Tremors of Doom* by Henry O——

Towards the end of the fire I sought refuge in the Jewish cemetery, or Mission Dolores Park. Actually, the graves had been removed in 1894, but everyone still called the park the Jewish cemetery. Right before the earthquake the cemetery ground, which slopes upwards from Eighteenth towards Twentieth Street, had been prepared for the planting of extensive lawns with the plentiful spread of horse manure. And so, exhausted, there I flung myself down, along with the other gray, drawn, spectral survivors, to sit in the fields of dung and mud, while the fire chattered like a billion maniac monkeys.

I could feel the monstrous suck of wind funneling down the Mission hills as it raced to feed the frenzied fire at the same time that up Dolores Street rushed waves of billowing heat and poisonous gases, which overcame retreating firefighters and fleeing refugees alike with its invisible surf of death. Great flakes of ash and large burning cinders rained down on the multitude, while I could occasionally hear a mother's horrified scream as she beat out a cinder that alighted on her baby's buggy or, worse, on her infant's head. I leaned back on my elbows, then felt in my pocket for the jewels, the cigars, the bottle of whisky, and the other oddments I had collected. All my loot was in order. I pulled out one of the cigars and lit it, puffing on my luxuriant Cuban. To the degree that I could think at all, I was not a little amused at the thought of smoking a cigar in the middle of such hellish flame and heat and smoke and hurricane. But many survivors were doing stranger things than I, and no one thought it too odd that I should puff away in the midst of a great conflagration. It certainly got less notice than the gentleman who seemed to be wearing his bed sheets from the morning of the first shock as he wallowed in the manure, beating his breast and praying to God to forgive San Francisco its sins.

Along Twentieth Street hundreds of firemen and volunteers tried to form a firebreak by pulling apart the wooden buildings with their bare hands. But there was no water, except for the little to be found in cisterns, and it seemed perhaps one more hopeless attempt to contain the flames. All the hydrants were checked again and again to see if any would work, but to no avail. I felt that the Jewish cemetery would afford little protection if the flames were to attack the break, so after a while I pocketed my stub, got up, and climbed to the corner of Twentieth and Church streets. From that height I would have a good view of the approaching firestorm as well as a headstart scrambling over the Church Street Hill to Noe Valley if the flames should cross the break.

I had lived as a child for a time in the Mission District, and I knew there were all sorts of wells and springs up around Dolores Heights. Boyhood legend had it that you could find gold in the craws of the ducks who drank from those streams, and we spent many an afternoon trying to capture those ducks for their treasure or trying to find gold with old pie pans. We never succeeded in discovering any nuggets, but the legend stayed alive nonetheless. Now, although the springs were paved over, I was not altogether surprised when a blacksmith from the neighborhood gave three turns to the valve and water gushed out. The hydrant apparently had tapped into one of those underground springs, divining its own source of water despite the general collapse of the mains.

A roar shot up at the sight of such precious water, and the firemen rushed to get an engine up the Dolores Street Hill to the hydrant. The exhausted horses, however, could not budge up the steep incline, no matter how hard they worked. I, along with hundreds of other men, raced to the engine. "Push! Push! Push!" we shouted, and inch by inch we forced the fire engine up the hill as the horses strained against the harness. When at last we reached the level plateau on Twentieth Street we fell to the ground with whoops and hurrahs while the horses took over to reach the hydrant. Other engines were then positioned to pump in tandem, while every inch of hose was stretched out to reach the final engine on Mission Street. Our little spring finally fulfilled its promise of treasure, although in a very unexpected manner, as the water pumped out to hold back the advancing fire. If it were not for that hydrant all of the Mission District would have been devoured by the beast.

Once again I stretched out in the ashes, mud, and manure. I believe I had used every last ounce of strength to help push that engine up the hill. I was so tired that if the flames had come to lick my face like a dog just then, I would not have been able to flee. Flat on my back, I could hear the chattering of the fire, the crash of collapsing walls, the shouts of the firemen, the screams of the mothers, the cries of the children, all of which combined with the piercing wail of the madman wrapped in his bed sheets praying to God to forgive the wicked city. There, sprawled in the Jewish cemetery, we had all been turned into crazy Jobs. Unable to move, I looked up at the howling sky, my mind emptied of all thoughts, my skull denuded of all philosophy, my heart, like the hydrants, withered. In the midst of that din, I simply fell asleep.

I awoke especially early on that Wednesday of the earthquake in order to breakfast with George Holmes, the head of the

San Francisco "Wobblies," before he began his hectic day. I was no revolutionary proletarian myself, but I was engaged in a project that I had hoped would contribute significantly to the Victor Archives. I had been interviewing the socialists and the unionists as part of documenting life "south of the Slot." Although I had spent part of my youth in modest circumstances in the Mission District, my father's business success allowed me the hobo's luxury of living without needing to work. After attending the University of California, I continued to teach there occasionally, although I would spend most of my time deeply engaged in my own independent social and moral research.

As I said, I was not a socialist, but I did enjoy life among the true intellectuals, those leaders of idealism and reforms, those unfrocked priests who could no longer lead the herds to Mammon, the broken professors driven from their university chairs, the passionate autodidacts, the "class-conscious workingmen." I preferred them to the businessmen, who were alive but were also crude and unclean, and I much preferred them to the university professors, the editors, and preachers, who were noble and clean but whose ideal was, as Jack London said, "the passionless pursuit of passionless intelligence." I may have spent my time in the parlor, but now it was the foundation of the social edifice that interested me.

As I began to knot my necktie in the early light, the tremor suddenly struck, its violent twisting motion tearing the cravat from my hands. In an instant I was flung across the room, my bed rocking to and fro. From all around I heard the screech of metal, the roar of bricks falling, the splintering of glass, the tearing of wooden houses like tissue paper, and beneath it all the uncanny sound of the earth itself reverberating like a deep gong. It must have lasted only twenty seconds, but the violence felt interminable. Then, just as suddenly, the shaking stopped. I lurched towards the door, but after a pause of a few seconds the seismic horror resumed its ferocious dance, hurling me against the wall, then down to the floor again, while great masses of plaster fell all about me. I could feel the building tearing apart, the earth actually seeming to jump vertically with a rotary twist, causing the rear three stories of the building to shear off and crash into the wooden houses in the alley below.

Even as I clung to the floor, I had a feeling of finality, of witnessing my own death, although I felt strangely distant, not at all frightened of doom. While the shaking probably lasted no more than a minute, I had the odd feeling that time had stopped, that the earthquake was all of eternity. I also had an even stranger sensation, the bizarre perception that the great power that was then tearing my house to pieces radiated from deep within me. That was the most unnerving feature of the first jolt, and even of the subsequent, smaller earthquakes, a sensation which I have yet to be able to describe adequately: that such enormous power came from nowhere else but within myself and not from without. I did not feel, as others have said, that the tremor pounced upon the earth like a giant bulldog, that I was being shaken by a huge beast or struck by some external force. Rather, I felt as if the shaking came from deep within my own abdomen, that it radiated outward with incredible violence from my chest, my navel, my genitals. Although, in that minute of interminable shaking, my own demise did not frighten me, this uncanny sensation brought me unspeakable terror.

Do not misunderstand me. This was not some kind of megalomania or solipsism. Of course, even then, in the midst of this crashing chaos, I realized that I was a part—a minuscule, fragile part—of a huge seismic performance; I realized that I was feeling an illusion of power within me precisely because I was in the grip of the unimaginable, overwhelming earth itself. And yet the sense that I was the one producing such incredible violence was overpowering, undeniable. In those few seconds, the difference between the objective and the subjective seemed impossible. I suppose I had suddenly perceived the great Oneness of which mystics speak—and it was horrifying! I was the one shaking my own house to pieces, and if I could not halt my horrible emanations, all of reality would crash. "STOP! STOP!" I screamed again and again, clutching my guts. A pathetically ludicrous gesture, I suppose, but eventually my command was obeyed, the lurching did stop, the deadly motion of the earth ceased.

Then there was silence, an eerie hush. I pulled on my jacket and hat and scrambled down the front steps, which miraculously remained intact. Seventh Street was filling up with people in a fantastic array of attire—half dressed, nightclothes, entirely nude—each dazed and soundlessly stumbling. No one cried out, no one screamed—there was nothing but utter silence. This strange interlude lasted but a few minutes—perhaps only seconds—before muffled screams and moans tore the morning air. Those who were buried beneath the wreckage of collapsed buildings began to call for help, and the mesmerized parade of silent survivors suddenly awoke as if from a dream. The throng still remained subdued, but now sound had been restored to the world—sobs and shouts and even nervous laughter could fill the air again, although for a time people spoke in hushed tones as if it were impolite to be too loud. Soon groups of men began to cluster around various piles of wreckage from which the cries could be heard, the rescuers madly pulling boards and bricks apart. I could smell smoke—the fires had begun almost immediately—and within an hour much of the area south of Market Street would be enveloped in flames.

I decided to make my way to my appointment at the I.W.W. headquarters a few blocks away. Blazing buildings, fallen telegraph poles, and live wires were all around me. The headquarters was in a horrible condition, the sidewalk had fallen in, and the building was leaning toward the street. There I saw George Holmes, and I joined him as he gathered the metal-workers' charter of the I.W.W. and a few other official books of the organization. Soon, however, the building was in full possession of the fire.

We went over to the Brunswick House on the corner of Sixth and Howard. Actually, the block consisted of several hotels, mainly for transient workers, and it seemed that each toppled over like a row of dominoes—the Nevada House ramming into the Ohio House, then the Ohio House flattening most of the Brunswick House, pushing it into the middle of Howard Street as far as the car tracks and trapping hundreds of people beneath the collapsed building. It caught fire, and the screams of the imprisoned people who were roasting to death were agonizing.

We joined the throng attempting to pull people out before the advancing fire. Blankets were held up to keep the heat from becoming intolerable. We pulled out a man and wife who were clutching each other in their bed. The man was dead, a pile of rubble crushing his head, but his wife still lived. As I frantically pulled more boards away, I saw a single hand stretched out and heard the muffled moans of a young woman beneath a jumble of beams and boards. We scrambled to lift the wreckage, but the beams were too heavy. By this time the heat was impossible, and one rescuer after another had to flee the flames. I could hear her whimper and plead for help. I pulled her hand, thinking that I could yank her free. I could barely breath because of the smoke and intense heat, but I pulled again and again, cursing the boards and the fire. Finally, my hands slipped free and I landed on my back as George hastily pulled me away.

I could hear her cries—I can still hear her cries—as the flames burned her alive. I stumbled to my feet, my fists still clutching tightly, tears lashing my burnt face. When I could no longer stand the horror, I turned to walk away. Only then did I notice that there was something in my clenched fist. I opened my hand to see a thin, gold band. I had strained at her hand so hard that I had yanked her wedding ring off. I had no idea of her name, her age, anything. I could not save her, but I did manage to save her ring. I felt like a ghoulish thief. For a second I considered tossing the ring back into the fire, but thinking that would somehow be killing her again I simply stuffed it into my pocket. Thus began my career as a looter.

Soon soldiers from the Presidio were seen on the streets, martial law appeared to be in force, and word spread that all looters would be shot on sight. George and I saw proof of the brutal rule General Funston had swiftly imposed on the city. We came across several men carrying away provisions from a grocery when soldiers arrived on the scene, suddenly leveled their rifles, and shot four of them dead. The store owner came out protesting that the men were not looting, that the building was going to burn soon anyway, and that he was giving the food away. "Get going," one of the soldiers yelled, "or you'll be next!" George and I just eyed each other and quickly but silently put some space between us and our so-called public guardians, only to get separated from each other in the melee.

⚜

Alone, I meandered aimlessly through the wrecked and burning city. I heard that the soldiers were ordered to destroy all drink, that a forced prohibition was imposed upon the town. I saw a company of soldiers storm into one saloon, breaking barrels of beer to drain in the street, smashing bottles of wine. I also noticed that the soldiers had downed enough whisky and beer themselves to produce a raucous two-step when they marched off to their next assignment.

Turning a corner I spotted an empty saloon in an alley. It

looked like just about everything had been carted off by looters previously, but I did find four pints of whisky that had been
carelessly left behind. I put two of the bottles in my pockets,
picked up one of the chairs and sat with the other two bottles
before me. I vaguely realized that if the soldiers saw me just
then that I might be shot, but I didn't care. I had to collect
myself somehow, and the whisky served a welcome medicinal
purpose. The alley was entirely deserted; not a sound could be
heard except the fire. That was the first time, sitting in that
barren saloon, that I observed the fire's uncanny, chattering
voice. I just sat there listening, finishing off the whisky, as the
chattering grew louder and louder.

Fortified, I finally left the ransacked saloon to resume my
peregrinations, eventually wandering across Market Street to
Union Square, where I was hailed by my friend Willie Collier.
"Bully way to welcome a new century, this," he joked, and we
exchanged the inevitable stories of "Where were you when" as
we tossed off a flask of brandy he had on hand. He seemed
quite jolly, so I refrained from giving him details of the horrors I had beheld south of the Slot. I saw no sense in upset-
ting his elan. He seemed quite comic sitting in his bedroom
slippers and flowered dressing gown.

Another friend, Dalton Chambliss, the theatrical agent,
stood beside him, and he told us the story of Enrico Caruso's
command performance. Chambliss was milling with the
crowd outside the Palace Hotel shortly after the shock when
Caruso, abruptly sticking his head out of one of the hotel's
windows, began to sing an aria. Apparently, the tenor had
been frightened into thinking that the earthquake had stolen
his voice, and he was singing to make sure that the precious
vocal gift was still his. There, above the dazed, incredulous
crowd, Caruso sang. His audience stopped in their tracks and
looked up, transfixed, listening as if they had received a gift
from God. "I'd pay anything for an audience like that,"

Chambliss sighed. Suddenly Collier noticed someone coming into Union Square and called out, "Go West, young man, and blow up the country!" The young man was John Barrymore, the actor then appearing in *The Dictator*, who cut a singularly striking figure in white tie and tails. "My, my," Chambliss remarked, "you certainly know how to dress for an earthquake." Barrymore assured him that he had been reveling the night before and had only dropped, fully clothed, on his bed an hour before the quake. "No need to apologize, my good man," Chambliss mockingly responded, "I know good taste when I see it." Meanwhile, Barrymore had noticed a charming lady dressed only in her nightgown sitting calmly on her trunk as her excitable French maid hovered about her. The actor veered towards her, charmingly introduced himself, offered the lady his evening jacket, and invited her for a drink. We watched as the overdressed actor and the scantily clad lady strolled together to the edge of the square before Barrymore set off for the Bohemian Club to retrieve some more brandy.

I learned afterwards that Barrymore would discover that there was more than one way to loot. Later that day he made his way to the home of mutual friends near Van Ness, where he drank steadily for the next three days and continued drinking even after they bundled him off to their house in Burlingame. There he wrote a completely fabricated eyewitness account of the earthquake and fire in the form of a letter to his sister Ethel. Despite the fact that he was drunk in his room almost throughout the entire disaster, he set down the story of "what I had seen in those harrowing days and what I myself had been through—people shot in the street, spiked on bayonets, and other horrors so great that the imagination was almost blunt from contemplating them." John Barrymore's imagination was quite blunt, indeed, from alcohol, according to my friends, but the actor was sure that the letter, when published in an Eastern newspaper, would be "worth at least a hundred dollars." The publicity alone brought him a thousand times that amount.

I was struck by this theatrical crowd. To them, even this disaster was a type of theater: the earth's performance merely giving them the cue to provide their own. A few years earlier I would have been delighted to have sailed through the destruction of the city with such a gay crowd, but I suppose that my chumming with all the overly intense socialists left me with little tolerance for seeing the world as a stage, unless, of course, as a stage for the Inevitable Drama of History. In any case, I bid my friends adieu.

＊＊ ≡✦≡ ＊＊

I wandered across Market Street again. Heading towards the fire while refugees fled in the opposite direction, I witnessed yet another incredible scene. About a block away from the flames I came across a crowd of people trying to rescue a man pinned beneath some wreckage. He was free from the chest up, but he seemed to be inextricably jammed in from below. The crowd seemed to have been working for some time, and the fire appeared less than a half hour away. He began to cry that he shouldn't be left to die a horrible death in the flames, and he begged repeatedly for someone to kill him. No one seemed prepared to take such a step. But after his rescuers retreated from the heat, a large, middle-aged man without a hat went up to the unfortunate prisoner. He talked with him for a few moments, then whipped out a revolver and shot the trapped man through the head. The man then turned to the crowd, his face contorted by pain, and requested to be taken to the police. The crowd was confused, since very few police were to be seen, and no one wanted to bring him to the sol-diers, since they felt the poor man should be commended and not executed. Finally, a few of the witnesses accompanied the distraught man to the Hall of Justice.

＊＊ ≡✦≡ ＊＊

I staggered away, this time heading towards Van Ness. I came across men looting a cigar store, each running out with boxes of cigars under his arms. A box had fallen to the street, scattering its contents before my feet. I bent down and grabbed fistfuls of cigars to shove into my pockets. "Drop that, or I'll shoot!" I heard. I whirled around to see a soldier leveling his rifle directly at me. I froze in terror, unable to release the cigars, as the other men began to scatter like insects. Just then a huge explosion threw me to the ground. When I looked up, the air was filled with dust and smoke. I could not see the soldier. Apparently, one of the dynamite charges the soldiers had been setting to clear a firebreak nearby had just gone off. The cigars were still in my hands, so I shoved them into my pockets and began quickly crawling away on my knees before the dust cleared. If it were not for that blast, I have no doubt that I would have been shot.

<hr>

I had had enough bizarre adventures for one day, so I made my way to Lafayette Park to spend the night. There, quite by chance, I was reunited with George Holmes. Keeping each other company, we stood in the lurid light on the hillside to watch the city burn through the night. He showed me a copy of the proclamation issued by Mayor Schmitz: "The Federal Troops, the members of the Regular Police Force and all Special Police Officers have been authorized by me to KILL any and all persons found engaged in Looting or in the Commission of Any Other Crime."

"Astonishing, isn't it?" Holmes remarked after I read the handbill. "And to think, the whole damn country thinks we got a Red government in San Francisco because of that sell-out Union Labor mayor. Do you know that Schmitz has rounded up all the big capitalists? No, he's not planning to put them all in jail, but he's formed them into a 'Committee of

Fifty' to try to save the city. He even brought in Spreckles and Fremont Older, the very same 'clean' capitalists who've sworn to pursue him into Hell with graft investigations. But with all of his notables and such, there's not a single labor representative, not a one. I suppose the city will be rebuilt without workers.

"Now we have that martinet General Funston, that master of water cures and murderer of Filipino goo-goos, joining up with that charming fiddler and boodler Schmitz—between the two of them we have the makings of a right good massacre on our hands! Mayor Schmitz is so fond of private property that he's been caught red-handed changing a whole lot of public property into private property for the benefit of himself and his friends. Sure, when he and Boss Reuf loot, none of the military will take a shot at them. But the poor little looter, trying to scrape together a mouthful to live on for a few days longer, he's shot to death. The big looters, the Reufs and Schmitzes, those who have amassed plenty of public plunder just to lay by a store of luxury, they're allowed to go free. Well, one of these days, law for the little looter will become law for the big looter.

"See, Henry, even this disaster takes on the character of the class struggle. The earthquake alone is simply a natural calamity, but the earthquake plus the profit system is a fearful, a horrible disaster. Think of all the lives lost in those miserable shacks south of Market Street—lives sacrificed through the greed of the proprietors of those dens. I don't believe they'll even be able to count the victims, the hovels burned up so quick. Then think of the comparatively small death rate in the bourgeois quarter. Oh, it burns me up more than the fire, Henry. Like the old question goes: Working stiffs, why do you build palaces when you live in hovels?

"Just think of it, Henry. While so many suffer, the calamity comes as a godsend to the great capitalists. It affords them the opportunity to invest hundreds of millions that lately have given them increasing difficulty finding places to invest at a good rate of profit. Now they can make money rebuilding, while the middle-class businessman will be down and out—tomorrow he'll be a wage slave. How many people who thought they owned their homes will now become renters? There's one thing an earthquake can't shake out of a house—a mortgage. There's one thing that fire can't burn—a mortgage. No, this calamity has wiped the economic slate clean, and now the big capitalists can write in larger letters than ever before, 'Greater consolidation, greater concentration of industry and ownership and control of the means of life.' I tell you, it makes me sick.

"But this earthquake is nothing compared to the social earthquake that is sure to strike. When this rotten class system shudders from the power of the workers, we'll see bigger fires than the one we watch tonight scorching all the capitalist vermin."

George went on. I knew he believed every word he said, but I also could tell that he had become so voluble because he was trying to talk his way out of remembering the many horrors he had seen that day. On and on he painted pictures of the social earthquake to come and the equitable commonwealth that would rise from the wreckage. I let him talk.

"But, George," I finally interjected. "Aren't you afraid that such a social earthquake will destroy so many innocents along with the guilty? Aren't you afraid that the edifice that rises from those ruins may be utterly different from the one drawn up by its architects? Aren't you a little afraid that you may be swallowed up when the fissure closes up again?"

A succession of dynamite blasts rent the air before he could respond. At last, he said, "Yes, the Revolution can be a beast, an uncontrollable beast that can devour its own keepers, and the job of the class-conscious workers is to give that beast some brains—but it's not as if we have any choice. I welcome such an earthquake—even if it swallows me up alive!"

"Frankly, George, I'm not at all sure that I am ready to be swallowed up by anything—although I do have something which perhaps both of us might much prefer to swallow instead." I pulled out one of my bottles of whisky; we both took big conspiratorial gulps, making sure no public-spirited soldiers spotted us, before resuming our watch over the burning city.

"Excuse me," a tall, imposing figure in a black frock coat and striped trousers said in an English accent moments after I returned the bottle to my jacket, "I am a physician, Dr. Howard D'Arcy Power, and I wonder if I may take each of your pulse."

George and I looked at each other quizzically, then assented to the doctor's request.

"Well, doctor, how are we doing?" I asked after he dropped my wrist.

"Just fine, my good man. Both of you are in splendid shape. Thank you so very much."

"Wait a minute, Doc," George called out as Dr. Power turned to hunt for other wrists. "What's the point of taking our pulse? What the dickens are you doing?"

"I am a student of psychic effects, and I am studying how such effects manifest themselves in a mass of people under such extreme duress."

"And what have you learned?"

"I've determined that those people who managed to keep control of themselves show signs of good health. Indeed, I'd say excellent health. People have been deprived of car service, alcohol, luxuries. With nothing but simple food, they have been compelled to take physical exercise in the open air. Most men have found it possible to survive without cigars or whisky, and the ladies, without candy. In short, they have had the enforced benefits of a sanatorium."

"Come again?" I asked.

"The earthquake has actually been good for your health!"

George and I just stared at each other in amazement, then burst out into laughter, as the good doctor continued on his rounds.

─────

At daybreak I took a stroll through the crowded park. Some were still sleeping fitfully under makeshift tents, while most spent the night like myself watching the eerie glare of the flames. Of all people, I came across Sam Wong, Mrs. Margaret Warner's houseboy. Even in the midst of such chaos he had the wherewithal to pack some provisions and was now keeping busy over a small campfire preparing breakfast for the widow, who slept several yards away. After expressions of pleasure at seeing me well, he graciously offered me biscuits and a cup of hot water —"white tea" he called it, but any drinking water was precious at that moment—and I much appreciated his hospitality.

Perhaps it is like this at all times, but only now, by means of calamity, can we discern the complete arbitrariness of everything, can allow that anything can happen, that chaos, always present just beneath the surface, creates strange conjunctions and dissociations. The calamity is so immense, so all-consuming, that boundaries dissolve, moral divisions become porous, surfaces crack, familiar relations reverse: The soldiers protect against looting by committing murder, while all the time looting themselves; General Funston decides to save the city by blowing it up.

At the same time, unusual acts of kindness fill the air: Strangers risk their lives to save trapped victims; thieves, cut-throats, and prostitutes from the Barbary Coast gently escort lost children to makeshift refugee centers. "When Altruria Awoke," one friend of mine titled his little memoir: Aroused by disaster, the whole city is marked by unaccustomed altruism; no matter their class or social condition, people help each other, are drawn together, rich and poor, shoulder to shoulder—catastrophe creating an unexpected foretaste of Utopia!

Mrs. Warner awoke. She greeted me effusively, happy to see a familiar face in the crowded park. "Mrs. Margaret Warner, may I introduce you to an old friend, George Holmes. Mr. Holmes is, uh, a very respected industrial architect."

George smiled at my tact, bowing suavely, and accepted a biscuit and some white tea from the houseboy. "You architects are sure to have much work when we start rebuilding, Mr. Holmes," said Mrs. Warner.

What a tableau—Chinaman, wealthy widow, Wobbly, ne'er-do-well intellectual—all sitting down to break biscuit together in the morning light.

Mrs. Warner was going to set off for San Mateo, and she invited us to join her; but we demurred, explaining that we had other responsibilities, other plans for refuge. After some more polite exchanges and many thanks for the repast, we went our way.

"Hell, Henry," George whispered to me, "next time I get arrested by the police I'll tell 'em I'm a fine and dandy industrial architect. I'll tell 'em they should get my references from my dear friend Mrs. Margaret Warner." He slapped me on the back, mightily enjoying the humor of the situation.

"I'm going to try to get to the Ferry Building, Henry. No sense in me sticking around here. I imagine General Funston is not about to organize relief for the Industrial Workers of the World, so we'll have to do it for ourselves. I'll be of more use in Oakland. Want to join me?"

My parents and my sister had long ago moved to New York, so I had no family to be concerned with. Nothing tied me to San Francisco, yet nothing compelled me to go to Oakland either.

"Thanks, George, but I think I'll stay—and loot."

⊷ ⋈ ⊶

At the edge of the park I encountered ———. A biologist, he had joined with the medical relief volunteers organized by Dr. Marcus Herstein and the others for the mayor's Committee of Fifty and was now briskly marching to Golden Gate Park to assess the sanitary conditions of the refugees. I asked if I could accompany him. He consented, but as I joined his swift pace, I noticed that he seemed highly agitated, almost shaking with rage. No, he was not at all irritated with me, but he was reluctant to share the cause of his anger. When I pressed him, he agreed to tell me—I believe he was relieved to unburden himself—but only under condition that I swore to keep silent.

My friend related how he had joined with Dr. Herstein in an early morning meeting with Mayor Schmitz and his Committee of Fifty to warn of the danger of rats. I had observed the rodents clawing out of broken sewers, running from cellars, scampering across the ruins, but to the degree that I even thought about the pests at all it was just to note that even the rats were fleeing the sinking ship. But the Medical Committee, deeply alarmed over the potential spread of disease due to unsanitary conditions, was especially troubled: If the rats were left uncontrolled, bubonic plague would very quickly menace the city.

Fearful that even rumors of the plague would cause panic and frighten away efforts to rebuild, the Committee of Fifty simply denied the problem.

"But, gentlemen," Dr. Herstein appealed, "if we do not immediately concern ourselves with controlling them, the rats

⊷ ⋈ ⊶

will rule the ruins, the city will be quarantined. Then we shall have all of your fears come true!"

"Bubonic plague is an affliction of the Chinese, an Oriental disease," one of the committee members replied.

"But the rats will use the open sewer pipes as boulevards throughout the city. The plague will spread. White people will become victims as much as the Chinese."

Yet Dr. Herstein's appeal fell on deaf ears. The mayor's committee was distracted by the more pressing matter of the fire. The military requested more dynamite, and the committee granted the request. Dr. Herstein and his colleagues left to cope with the dangers of plague and epidemic on their own.

My friend was trying to exhaust his rage by his forced march to Golden Gate Park. "Fools! Idiots! To think that they can ignore something like the bubonic plague! 'It's an Oriental disease'—posh!"

He fell into a sullen silence as we marched on. At last spotting the army tents and the jumble of other hastily constructed structures of the refugee camp, he cursed aloud, "Damn! No latrines, no drinking water, but plenty of rats—and more stupidity than we know what to do with!"

—◦—≣◆≣—◦—

I was not content to stay in the teeming refugee camp, so I resumed my aimless wandering, inevitably gravitating towards the flames like a moth. The fire was encroaching steadily on the Mission District, and I walked up and down its streets, pausing occasionally to drink discreetly from my bottle of whisky, as residents hastened to salvage a few remaining belongings before the onslaught. On Capp Street, I noticed a house that tilted at a particularly crazy angle, the front of it having collapsed into a pile of sticks.

Seeing no one within a block, I quickly slipped through an overhang of wreckage to the back door, which, because of the strange slant of the building, had been wrenched ajar. Although in disarray, the kitchen seemed to have been unmolested by looters or by occupants trying to flee. I found some bread, a little stale but edible, and, most gratifying, I spotted a bottle of brandy, which I downed so quickly I almost fell down from the sudden ingestion of alcohol. The staircase still seemed sturdy, so I gingerly made my way upstairs. At one end of the hallway was the front bedroom, which had been entirely shorn off and exposed to the elements like a dollhouse. The rear bedroom was fully intact, however, and I pushed open the door to enter what was obviously a lady's boudoir.

I picked up a fallen chair, pushed off plaster from the bed. A photograph had fallen from the bureau, a young girl and her mother—evidently I was now in the young girl's room. I rifled through the drawers, coming across a small box that contained some jewelry and a small packet of letters tied with a ribbon, along with a cameo photograph of a young man in an army uniform, presumably her beau. I dumped them all into my jacket pockets. Then I came across underclothes, garters, stockings, nightgowns. I smelled them—I could still perceive the faint, delicate odor of a woman—and I gently pressed them against my cheeks. In the closet I found dresses, and I spread them out on the bed. By her photograph and the shape of those dresses I could tell that the young lady was petite and quite pretty. I stretched down on her bed and pulled the sleeves of one of the dresses around me. I could feel her presence all around me; I dreamt that I was the young man in the cameo, and my darling was embracing me in her arms . . .

I awoke with a start when her sleeve turned into the roasted hand of the woman buried under the Brunswick House. Smoke filled my nostrils. I had no idea how long I had been dozing on the bed, her gowns all about me. Evidently the fire was very near, and I had to flee the young lady's doomed bedroom or myself be consumed in the conflagration. I jumped up from the bed, but, whether from the brandy, the sudden motion, or the smoke, I fell down to the floor, retching violently. The smoke became denser, more acrid, and the thought that I would die of a sort of bizarre romanticism made me giddy despite my nausea. I managed to pull myself up and stumble down the staircase and out the door. The fire seemed very close as I squeezed through the overhang of wreckage to Capp Street again.

A man in civilian clothes and a rifle stood at one corner—I imagine he was one of the "Special Police" vigilantes sworn in by the mayor.

"What were you doing in there?" he gruffly demanded.

I walked up to him and stared at him mutely.

"Answer me, or I'll blow your brains out!"

"I raped your daughter!"

Ordinarily this would be the end of such a tale, but, as the handbill from "the Committee on History appointed by Mayor Schmitz" announced, "We Want All the Facts." But "all the facts" of my experience only became apparent months after the end of the fire.

Actually, the mayor's Committee on History requested "an accurate account of their experience" from all persons who survived the earthquake and fire. The Victor Archives, however, taking little stock in the mayor's announcement or the efficacy of his committee, decided to gather its own documentation of the disaster. I took up where I left off, interviewing the proletarian revolutionaries again, but now in the context of what they considered to be "the great field for socialist agitation" provided by the earthquake.

By August, thousands still lived in the camps, suffering from lack of relief, misappropriation of supplies, inefficiency, cheating, intimidation. There was to be "a monster meeting of protest and indignation" by "a great army of the homeless" led by Mrs. Mary Kelly, one of the tenters in Jefferson Square and chairman of the complaint committee of the united refugees. The throng—twenty thousand, the *Socialist Voice* assured readers—would march to the St. Francis. There Dr. Devine of the Red Cross was to hold a feast for officials and other important personages. Inside, they would banquet on blue points, potage mongol, and filet of beef, then discuss how the refugees were being fed and clothed; outside, the refugees themselves planned to stand just across the threshold pleading for bread. I went to visit Mrs. Kelly the night before the "monster meeting."

"We are going to march to Union Square, to say to those smiling and fawning upon Dr. Devine, who calls us paupers, that we want bread; that we want shoes; that we want help to get back our independence, the help that was sent to us and that has been misappropriated. We go to that meeting in peace. We shall not carry ropes or stones; we shall not threaten anybody. We will not wave the red flag. But unless things change—unless things change, and soon—something terrible will happen. I pray it may never happen. But how long will these men, do you think, be content to spill only words while their wives and babies suffer?"

Mrs. Kelly was remarkably good-natured and not at all grim as she spoke, and I wished her much luck in achieving the aims of her "monster meeting." I was scheduled to meet a new associate of the Victor Archives in Jefferson Square to discuss further documentation, so I excused myself after a while. At the appointed spot, a young woman introduced herself. Ann —— was staying in the camp, taking dictation from its inhabitants, and she had accumulated a sizable pile of notes, which I was supposed to bring back. She looked vaguely familiar, yet I was sure we had never met. She was speaking to me with vivacious animation about her project when, her face turning at a certain angle, I was suddenly mortified, struck dumb with terror. It must have looked as if I had just fallen victim to a stroke, for Ann ——— was quite alarmed, taking my arm, shaking me and asking what was wrong again and again. *How could I tell her that I had crept into her very bedroom, embraced her image, stolen her precious belongings, violated her dreams?*

"Are you planning to go on the march to the St. Francis tomorrow night?" I finally stammered.

"Yes."

"I hope I am not too presumptuous, but would you be so kind as to join me at the monument to Admiral Dewey after the meeting? There is something important I must tell you, but I cannot now."

She readily agreed, and I tore off as quickly as I could. My stomach quivered with alternating tremors of shame, fear, humiliation, and guilt throughout that night, as I contemplated confessing my crime to my victim. My anonymous woman of fantasy had become flesh and blood, someone very real, very attractive, and of great intellect, and my soul, as a consequence, was cast into the inferno. The packet of letters, all by the soldier in the cameo, her fiance, were written when Joseph ——— served in the Philippines. Filled with tenderness, remembrances of lovers' delights, with longings to be home and to be with Ann, the letters also spoke frankly of the war, of atrocities he had witnessed, of ambushes by the "bolo men," and of fear when his company had to pursue Filipino insurgents into the "boondocks." The packet concluded with the sad, official telegram from the War Department announcing his death in combat in 1899. I thought the letters were all so touching when I read them for the first time in the Jewish cemetery that even there, wallowing in ashes and manure, I shed a tear. I planned to give the packet to the Archives. But now, with the reader for whom they were actually intended right before me, I realized that not only had I violated her, but that I had also desecrated the sacred relics of the dead. There was no question in my mind that I had to confess, if only to see my perverse act to its logical conclusion.

I cannot reproduce what happened the next night. The demonstration was a success, although numbering about two thousand, and not the twenty thousand promised by the *Socialist Voice*, but I hardly noticed as I waited for our rendezvous. I met her under the towering column memorializing the hero of Manila Bay, and as we walked away I hastily blurted out the whole story, confessed to everything—her room, the garments, even the packet of letters—in an almost incoherent flood. I will not describe her surprise, her disbelief, her agitation, her anger, when the packet of letters and the cameo and the jewels suddenly appeared before her eyes. When I placed them in her hands, she looked as if the dead had returned, her face torn between joy and horror. Then, when she grasped the full extent of what I was saying, she exploded with epithets—"Ghoul!" "Monster!" "Necrophiliac!"—and others far worse than these. I stood there as if before a firing squad. But just as suddenly as she had begun, she quit her rage, as if realizing it was useless, would never bring Joseph back again, and she began to sob. I stood there with my head bowed, mumbling, "There is no punishment too strong . . . such shame . . . expunge my guilt . . . dishonorable trespass . . ."

Then, to my surprise, she composed herself after a few moments, dried her tears, and said without rancor by the ruins of Market Street, "You have gotten to know Joseph. You have forced yourself upon me, upon my memories, by stealing these faded letters. I thought they were gone forever, burned in our house. In a way, I should be thankful—because of your obscene perversity, they have been saved." She considered this for an instant, the peculiar intimacy we shared, the fact that I too had come to know her dead love. "What a waste," she sighed. Then, recalling my violation, she continued, "Well, I suppose that you have also come to know *me*—in the disgusting fashion of a man driven to debasement. Now that you and I are supposed to work together for the Archives, fate has drawn a loop—or a noose—around us. I could protest, refuse to collaborate with such a worm, such a criminal—but I believe I will not. Instead, I will force myself upon *you*, I shall begin to know *you*—in my own fashion—if only by way of punishment."

What an odd way to meet one's future wife.

About the Author

Hilton Obenzinger is the author of *New York on Fire*, a history of the fires of New York in verse; *This Passover or the Next I Will Never Be in Jerusalem*, winner of the Before Columbus American Book Award; *The Day of the Exquisite Poet Is Kaput*; and *Bright Lights! Big City!* He is featured in *Five on the Western Edge*. He has taught on the Hoopa Valley Indian Reservation and at Stanford University. He lives in San Francisco.

Cover Designer:	Sharon Smith
Cover Illustrator:	Jim Pearson
Handlettering:	Robert Schwarzenbach
Text Designer:	David Peattie
Production Coordinator:	David Peattie
Copyeditor:	Amy Einsohn
Proofreader:	Heidi Fritschel
Text/Display Type:	Adobe Caslon/Madrone
Composition:	Philip Bronson
Printing/Binding:	R.R. Donnelley & Sons